Joey and the Magic Map

Tory C Anderson

Cover Art by Sarah Hunt

DEDICATION

To Tory, Cory, Rory, Clory, Lory, Jory, Glory and Story, my inspiration. To my sweet wife, Barbara, who believes in me.

Chapter 1

Just outside the little town of Stoneybrook, Tennessee, past Katy Mills' Homemade Pie Company, and up a dusty lane lined with tall poplars is an old mansion. People call it the Mansion on Katy Mills' Road. It's not a typical mansion as old Southern mansions go. Some would say it isn't a mansion at all, just a big house. Two stories rise above the ground and on top of these sits an attic with dirty dark windows looking out in four directions. It does have three tall pillars out front with white paint peeling like somebody's sunburned nose. Untrimmed shrubs reach toward the windows. Fat oak trees shade the lawn so much that it isn't green but only brown grass mixed with patches of dirt.

Colonel Orson T. Horsebaum built the mansion before the Civil War with his great fortune made in slave-grown cotton. Tales say that Horsebaum boasted of building the mansion to last five hundred years. Fifteen years after building it the Union Army burned it to the ground. Well, it would have burned to the ground if it hadn't been for the rain which saved the pillars out front. Colonel Horsebaum, a stubborn man, with a little gold he had hidden, rebuilt his mansion in hopes the South would rise again. His money ran low; he ended up with only a large house with pillars. The South didn't rise again either, at least not to its former glory.

The little mansion is 160 years old. It stands as stubbornly as Colonel Horsebaum lived. It could be that it leans to one side just a little, but to which side depends on who you ask. Like a lot of old houses it seems alive at times. The floors creak and the walls groan. When the wind blows, even with the windows closed, the curtains dance and papers shuffle. Everybody within twenty-five miles, child or grown up, has talked of the mansion being haunted. The grownups don't actually believe in haunted houses. The children know better.

The first time Joey laid eyes on the mansion on Katy Mill Road he knew it was haunted. It was early Thursday afternoon. His mother, Mrs. Molly Wilhelmina Johanaby, drove the old, extended-cab, pickup truck pulling a U-Haul trailer up the dusty lane. With brakes squeaking she stopped in front of the house. Mrs. Johanaby, Joey, and the twins stared silently at the mansion. They had come from five states away and knew nothing of the mansion's history. The mansion seemed to speak for itself.

"This is the place," Mrs. Johanaby finally said, breaking the silence.

The two back doors flew open and the twins Glory and Story leaped out. They ran to the front door, tried the handle, and then began banging on it.

"It's locked, Mom!" Glory yelled.

"Back door!" Story said and took off along the porch with Glory one step behind him. As they disappeared around the corner of the mansion silence descended on Joey and his mother once again.

Mrs. Johanaby's mouth hung open, the words "I've got the key," right on the end of her tongue. The twins moved too fast. She shut her mouth slowly.

Joey and his mother showed none of the twins' energy or enthusiasm. They continued to sit in the truck. Mrs. Johanaby sat because she was tired. Joey because he thought the mansion, or something in it, was staring at him. Goose bumps rose on his arms. The hair on his neck stood up. The feeling had come over him the moment they turned into the lane and he caught sight of the house. It was the same sudden fear you might feel when you are walking home at night and suddenly an unseen dog growls at you from the shadows. He almost told his Mom that they should leave, now, and never come back.

Before he could speak, the panic drifted away like the smoke from an exploded firecracker. It was replaced by a kind of excitement which was like fear, but more hopeful.

"Mom," he said, his voice trembling a little. "There's something about this house . . ." He stopped, not knowing what words to say.

"Yes," she said. "It's a wonderful old house, isn't it."

His mother wasn't feeling it. He could tell. He knew better than to try to explain.

"Are you going to get out?" his mother asked.

Joey nodded, taking his eyes off the house for the first time since they had driven up the lane. By the time he and his mother got the front door opened, the twins had completed their round of the house. They stood behind Joey panting happily.

As soon as Mrs. Johanaby opened the door a crack the kids pushed past her. Yelling excitedly they began exploring the mansion at a run. Joey wanted to follow. He hesitated. "Do you want to start bringing in stuff now?" he asked his mother.

"No. Let's have a look first," she answered.

Joey stepped into the house. He found himself in a dim entryway. A wide staircase with wooden banisters rose in front of him. On one side of the stairway was a dark hallway. In front of the staircase, on either side, were doors leading into other rooms. Joey realized he was holding his breath and let it out in a puff. His first breath of the old mansion was of things old and musty. He expected this. Then his nose detected something unexpected. The scent was faint—the ghost of a scent.

"I smell lilacs," Mrs. Johanaby said.

Yes, that was it. "Lilacs? In the house?" Joey asked.

"Maybe someone left a bouquet," she said, raising an eyebrow in doubt.

Joey turned and walked into the room on his left.

"It's a formal living room," his mother said, walking in behind him. The wooden floorboards were warped and uneven. Dusty couches and chairs sat on a rug that covered all but the edges of the wooden floor. The furniture looked old and used like furniture Joey had seen in thrift stores where his mother liked to shop. The ceiling was high in this room. Paint on the walls near the ceiling peeled back in delicate curls. The room was painted a light blue.

Behind him Joey heard his brother and sister run down the hall and scurry up the stairs. Curious he turned and climbed up after them. There was another long hallway lit by two windows in the west wall. There were four doors on the right. There was one more door facing them at the other end of the hallway. Joey found Glory and Story in the first room. It was a large bedroom with windows facing north and east. The room was nearly bare. A queen size bed stood at one end of the room and a large oak wardrobe at the other end. Glory was bouncing on the bare bed making it squeak furiously. She executed a forward flip landing on her bum. Story opened the wardrobe door and climbed in.

"Wow, it's huge," he said from the darkness inside. Sticking his head out the door he added, "It'll make a great fort."

"This is my bedroom," yelled Glory. She wasn't expressing hope, but staking her claim. It would take a formal eviction notice to get her out now.

Story, a bright kid, stood for a moment preparing to argue with Glory. Before he spoke his eyes lit up with an idea. He ran out the door. A moment later the same thought occurred to Joey. It was too late.

"This is my bedroom," Story yelled. His voice echoed faintly down the hall. Joey found him in a bedroom just like the first except the two windows faced south and east.

"Get out of my room," Story said as Joey stepped in. "Trespassers will be violated." He quoted from a sign he had seen on a junk yard gate. The sign had an outline picture of a big, snarling dog.

Joey didn't argue. He never argued with the twins. They always got what they wanted no matter how unfair it was. Disappointment growing, Joey checked the two doors in the middle. He found a bathroom and a small bedroom with only one window facing east. The bed was small and dumpy looking. There was no wardrobe at all, just a chest of drawers.

Joey knew this would be his room. The twins had staked their claims. They would get what they wanted. As the oldest child he should have some clout. For some reason he didn't get much respect. Respect slunk away from him like a strong-willed dog from a weak master.

He was thinking of how he could make his case for one of the bigger rooms when Mrs. Johanaby stepped in behind him.

"It isn't fair," he said. "Their rooms are ten-times bigger than this, and they'll just end up sleeping in the same room anyway like always." Joey made some good points, but even he heard the lack of energy and conviction in his voice. He had lost already.

Joey looked up at his mom as she eyed the room. Ever since his dad died she looked tired all the time. Underneath the tired she was still pretty.

"This used to be as big as the other two, but it looks like they took part of it when they added the bathroom," she said.

"I want one of the big rooms," Joey said. He heard the whine in his own voice. He blushed, ashamed. He had promised his father he'd be the man of the house.

Mrs. Johanaby looked at him and sighed. "I'll see what I can do," she said. "Give me a hand with the stuff from the trailer."

Hearing his mother sigh made his face grow even redder. Wishing he could take back his complaint Joey followed her down the stairs.

They didn't have to bring their furniture because Aunt Winocha had left all hers. There were couches and beds and end tables and funny looking dressers with long legs. They sat like obedient dogs in rooms where Aunt Winocha had left them. It's possible that some of the furniture was still sitting where Colonel Horsebaum left it. Aunt Winocha had inherited the house from him.

Aunt Winocha lived more than one hundred years—longer than most of her relatives. She had to search long and hard before she found Mrs. Johanaby—her cousin three times removed—to whom she left the house. This was lucky for the Johanabys. Eight months earlier Mr. Johanaby had died from cancer. Mrs. Johanaby couldn't make the house payments. The same day the foreclosure notice from the bank arrived Mrs. Johanaby received a call from Aunt Winocha's trustee.

When Mrs. Johanaby realized she had a place for her family to live she cried. The twins cried when she told them they were moving. Joey didn't, not then.

"This is where Dad lived, and this is where I want to live," Glory said.

"Dad bought this house for us so why can't we stay here?" added Story.

Joey wasn't feeling much at all. His dad had died. Nothing mattered anymore.

Mrs. Johanaby explained that the house wasn't paid for. She couldn't make the payments. The bank was taking it back

"Well, then, get a job like Dad so we can still live here," Glory said. Joey saw hurt in his mother's eyes.

"I'm doing the best I can," she said.

There were more tears and mutinous exclamations as they packed the trailer. Glory was going to lock herself in the bathroom. Story was going to run away from home. They weren't far down the road on the way to Stoneybrook, Tennessee, when the twins began to forget about their old home. They started talking about the mansion.

Glory and Story were like that. They could move from one thing to the next as if nothing really mattered. They were only eight. It helped that they were Mr. and Mrs. Johanaby's babies. They were spoiled. That's the way Joey saw it. Joey would have cried if he had had the energy. That was the only house he had ever known. Driving away made his dad seem deader. He wondered what his mother was feeling. She wore sunglasses. He couldn't see her eyes.

At dinner, after the trailer had been unloaded, the twins asked him where he was going to sleep.

He ignored them as if it wasn't an issue.

"Well you don't get my room," Glory said. She was only eight and yet spoke like she was his big sister. Somewhere in her eight years she had taken his power from him.

"You can't have my room either," Story said. His voice wasn't nearly as bossy. He folded his arms for emphasis. Story couldn't argue like his sister. To her credit Glory would defend Story's interest as her own—that is unless his interest conflicted with hers. Toward Story her motto was, "You first . . . after me!"

6

Joey gave his mother a quick glance. Even though the odds were the same as winning the lottery he hoped she might stand up for him here. The thought of taking the little, middle room while his little brother and sister got the big rooms made his blood boil.

It wasn't really about the room. It was about how he was always expected to give in to them. If he went somewhere they had to come along. If there were only two cookies left they got them. They didn't seem to think about him getting none. Or maybe they did—Glory sometimes grinned at him at times like that. He had learned that justice in the family was arbitrary.

His mother didn't appear to be listening. Her eyes wandered around the old, rather bare-looking kitchen as she ate her spaghetti. It was the mushy kind from a can. The empty cans were still sitting on the counter next to the massive, old stove.

Feeling more cantankerous than courageous, Joey said, "I'll take whatever room I want." This was unexpected. Glory and Story stopped chewing and stared at him. Glory pulled herself together and went into action.

"Mom!" Glory said, in that sharp way of hers. That was all she said. Just one word, but it was her shot across the bow. She had given warning and waited to see the response. Giving in to her was so much easier than fighting her. She knew this and so did everyone else. If she didn't like the response she would start in on one of two strategies—extreme annoyance based on reason (I called it first!) or extreme annoyance based on sheer defiance (It's my room and he can't have it!).

Mrs. Johanaby's tired eyes came to rest on Glory, then Story, and finally on Joey. She pushed her chair back and got up. For one fearful moment Joey thought she was just going to walk away and leave him and the twins to it. But then she said, "Follow me everybody." There was a tired smile in her voice.

Leaving the mushy spaghetti in red sauce, they pushed away from the table and hurried to catch up with their mother. They caught up with her in the hallway and followed her up the stairs. She walked past the bedrooms in question to the end of the hallway and stopped at the fifth door. This was a mystery door. The kids had tried to open it earlier. They found it locked and the door solid.

Mrs. Johanaby produced a key—an old-fashioned one that had an ornate ring at one end. She worked at the lock until it sprung with a "click." The door opened noiselessly to reveal a very narrow stairway that led up sharply into total darkness.

"Whoa," said Story. He stepped closer to his Mom.

"Where does it go?" asked Glory. She nervously pulled at her bottom lip with a finger as she peered doubtfully up into the darkness.

Mrs. Johanaby looked at Joey and smiled. She raised her eyebrows as if to say "isn't this exciting."

"Follow me," she said as she disappeared into the darkness.

Glory and Story didn't move. They just stood staring. Joey was inclined to stay with them.

His Mom called down, "Joey, you will want to see this."

Joey put his hand on the wall for support and started up. He was halfway up when a light turned on making the rest of the steps easy.

"We'll have to get a switch or something at the bottom of the stairs," his mother said from somewhere up above.

At the top of the stairs Joey stepped into the happiest room in the house. It was the attic, but an attic made to live in. It was a large square space with a ceiling that was high in the middle, but sloped gently on all four sides. There was an old eight-paned window in the center of each wall. The windows were open. A sluggish evening breeze disturbed the hot air in the attic only slightly.

Unlike the depressing blue of the rest of the house the walls were painted in a kind of gold. The floorboards had been painted brown. A bare bulb hanging from the middle of the ceiling lit the room.

Joey stopped in the doorway, his mouth open. Glory and Story pushed by him.

"Out of the way, bro," Glory said. She took two steps before she suddenly stopped. "Whoa."

The room was empty except for a brass bed sitting right in the middle. And unlike the other beds in the house, which were still bare this one was made up with sheets and a quilt. At one end there was a pillow that looked inviting. Mrs. Johanaby stood on the other side of the bed smiling at Joey.

"This is the attic?" Joey asked.

"Well, it should be," said Mrs. Johanaby, thoughtfully.

"But where's all the stuff?" asked Glory. "Attics are always full of stuff."

Story took off and did a lap around the bed. "We could play up here," he said.

"No," said Mrs. Johanaby. "This isn't a play room; this is Joey's bedroom—that is, if he wants it."

"Not fair!" yelled Glory.

"What's not fair?" asked Mrs. Johanaby

"Well, that he gets this room," Glory said, less certain of herself.

"We need it to play in," Story said, turning from the window he was peering out of.

"Nope," Mrs. Johanaby said. "This is Joey's room. Right Joey?"

Joey walked to the window Story was at. He looked down at the tops of the oak trees in the front yard. He could see the pickup and trailer through the limbs. Lights of a lone car on the old highway made a bubble of light as it drove past their lane. On the other side of the highway, beyond the woods, he could see the dying glow of a sun long set. He turned and gazed again at the happy bed in the middle of this golden room. "Yes, Mom. It's perfect."

Joey ran downstairs to the living room and began hauling his things to his new room. He had a suitcase of clothes, a box of books, a telescope, model airplanes and ships with gluey fingerprints, and a model rocket that really flew.

His mother helped him bring up the chest of drawers from the little bedroom. Next they brought up a coffee table from the parlor that would serve as a desk if he sat on the floor.

"I'll get you a pillow to sit on," Mrs. Johanaby said.

After they had finished they both stood admiring the arrangement.

"This is so cool, Mom!" he said and put his head against her chest and hugged her tight.

"It is, isn't it," she said. "I'm glad it's working out this way. You've been trying so hard with Dad gone and all—you deserve it." She tousled his hair.

"Where did you find the bed?" he asked. The brass was shiny and the springs were firm. It was a great bed.

"It's kind of funny," she said. She backed away from the bed a few steps for space to tell her story. "When I was making supper the house keys were sitting on the counter. This old key was sticking out from the rest. I hadn't noticed it before. It occurred to me that it might be the one to the locked door at the end of the hall. So I took the keys," she was pantomiming now. Mrs. Johanaby, when she was happy, would speak with her whole body. "And I went upstairs. I put the key in the lock . . ." Mrs. Johanaby showed him just how she did it, "and it didn't go in. That made me mad." She pursed her lips. "But then I wiggled it and it went in. I opened the door. It was so quiet. Did you notice how quiet the door is?" she asked. She waited for Joey to respond. He nodded. "Then I came up the stairs and there it was." She spread her arms in front of her.

"My bed?" Joey laughed. This was the most playful his mother had been since his dad had died.

"Yes, right there." She lifted her hand and poked her finger at the bed.

"You mean, right here?" Joey said, patting the bed.

"Sitting right there as if it were waiting for you. It wasn't even dusty."

Goose pimples ran up his arms in spite of the heat of the room. He remembered the way he had felt that morning when they had first pulled up to the house. It was as if the house had recognized him. The feeling had gone away. Now his Mom had said the bed had been put here for him? Well, she hadn't said exactly that, but there was something strange about this house.

"It's way old," Mrs. Johanaby said, referring to the house. "But I feel there is something good about this place. I think things will get better here." She said the words so confidently that Joey's goose pimples slowly sank back into his arms.

"Yeah, Mom, I think you're right."

Later that night the moon rose. It was nearly full, just one day more. The house and grounds were lit with bright, soft light. The windowpane pattern crept across the attic floor. Eventually it rested on the foot of Joey's bed. The pattern disappeared as a cloud rolled in front of the moon. More clouds came. A breeze picked up and danced softly through Joey's open windows. In his sleep Joey sighed at the relief the breeze brought.

Lightning flashed a long way away. Thunder followed rolling softly along the horizon. The lightning drew nearer with the thunder in tow. While the thunder grew louder it never grew sharp, but instead purred like a giant cat.

The breeze, the flashes, the rolling rumble gently roused Joey from sleep. It was that other sound that woke him entirely—something in the thunder, or was it in the breeze—chimes. They tinkled softly. It was a pleasant sound. Joey opened his eyes unafraid, but curious. He sat up in bed and listened more closely. He heard a large drop of rain plunk against the west window. Joey got up to close it a ways. As he slid the window down lightening flashed. As clearly as pen on paper he saw the words on an upper pane, "Welcome Joey."

He sucked in a breath and stepped back. It had been written with a finger in the dust on the window. The letters were rounded and pretty, like how his mother wrote. Of course, his Mom had written the message. Joey's fright changed to pleasure. He didn't notice that the words were written backwards on the outside of the window.

Joey smiled as he lowered the other three windows and went back to his bed. He closed his eyes and listened to the erratic patter of the rain. Soon it made a steady drumming that lulled him to sleep. In just a moment the dust on the outside of the window was washed away and with it the welcoming words.

Chapter 2

The sun shone brightly through Joey's east window. He opened his eyes to the dazzling goldenness of his room. He squinted in the brightness. It filled him with happiness. For just a moment he felt a perfect peace—like nothing had ever gone wrong in his life. Then, he remembered. His father had died. His mother had been laid off. They had been forced to move. Inside him the golden color slowly faded to grey. When he sat up and looked around his room the colors started to glow again. He had a golden room in the attic with a brass bed in the middle and a window in each wall.

Joey slipped out of bed and looked through the south window. Outside stood a large, weeping willow tree. The tree filled the entire view with branches dangling long, leafy, willowy whips toward the ground far below. The branches reached toward his window, but stopped too far away to touch. If he stood on the windowsill and leaped he was pretty sure he could grab the ropy willows and swing like Tarzan then slide to the ground. Something told him that trying that would probably be a bad idea.

Down through the limbs of the tree Joey could make out a low building that sat on the other side of the driveway. Mrs. Johanaby had said it was the garage. Joey wondered why it sat on the other side of the driveway instead of at the end of it. Joey heard a door shut followed by the soft, but incredibly clear, tones of a wind chime. The sound of the door came from the garage, but the chimes—were they up in the tree or coming from the front porch? He couldn't tell. Their gentle sound carried softly on the morning air like a downy feather. Hadn't he heard these chimes last night?

Joey noticed movement down below. Briefly, through the limbs, he saw a figure. A balding man walked beside the garage. Just before turning behind the garage the man stopped and looked over his shoulder. He looked up through the limbs into Joey's eyes. Frightened, Joey backed away from the window.

"Who was that?" Joey thought he should tell his mom. Needing to use the bathroom Joey hurriedly pulled on his clothes. Before he went to the stairs he opened each window. It was going to be a warm day. At the west window he remembered the message written there last night. He looked for it as he pulled the window up. It wasn't there. Stepping back Joey stared hard from one angle then another trying to get the light right so he could see the words. They were gone. "How . . . ," he thought. Had it just been a dream? No, he was sure the words had been there. A shiver ran through him. He quickly made his bed and ran down the stairs.

After using the bathroom he looked in Glory's room. It was just as he thought. He found the twins asleep in Glory's bed. Glory was sleeping on her side, her arm around a doll pulled tightly to her cheek. Story slept on his back, mouth open with his hands behind his head. He had kicked the covers off like usual. They were cute when they were asleep. He left them and went downstairs.

His mother was in the kitchen stirring a pot of Cream of Wheat on the stove. She was in her pajamas—cut off sweat pants and a loose t-shirt advertising a long-ago country music festival.

"Hey, Joey," she said. "I see you survived the storm. Did it wake you up? Were you afraid?"

"There's something—" he thought for a moment wondering which story to tell. Then he decided. "There's something not scary about that room," he said.

His mother gave him a long, considering glance as she turned off the stove. She nodded. "Yes," she said. "It's a happy room." She took the pot of hot cereal to the table.

"Why is it happy?" Joey asked.

"The paint color, the windows, the brass bed," she said, hunting for the brown sugar. "I think it's called Feng Shui."

"I think it's something more than the paint," Joey said, thoughtfully. He wanted to talk about it more, but Mrs. Johanaby's mind was elsewhere.

"Get the bowls, okay? I think they're in that box over there." She pointed with her elbow. "Then go get the kids before this gets cold and gunky."

Joey was setting the bowls on the table when Glory and Story dragged into the kitchen. Glory's shoulder length hair was all a tangle. It reminded Joey of the Greek Medusa he had seen in a book with writhing hissing snakes coming out of her head. She held the doll tight to her chest. There was sleep in Story's eyes. He had bed hair, too.

"It's the Dynamic Duo," Mrs. Johanaby said. Glory and Story stood in sleepy silence. "Have you used the bathroom yet?"

Joey rolled his eyes. They were eight and shouldn't have to be reminded to use the bathroom. Glory shoved her doll into Joey's hands.

"Hold her," she said. She turned to run toward the kitchen door. She stopped and looked over her shoulder. "Nicely!" she ordered when she saw Joey holding the doll at his side by one leg.

Joey wanted to throw the doll at her. He didn't. Story ran out of the kitchen after his sister in a race to get to the bathroom first. Joey heard a scuffle on the stairs, an exchange of complaints, then running footsteps down the hallway.

At breakfast Mrs. Johanaby delighted them all by bringing out a bag of gummi bears to put in their cream of wheat. If the cream of wheat was hot enough the gummi bears would melt and make multi-colored polka dots in the cereal. Mr. Johanaby had started the gummi bears tradition when he heard the kids complaints that hot cereal was gross. The gummi bears brought Joey mixed feelings of delight and sadness.

Glory and Story cleaned their bowls and got up to leave. "Let's go explore outside," Glory said.

"Beat you there," Story yelled. He bolted for the door.

"First you have to take your bowls to the sink," Joey said.

They both stopped. "You're not our boss," Glory said. "Right, Mom?"

"You know he's right," Mrs. Johanaby said. "And after you take your bowls to the sink I want you to go to the library and sit on the couch. I need to talk to you all together," she added.

"Aw," Story said. "We wanted to go outside."

Glory stuck her tongue out at Joey as she passed. She somehow communicated superiority and dominance when she did that. Joey hated her tongue.

The library wasn't a big room but the walls had built-in shelves that were filled with old books. There were fat books, skinny books, tall books, short books, red books, yellow books, and lots of brown books. Although the books were pretty, the kids weren't interested in them. There didn't seem to be a kids' section. Joey noticed a long series of books each with letters of the alphabet on them in perfect order—the *Encyclopedia Britannica*. They were old. Some of the spines were cracked. Mrs. Johanaby liked the room. Joey watched as she ran her finger along a row of books as she passed by. She smiled in pleasure.

A lamp, a big reading chair, and a couch sat in the middle of the room. The black leather couch was big. It looked like it weighed more than an elephant. It had big sloping arm rests the kids tried to slide down.

"Stop it," said Joey. "This is a library, not a playground. And you might break the couch."

The twins laughed. They were about to climb up again when their mother gave them the evil eye.

"Everyone sit on the couch properly," she said.

Joey sat down on one end of the couch. Trying her mother's patience Glory did a somersault over the arm of the couch onto Joey before scooting to the other end. Story followed Glory landing on his back on Joey's lap. He laid there for a moment grinning up at Joey.

"Hi! Just dropping in," he said.

Joey grinned in spite of his annoyance. Glory patted the space next to her and Story scooted over.

Mrs. Johanaby sat in the chair across from them.

"Well, how are you going to like living here?" she asked.

"It's gonna be great," said Glory.

"Yeah, love it!" agreed Story.

Joey shrugged. His Dad wasn't here so how could he like it? When he thought about his room a warm feeling betrayed him.

"Well, I think we are going to do all right here," Mrs. Johanaby said. "We've got plenty of room inside and almost too much room outside. You kids shouldn't get bored all summer."

"We'll never get bored here," said Glory.

Joey didn't believe it for a moment. She could get bored at Disneyland. She could make you miserable when she was bored.

"No, this is better than Heaven!" Story said. "We won't ever get bored." Both Mrs. Johanaby and Joey gave Story a long look.

"NO! It's not," Joey said. Heaven was where Dad was. Dad wasn't here. This wasn't Heaven.

"It's okay, Joey," Mrs. Johanaby said. In her eyes Joey saw, *"He's only eight."*

Mrs. Johanaby cleared her throat. Joey could tell this was going to be official. "As you know with your father gone I need a job."

Joey and the twins stared and said nothing. They always did this when she brought up the loss of their father.

"Well, I have the possibility of a good job, but I have to pass this course on medical transcribing first."

"Medical what?" asked Glory

"Writing boring stuff," said Joey. His mother had told him a little about this already.

"Well, yes," said Mrs. Johanaby. But if I work hard I can get certified by the end of the summer and we'll be on our way," she said, happily.

"*Well,*" Joey said, mimicking his mom's overuse of the word. "On our way to where?" He was feeling mean suddenly.

Mrs. Johanaby meant getting back on their feet after the loss of Mr. Johanaby. Joey knew that. He knew she was right. His mother was strong. Joey knew she missed his dad, but was learning to move on without him. Even though he knew this was right and good he still had to fight feelings of rebellion at the idea of moving on without his dad.

Mrs. Johanaby set her jaw and looked at him. She said nothing. Story, feeling the tension did the only thing he knew how—he whacked Glory in the head with the couch pillow.

"Stop it," Glory said, slapping his arm with each word.

"I'm going to need total concentration to do this," Mrs. Johanaby said sharply. "I need a system to look after you kids. There is so much room in this house and too much room outside. I won't be able to keep track of you."

I know!" cried Glory. "We could each carry a walky-talky like the FBI and check in with you every fifteen minutes, Mom."

"We would each have to have a watch, too," added Story, liking the idea very much. They both bounced up and down on the couch making dust rise.

"Hey, that's a great idea," said Mrs. Johanaby, "but you know what? I think instead we are going to use a system that has been in use for thousands of years. It's called Big Brother."

"Big Brother? What's that?" asked Glory dubiously. She raised one eyebrow glancing unhappily at Joey.

"It's Joey," said their mother.

"Joey?" Glory and Story spoke in unison.

"Ohhhh," said Story hitting himself on the head with the pillow. Glory just glared at him.

"Yes, Joey," their mother answered. "He's twelve-years-old and a very responsible young man. During the day while I'm studying he is going to be chief."

"What does that mean?" asked Glory, looking suspicious.

"It means when I'm not around you have to obey him like you obey me."

Glory's mouth dropped open. Story hit himself in the head with the pillow again. As for Joey, his stomach dropped. His Mom had always taken care of Glory and Story. He didn't get along with them very well, especially Glory. Mrs. Johanaby had always been a buffer between them. Now she wanted him to take her place? Just like that?

Glory was staring hard at Joey in a way that scared him a little. She looked like a rattlesnake about to strike.

"*We* don't *need* him," she said, dangerously. She spoke to Mrs. Johanaby; she looked at Joey.

"Oh yes, you do," said Mrs. Johanaby decisively.

"Now you two run along outside and play while I speak with Joey."

The twins were gone in a flash. Their feet sounded in the hall followed by the slam of the screen door on the back porch. Silence took the twin's place.

Joey remained on the couch. His mother sat in the chair. Joey laid his hands in his lap. His mother crossed her legs. They looked at each other feeling awkward.

Joey's mother was pretty. Joey couldn't imagine a prettier mom in the world. Her long, dark hair was held back behind her head with a barrette. A strand of hair escaped the barrette and fell down along her face. Her dark-brown eyes reminded Joey of root beer. Her mouth was big. He liked her mouth. Dirk, one of his friends from his old neighborhood, told Joey that his mother's mouth was too big. Joey had slugged him and given him a fat lip. Dirk had slugged Joey back and given him a bloody nose. Slugging Dirk was the only brave thing Joey had ever done in his life.

"But I do have a big mouth," his mother had said when she was helping Joey wash the blood from his face. "When I was a kid my classmates use to call me Molly the Mouth."

"Didn't that make you feel bad?" asked Joey.

"I used to go home, throw myself across my bed and cry. Then I would look in the mirror and make my lips do this," she said pursing her lips, "so that my mouth would look smaller."

Joey laughed at the funny face she made.

"My Dad, your Grandpa Mulligan, asked why I thought my mouth was too big when maybe all my friends' mouths were too small? 'Think about it,'" she said, in a deep voice, imitating Grandpa Mulligan. "'You are more highly evolved than your friends. You can put more food in your mouth at one time. You can yell louder. It's easier for you to brush your teeth. Most importantly, nobody can smile as big. You just wait,'" he told me. "'That smile of yours will get you places that your friends will only dream about.' Ever since then I've been proud of my mouth. Grandpa was right—all the girls were in love with your father, but he chose me. He said my smile outshined them all."

Mrs. Johanaby smiled at Joey now. It was a big smile and made him feel good.

"So, what do you think? Do you want the job?" she asked.

"No," Joey answered.

"I need you, Joey," she said. "The family needs you. It may not be fair asking you to do this, but there it is."

"They don't listen to me," Joey said. "And Glory, she makes me so mad."

"They'll learn. You'll find a way." The smile on his mother's face faded and she got a far-away look in her eye. "You know as well as I do that ever since your father died it's been hard. Not having any money, losing our home . . ."

Joey saw his mom swallow. He swallowed too. It was a way to keep from crying that worked for both of them.

"But now I have this opportunity and we inherited this old house. It makes me wonder if your father's on the other side pulling strings for us."

"You think so?" Joey asked. He liked that thought.

His mother smiled again. "I think so, Joey," she said. "Anyway, we have a chance to pull our world together, and we have to make the most of it."

Joey felt proud with his mother talking to him like a grown up. Then he felt uncomfortable, because he wasn't a grownup. He was a kid.

Her face became serious. "I need to be honest with you, Joey. This job scares me a little bit. I'm not real good with computers and this whole course I'm taking is on-line. It's going to be hard for me. I need to concentrate. That's why your job of looking after your brother and sister is so important. If I have to worry about them getting hurt or in trouble I'll never get anything done."

"I'll take care of them," Joey said, resigning himself to the unpleasant task.

Mrs. Johanaby was silent a moment. Then she said, "I knew I could count on you."

Joey blushed.

Mrs. Johanaby went on. "Now the rules are that they are to be ready for meals at seven a.m., twelve noon, and six in the evening. They need to wash their hands before they eat. They need to rinse their plates when they're through. They are to play outside most of the day. If they play inside, they have to play quietly. They are not to climb trees, play near water, or cross the highway. Bedtime is eight o'clock and lights out at eight-fifteen."

"For me too?" asked Joey.

His mother thought a moment and then said, "For you lights out is at nine."

Joey smiled. He hesitated a moment and asked, "What happens if they don't obey me?"

"If they are being ornery and won't do what they're supposed to, you just tell me and they'll lose their dessert or some other privilege, okay?"

"Okay," Joey answered. He was skeptical about how well this was going to work out.

"You start immediately," said his mother.

Joey stood up and headed for the door.

"Joey," she said. He stopped and turned around.

"Come here." She stood and hugged him. She smelled like cinnamon. "I love you," she said.

"I love you, too," he answered. Reluctantly he left the comfort of his mother and went to find the twins.

Chapter 3

Joey couldn't help feeling a little excited as he stepped outside. He knew he had plenty of reasons not to. His father was still gone. The responsibility of looking after Glory and Story would lead to trouble. He was spending the summer, maybe the rest of his life, in an old house in a new place where he didn't know anyone. On the other hand Mrs. Johanaby's pep talk on a new life here sparked a small hope in him that things might get better. In the golden sunlight the colors of the world danced brightly. The leaves of the trees were a cool green, the dirt driveway was rusty brown, and the sky was turquoise.

Amid all this color there was only one problem—Joey didn't see the twins anywhere. He started around the house looking for them. He felt good and broke into a run. The morning air was cool against his face and rushed past his ears. He ran around the house three times before he tired and stopped. With hands on his knees he sucked in deep breaths of sweet air.

Out of the corner of his eye he saw movement. He looked up. Through the warped and dusty panes of the library window he saw his mother setting up her computer. It was an old computer that still had a floppy disk drive. A neighbor had given it to them before they moved. Mrs. Johanaby said it was something to be thankful for, not complain about. Joey smiled and waved at her and she waved back. Her voice muffled by the glass, he heard her ask, "Where are the twins?"

In all his running around he had forgotten who he was looking for. He took off running again, this time keeping a sharp lookout for the dynamic duo. The yard around the house was empty. They couldn't have climbed the oak trees because the lowest branches grew too high from the ground. An old weeping willow billowed high against the sky in the backyard. Its whip-like limbs cascaded down from the top of the tree like water from a fountain. Lower branches close to the ground made this tree easy to climb.

Standing next to the trunk he looked into the waterfall of yellow limbs and narrow grey-green leaves. It was a perfect climbing tree. There was nobody up there. He wanted to climb it right then, but he remembered his mother's rule about climbing trees. He wondered if that meant him too.

Leaving the tree, but not forgetting it, he walked across the backyard. Next to the screened back porch two, big, wooden doors lay on a slant covering the entrance to a cellar. He pulled on one. It wasn't locked, but it was heavy. Pulling hard and adding his own grunts to the groaning and creaking of the door, he opened it.

A wet, musty smell licked his nose. Crumbly brick stairs led down into blackness. Goose bumps, which were getting quite familiar by now, ran up his arms like ants. He knew he was never going down those steps. He let the door slam shut. The twins were too little to get those doors open. They wouldn't be down there.

East of the house was a rusty wire fence held up by rotting wood posts that tilted different directions. A field of tall grass and weeds grew on the other side. Beyond the field grew thick green woods. They could have gone out there.

Joey started walking toward the fence when he thought of the garage. Joey stopped suddenly when he remembered the man who had come out of the garage that morning. He hadn't told his mother as he had planned. Joey fought an urge to run straight to his mom.

"Get a hold of yourself," he mumbled. Taking a big, shaky breath he started for the garage. As he neared it he heard a BANG that made him jump. Frightened, Joey turned to run back to the house to get Mrs. Johanaby. He stopped when he heard giggling. It was the twins. They didn't sound like they were in danger.

Curious, but cautious, Joey walked to the big sliding doors in the front of the garage. They were open a crack—just enough for two skinny twins to slip inside. There were windows on the doors but they were too high to see through.

Joey heard another BANG followed by the excited laughter of Glory and Story. He pulled on the door and it slid further open with a horrible grating sound. The interior lay in deep shadow. He could hardly see a thing. Grimy windows on both sides of the garage let in dirty, gray light.

"Glory! Story!" he called. There was no answer—not a sound. The heavy smell of grease and oil hung in the air. He could almost taste them. As his eyes adjusted to the dimness he saw a large room with piles of stuff. He could make out an engine block hanging from a chain connected to the rafters. There was no sign of the vehicle it belonged to. Boxes of engine parts perched on a bench nearby. An old riding lawn mower missing its wheels sat forlornly on its belly. Four or five bicycles lay in a pile—petals and rusty spokes tangled.

The garage reminded him of his dad. Mr. Johanaby had taken the engine of their old pickup truck apart in their little garage back in Oakley, Idaho. He "rebuilt" it hoping to make it run better. It didn't run better but Joey had a good time helping his dad.

Some scuffling on the other side of a big pile of junk caught his attention. "Glory! Story!" he yelled again. "I know you're in here."

The scuffling stopped. There was no answer. Joey stepped into the garage and walked slowly between the piles of greasy parts. He almost tripped over the frame of a large motorcycle. The stuffing in the seat was pushing out through holes in the leather like filling does from a jelly-filled donut when you bite it. A chain from another motorcycle lay across the oil-blackened floor like a snake.

On his right was a stack of old crates, one of them filled with used spark plugs. Sitting on shelves on the wall were messy cans of paint and other things that looked sticky and smelly. Mayonnaise jars full of nuts, bolts, and nails appeared to be floating in the air just below the shelves. Joey knew they weren't floating. The lids of the jars had been nailed into the bottom of the shelves and the jars screwed back into them. His father had done this in their garage.

"Keeps the jars from getting knocked off the workbench and breaking," he had said.

An old mattress leaned against two wooden beams. Holding up the mattress were cardboard boxes full of yellowed newspapers. There was no sign of the twins. He felt the old annoyance rising in him. The twins were in here and they shouldn't be. It wasn't his fault, but somehow Glory was going to pin it on him. When there was a question of blame she always won. Always.

"Glory!" he called. "I see you so you might as well come on out. Don't make me come over and get you." Silence. Glory had called his bluff.

At the back of the garage was a heavy, wooden workbench. Odds and ends lay scattered across it. One item was a metal box covered with buttons, switches, and dials. It was old and the glass on the dials was smashed. Still, it was cool looking. He forgot the twins for a moment as he reached up and pulled it off the workbench to study it. It was heavy. There was a red button on the front of it. He pushed it.

BANG!

Joey dropped the gizmo and leaped back. He whirled around to see the twins standing beside the mattress they had been hiding behind. The remains of a popped balloon lay on the floor.

"We scared you. We scared you," sang Glory through her laughter.

"You almost hit the roof!" laughed Story.

They *had* scared him and, worse, they could see it. He hated them.

"What are you doing in here?" he asked.

"What are *you* doing here?" asked Glory.

"I'm looking for you," answered Joey. "I don't think you should be in here."

"You are not the boss," said Glory.

"I am too," Joey said. "You heard Mom."

Glory stuck out her tongue. Story was struggling to blow up a balloon. His cheeks bulged, his face red.

"Where did you get the balloons?" Joey asked.

"Found'em," Glory said. She pulled a balloon out of a torn plastic bag and started blowing it up. Story already had his going, but Glory quickly caught up.

"Now pop it," said Glory with a sinister giggle. Story pushed a nail against his balloon. It didn't pop. Instead it fizzled and hissed as air escaped.

"Ahh," Story said, disappointed.

"Here, let me," Glory said, taking the nail. Her balloon popped with a satisfying bang. She squealed with delight.

"I'm getting a headache," said Story, putting his hands to his head.

"At least you are scaring the rats away," said Joey.

"Rats?" asked Glory, looking around her nervously.

"Sure. There are always rats in dark old places like this," Joey said.

"There's no rats," said Glory still looking around her.

"Sure there are. See where the stuffing is coming out of the motorcycle seat. That's where rats have been getting stuffing for their nests."

"Oh," Glory said. She walked over to Joey and took his hand. She was scared now. "Let's go," she said, pulling on his hand. For a moment Joey felt the joy of victory. It was quickly replaced by guilt. When she wasn't being bossy and mean, she could be almost sweet.

"I'll get them," Story said. He went over to the motorcycle frame and took a swing at the seat with a broken shovel handle he'd found. Dust and stuffing swirled up into the rays of sunshine coming in through the open door. "Ha Haaa!" Story said, making his voice husky. "You don't stand a chance against my power." He took another whack.

"Hey, let me!" Glory let go of Joey's hand, forgetting all about rats. She tried to take the shovel handle away from Story. He resisted. A tug-o-war ensued with them both complaining that they had it first.

It was then that Joey noticed the door in the back wall of the garage. Leaving the twins to their battle he walked over and turned the handle. The door opened noiselessly. Joey found himself staring with wonder. The room was bright and colorful and clean.

It was lit by sunlight streaming through three large picture windows on the other side of the room. Through them Joey could see the long grass of the field and the woods beyond. Then Joey saw what was in the room.

"Oh, wow," he whispered.

On tables and shelves lining the large room were models of ships and planes and rockets and trains. These weren't the plastic kind of models that Joey put together, but models made of wood and steel. In the corner was a rocket that stood higher than Joey. It was the kind of rocket that shot high into the air, higher than any of his rockets. It had been carefully painted and had official numbers on the side. Hanging from the ceiling were several models, put together and painted with the same care as the big rocket. Joey's models always ended up with glue smears on the plastic, cracks between the parts, and decals that were crooked.

There was a B-29 flying super fortress with its long wings and four powerful engines. Flying escort around it was a sleek P-51 Mustang; a powerful P-48 Thunderbolt; and a twin tailed, twin engine P-38 Lightening. Joey could almost hear the drone of their engines and the sounds of their voices over radios as they sighted, "Bandits! 12 O'clock high."

In the corner near the door was a gigantic balsa wood model of a Cessna 172. The wings and body were covered with thin paper. Joey could see each of the pieces of balsa wood that had been carefully cut out and glued together.

On top of a low table sat a British Man O' War. It was almost two feet long. Rows of cannons stuck out of little square hatches on the side of the ship. Sails were secured to tall masts. Strings representing ropes went every which way. On the deck were figurines of sailors. One was climbing the rigging and others were scrubbing the deck. On the poop deck the captain was talking to the First Mate. The helmsman was at the helm and the lookout was in the crows' nest. The lookout was pointing to a model pirate ship on the other side of the table. It was elaborate like the Man O' War. Instead of the Union Jack, it flew the ominous skull and cross bones on black. It wasn't nearly as well armed as the Man O' War, but was sailing boldly toward it anyway.

Joey smiled. Pirates weren't afraid of anything.

Suddenly the twins were pushing by him into the room.

"What is it?" said Glory with a shove.

"Whoa!" said Story, his arms hanging limply at his side as he slowly scanned the room. Glory, too, stopped with her mouth hanging open.

"Don't go any far—" Joey started to say. The twins scampered in before he could finish the sentence.

Glory found a switch and clicked it. A perfectly miniaturized train whistled, and began its journey across a highly detailed countryside. It was on a large table that took up almost a quarter of the room. There were miniature hills and trees, a lake with real water, roads with tiny cars, telegraph poles and wires, and a complete city with school, church, stores, houses, water tower, train station, and many other things.

"Wow!" Joey said.

"Isn't it neat," said Glory. Story rested his chin on the table on the other side and followed the train with bright eyes as it rolled past.

"Yoyo!" Glory yelled.

Joey turned to see Glory picking up a bright yellow yoyo off the arm of a couch that sat in front of the window. She put it on her pointing finger and gave it a whirl. The yellow yoyo spun down to the end of the string and hit the floor—the string was longer that Glory was tall.

"Dang!" she giggled.

"On Guard! Story said.

Joey turned to see Story confronting him with a detailed wooden sword. The curved, blunted blade was polished and shiny. Story danced forward a couple of steps like the sword fighters he had seen in old movies and poked at Joey.

"Hey," Joey said. He backed away from Story until he bumped into a shelf. He felt the shelf rock unsteadily. Before he could turn to steady it a replica musket fell into his out-stretched hand. He stared in surprise at the pistol. Doing the only natural thing he pointed it at Story and said, "Bang!"

Story had stopped in surprise at the sudden appearance of the pistol. Not one to miss an acting opportunity he quickly moved into his death routine. He groaned loudly, stuck his tongue out the corner of his mouth, spun around once and fell onto his back, dead.

Joey laughed. He felt the happiest he had been since his father's death. The bright room filled with wonderful things, Glory's concentrating on winding that long string back around the yoyo, Story playing dead at his feet—it was all so good.

The happiness Joey felt faded suddenly when Joey remembered the man coming out of the garage that morning.

"Guys, we have to get out of here," he said, with sudden urgency.

"You are such a pooper party," Glory said frowning at him.

"Party pooper," Story corrected, sitting up.

"I like 'pooper party' better," Glory said, making progress with the yoyo.

"No, I mean it." Joey said. "I saw a man coming out of here this morning. This must be his room."

"You mean him," Glory said. With a tilt of her head she indicated a man standing in the doorway. She continued winding the yoyo for a second more, then stopped, looked at the man, and screamed.

Her high, piercing scream would have hurt a dog's ears. Joey's heart thumped wildly. It was the man who had looked at him this morning. Story scrambled to his feet and squeezed between Joey and the shelf. Glory's scream stopped as she ran out of breath. As she prepared to scream again the man, who had put his hands to his ears and was grimacing in pain said, "Please don't."

His words distracted Glory and she stood silently with her mouth open. The moment to scream now gone, Glory turned and whispered loudly, "Joey!" She squeezed in with Story behind her big brother. The shelf rocked again and a little plastic figure sailed down in front of them on a parachute. They all looked up half expecting to see a tiny plane flying by. There was only the ceiling.

The man brought his hands down from his ears. "Thank you," he said. "You better be careful over there. An elephant might drop on you."

In unison Joey, Glory and Story took one step away from the shelf. It seemed in that room it could happen. The man's voice was strong and soft at the same time. It had earnestness to it like when someone is telling you a secret. The man was very short, not much taller than Joey. He had a soft, round face. He wore round glasses with thick, Coke bottle lenses that doubled the size of his hazel eyes. His glasses flashed as they reflected the light from the window. The kids couldn't decide whether to cry or to laugh.

"Now, what you young'uns doing in here?" he asked.

Nobody answered.

"Come on now. Speak up!" He made a strange sight with his clean blue overalls rolled up at the ankle, his hands on his hips, a band of graying hair around the back of his head. His big eyes darted from one child to another. "Am I going to have to hang you up by your feet until the blood runs out your ears?"

"We were just exploring," squeaked Glory.

"And you just happened to choose my dream room, huh? How did you find it anyway?" His eyes narrowed and he lowered his voice. "Did someone give you a *map*?" He said 'map' as if it were a powerful word.

"We were just exploring the garage when we found this door," said Story, taking courage from Glory.

The man cut him off, "You were exploring the garage?" He stepped forward and waved his arms. "Don't you know that's dangerous! There's rats in there with big teeth." He put two fingers up by his mouth to illustrate. "And the bats. Ohhhh, the bats. They're so big they'll take you out and hit you back and forth like a volley ball to warm you up before drinking your blood for dinner." As he was saying this something small and black flew into the room through the open doorway. Glory, whose courage didn't extend to bats, screamed again.

The man threw his arms over his head and dived to the floor. Joey and the twins did the same. Joey was the first to dare peek. He saw it was just a little sparrow trying to get through the window.

"It's just a sparrow," he said, as he sat up on his knees. "See." He pulled Glory's hands away from her face. He had to do this twice before she would look. Story looked from between his fingers.

"Gee whiz. You scared me!" said the man as he got up off the floor. Joey thought his face was a little red. "Actually, that is not a sparrow, but a dark eyed junco." He cleared his throat trying to get his dignity back. Walking to the door he whistled twice and pointed out the door. The bird turned from the window and flew out. "Windows confuse'em so."

"How did you do that," asked Joey.

"What?"

"With the bird?" said Joey.

"Oh, we have an understanding." He walked a few steps farther into the room looking around. "So, what do you think of her," he said with a sweep of his arm. "Isn't she a beaut."

The kids got back to their feet. Glory accidently touched the shelf. She jumped away from it.

The train, which had been dutifully making its rounds about the miniature countryside jumped off its tracks and came to rest in the little pond along side a tiny building that said, "Marlin's Bait Shop."

"Well," said the man. "The Twelve-O-Clock is going to be late today."

"Who are you," asked Glory.

"Who, me?" He cleared his throat importantly. "I'm Beezer," he said. He held out his hand to shake and Glory shook it.

"Well look at that," he said, reaching up and touching her hair near her ear. "Chrysanthemum maximum." He brought the flower down and handed it to her.

"It's a daisy," she said.

"You always carry one of those around with you?"

She shook her head and gently rubbed the flower against her cheek.

"And you," he said looking at Story. "Do you know how to use that thing?" Story still had the sword in his hand. Beezer went to the shelf and picked up another sword just like Story's. "Arrrrr," he growled in pirate brogue. Story grinned and attacked. They sparred back and forth until Beezer gave Story an opening. Story struck home. It was Beezer's turn to die. He rocked forward, then backward holding his stomach. "Arrr, Henrietta, he's killed me. Avenge my death." Then he fell on his back, dead.

Beezer sat up, smiling. Story, completely won over by this stranger, stepped over and hugged him. Joey was uncomfortable with this.

Growing a little more serious as he got up, Beezer said, "Now I know this room doesn't look too dangerous to you, but you'd do well not to come here without me," Beezer said.

"Why's that?" Glory asked, unafraid of Beezer anymore.

"You just never know what's going to happen," Beezer said. "The wrong movement, the wrong word—it could be a disaster." Beezer looked around him as if he were in a pit of snakes.

Glory and Story started laughing. Joey didn't think Beezer was trying to be funny.

"You mean if I stomp my foot—" Glory said,

"—and I yell abracadabra . . ." added Story.

"No, don't!" yelled Beezer, holding out his arm to stop them.

It was too late: Glory's foot came down and Story yelled the magic word at the top of his lungs. With a roar and a flame the four foot tall rocket tipped a little, lifted off the floor, and shot through a window pane with a crash. It continued at an angle up into the sky. It flew higher and higher leaving a white trail of smoke until it eventually disappeared from sight.

"Now you've done it," Beezer exclaimed, his hands on his head.

Glory and Story stood just for a moment with eyes wide and mouths open, then they ran around the table and out the door. Joey started to follow them.

"Just a minute, Joey," Beezer said.

Joey froze.

Beezer, shading his eyes with his hand, stood staring through the window up into the sky. He snorted once, then broke into a rolling laugh. "It gets 'em every time," he said.

Joey was confused. Beezer had just lost a beautiful rocket, there was a hole in his window, and he acted as if it were a joke.

"I'm sorry about the rocket," Joey said, quietly. "We'll find a way to pay for it."

"That'll be difficult the way things are now, won't it?" Beezer asked.

"What do you mean?" Joey asked. What did Beezer know about his family?

"Never mind," Beezer said. "Anyway, the rocket will be back down." He looked closely at Joey and changed the subject.

31

"I thought you might like this." He handed Joey an adjustable brass ring that had the letter 'J' on a round plate in the front. Joey stared at it, his mouth hanging open. His father had given him that ring when he turned nine. He had lost it on a family outing to Emerald Lake in Idaho. He had searched the bank of the lake where they had picnicked but hadn't been able to find it. He thought it was gone forever. He took the ring from Beezer's hand.

"Where—" Joey began.

"I found it by the truck last night. I figured it must be yours."

That just can't be, Joey thought. Joey stared at the ring unable to speak.

Beezer, after a moment's silence, said, "I'm the fix-it man around here. Been with the mansion for a long time. Tell your mother I'll come introduce myself this afternoon, okay?"

Joey slipped the ring on his finger, looked at Beezer, and nodded. "Okay," he said.

"It's your lunch time. You'd better go."

Joey nodded again and walked out the door.

"Try to keep your little brothers and sisters out of my room," He called. "I'd hate for a ship to sail away."

Joey looked over his shoulder and nodded. Short, bald-topped Beezer with the coke bottle glasses stood silhouetted by the sunlit windows behind him. In the mixture of light and shadow Beezer didn't look completely of this world.

Chapter 4

Joey squinted at his watch as he left the darkness of the garage. It was 12:30. Joey let the screen door slam as he ran across the porch and into the kitchen. Mrs. Johanaby was waiting for him. He knew the look on her face. He had seen it a lot since Mr. Johanaby had died. Joey had the nicest mom in the world, but lately his mom could go from happy to angry as quickly as a snap of the fingers.

"Joey Johanaby!" started his mother. "Will you look at your brother and sister. There's grease on their hands, clothes, faces, *and* in their hair. They tell me they've been in a dangerous old garage where there are time bombs, rats, bats, strange rooms, and loony old men. I entrusted you with their safety and I nearly lose them to who knows what, the very first morning. And what time did I tell you to bring them in to lunch?"

"Twelve o'—"

"Twelve o'clock, that's right," interrupted his mother. "And what time is it now?"

"Twelve-thir—"

"Twelve-thirty," his mother said. "I was worried sick. I couldn't see you kids anywhere. I went out and looked but had to rush back in because cheese sandwiches were on the grill. They burned. Well that's just the way we'll have to eat them. Now go clean up, and then hurry back to the table. I should make you all take baths."

Joey didn't just have to listen to his mother, but he had to watch Glory stick her tongue out at him while Story shook his finger at him as if he were Mrs. Johanaby. Sometimes he hated them.

They rushed to the bathroom and washed up. When they finished, the bar of soap was black. Dirty streaks ran down the outside of the sink. The towel lay in a stained heap under the towel rack. Joey was hungry but he knew his Mom would be angry if she found the bathroom like this. He rinsed the bar of soap until it was pink again and scrubbed the sink with a towel until it was clean. He threw the dirty towel in the clothes hamper and ran down the hall to the kitchen. Everyone was sitting around the table waiting when he came in.

"Are you trying to set a new record for late today?" asked his mother.

Joey slid into his chair and mumbled, "I had to clean the sink up."

"What was that?" asked Mrs. Johanaby.

"Nothing. I'm sorry I'm late," Joey answered.

Mrs. Johanaby stared at him, the hardness in her face softening. "You're a good boy, Joey," she said, with a sigh. Then, looking round the table she said, "It's good to have you all here."

Mrs. Johanaby dished up tomato soup while Joey and Story used their spoons to scrape the burned part of the bread off their grilled cheese sandwiches. Glory ate hers the way it was. She liked burned grilled cheese sandwiches. A black ring of buttery, burned bread crumbs formed around her mouth.

"So, are there really rats in that garage?" asked Mrs. Johanaby.

"Well, there could be rats in the garage," said Joey. "I mean, it looks like a place rats would like to live, but I didn't see any."

"What about what Beezer said?" asked Glory.

All the kids were silent at that question. Mrs. Johanaby looked at each of them.

"Who is this Beezer?" she asked.

"He's this man who has a room out in the garage," Joey said.

"You mean they are not making him up?" Mrs. Johanaby looked alarmed.

"I don't think so," said Joey. "I mean, I saw him too." The room and Beezer had been so fantastic that Joey actually wondered if any of it was real. He looked down at his spoon hand and saw the ring Beezer had returned to him. Yes, he must be real.

Mrs. Johanaby followed Joey's eyes and saw the ring. Her mouth dropped open. "Didn't you lose that ring in Idaho?" she asked.

"Beezer found it," Joey said. "He says it was by our truck." Joey could see the same thoughts of disbelief going through his mom's head that went through his own.

"Let me see," she said. Joey held his hand up. Mrs. Johanaby fingered the ring and looked closely. She touched the ring as if it were her husband's face. Suddenly she came back to herself. "Is he still there? Did he threaten you? I'm calling the sheriff!" She started to get up.

"No, Mom!" All three kids spoke at once. Their earnestness stopped her.

"He's okay. And besides, he says he comes with the house," Joey said.

This statement made Mrs. Johanaby think.

"Just a minute," she said.

She left the kitchen and came back with a paper in her hand. "It does say here that there is a caretaker for the mansion. I remember the lawyer telling me now. It's strange because part of the agreement for us to inherit the house is that we can't fire the caretaker or make him move. He must have been pretty special to Aunt Winocha." Mrs. Johanaby sat down pursing her lips in thought. "So you met this caretaker and his name is Beezer. What did this Beezer say about the rats?"

"He said there were rats so big in the garage that one of them could eat all of us and still be hungry," said Glory.

"He said the bats would play games with us," added Story.

"Games?" asked Mrs. Johanaby.

"Volleyball," said Story.

"Oh, volleyball," answered Mrs. Johanaby. Joey could see his mother trying to decide if Beezer were crazy, eccentric, or just full of tease. Joey was still trying to decide that.

"Is it true?" asked Glory.

"Well, I don't think bats know how to play volleyball. Rats can get big and nasty but not that big."

"I knew it!" exclaimed Glory. "Beezer's just an old fart."

"Glory, you don't call anybody that," said Mrs. Johanaby angrily.

"You called Grandpa Johanaby an old fart when he told his fishing stories," said Glory.

"That's . . . that's different," said Mrs. Johanaby.

"How—"

"It just is. Now I don't care if this Beezer does tell stories, don't call him that anymore. Understand?" She gave Glory that look that said 'You better understand!'

Glory nodded reluctantly.

Joey, happy to see his sister getting it from his mom took a big bite of his sandwich and watched the cheese stretch from his mouth back to the plate when he set his sandwich down.

"Maybe Beezer tells stories," said Glory, "but he's real nice." She brought the daisy from her lap and laid it on the table next to her bowl.

"Did he give you that?" asked Mrs. Johanaby.

Glory nodded.

"I wonder where he picked it."

"He found it in my ear."

"In your ear?"

Glory nodded. "He reached into my ear and pulled it out."

"I should look harder when I clean your ears," Mrs. Johanaby said with a smile.

Glory started giggling. Story rolled his eyes. He knew once his twin started giggling she can't stop. True to form Glory giggled until red soup ran out her nose.

"Ugh!" said Story. "That's disgusting." He put his spoon down and said, "I don't want any more soup." This made Glory giggle even more.

"That's fine," said Mrs. Johanaby. "But don't come crying to me when you're hungry. And Glory, keep the soup in your mouth and out of your nose."

It took three minutes of threats from Mrs. Johanaby before Glory could stop giggling.

"Sounds like I need to meet this magic Beezer," Mrs. Johanaby said.

"He seemed to know we moved into the house," said Joey.

"He probably saw us move in," Mrs. Johanaby said. She pressed her finger against a bread crumb on the table and put it in her mouth.

"I mean, he seemed to know it was us before we got here."

Mrs. Johanaby raised an eyebrow quizzically.

"Anyway," Joey said, not knowing how to explain, "he said he would come meet you this afternoon."

"Meet me?" said Mrs. Johanaby. She looked uncomfortable. "Yes, of course we need to meet." She spoke absentmindedly.

"He found my ring," Joey murmured, still wondering how that could be.

The Johanaby children sat on the back steps just outside the screened porch, eating their ice cream cones. Story attacked his from the top, taking big bites and chewing the chocolate chips. Glory bit the bottom out of her cone and sucked her ice cream like it was a milk shake. This was risky. She had to keep up with the melting ice cream from the top and the bottom. Joey simply licked all the way around his cone catching the ice cream as it melted.

Story finished his cone first. He stood up, held out his arms and started spinning around while looking straight up in the sky. He turned tightly at first, and then started to stagger. Finally he tumbled dizzily to the ground.

"Ugh, the world's still spinning," he said lying on his back. "I wonder why that happens after you twirl." He added. "I think I'm going to be sick."

"Mom'll be real mad if you throw up lunch," said Glory. She had ice cream dripping down her chin and running down her arm.

"Hey, what's that?" asked Story. He pointed to the cellar doors. He got up, staggered over, and began tugging on them.

"I wouldn't mess with those," said Joey. "They lead down under the house. It's probably dangerous."

"That's what you said about the garage," answered Story. "Come on Glory. Help me." But even with Glory's help they couldn't lift the door high enough to open it.

Joey finished his ice cream as he watched them try again and again. He would have given up a long time ago; the twins didn't know when to quit. It was clear one or both of them were going to smash some fingers. He would really get it from his mother then. Joey got up and went over to help them open the door. Once they saw how dark it was down there Joey knew they would lose interest.

The door fell open with a bang. Joey noticed Glory's nose twitch at the musty smell..

"Wow," said Glory. "Creepy."

"What do you think is down there?" asked Story.

"Dead bodies," said Glory matter-of-factly.

"Probably more bats," said Story.

"Maybe there are hidden tunnels to hidden doors in the house," Joey said. That was a mistake.

"Cool," said Glory. "Let's go see!"

"What are you, nuts?" said Joey, eyeing the darkness with trepidation.

"Oh, she's nuts all right," said Story, nodding.

"Maybe I am," she said. "But at least I'm not afraid. Come on, Story." She grabbed his hand and took a step.

"Okay," Story said. In spite of his verbal willingness he jerked his hand from hers and stayed where he was.

"You are not going down there," Joey said.

"You going to come down and stop me?" she said, going down four more steps getting closer to the blackness.

Joey knew that if he bolted after her now she would run into the darkness even if she didn't really want to. He most definitely did not want to go down there after her. He stayed where he was hoping she was bluffing.

"Mom wouldn't want you to go down there," he said. He was embarrassed that he had to lean on his mother's authority because he was too afraid.

Behind them a voice said "You'd better listen to your big brother. There's some mighty strange goings-on in that there cellar." It was Beezer. He was standing right behind Joey and Story. They hadn't heard him approach. All three kids jumped and yelped.

"Come up out of there," he said. The urgency in his voice had Glory running up the steps as fast as she could. She squeezed between her two brothers as if she were cold. Beezer stared down into the cellar as if he could see something they couldn't. Quite suddenly he turned to the kids and spoke.

"Over a hundred fifty years ago Henrietta Calhoun—she was niece to Colonel Horsebaum—used to hide runaway slaves in that cellar."

"Slaves!" Glory said. All three kids looked back down into the darkness.

"But wasn't Henrietta Southern?" asked Joey. "Weren't they the ones who kept slaves? I mean, why would she hide them?"

"Oh she was Southern, all right. But some Southerners didn't believe in slavery—Henrietta was one of them. She was part of the Underground."

"Underground," said Story. "That's why they hid them in the cellar." It made sense to him.

"Well, kind of," said Beezer. "The Underground was a network of courageous people who helped slaves escape to freedom in the North." Beezer's glasses glinted in the sun as he spoke making the kids squint. "Henrietta helped many slaves escape by hiding them under her uncle's mansion. She was a bold one she was. She was helping a new group when Colonel Horsebaum discovered her nefarious designs.

"One dark night, right here in the back yard, he overheard her speaking to a brave fellow called Applegate. He was a member of the Underground, too. Applegate was going to take the slaves from the cellar and lead them to the next station on their way North."

"What happened?" asked Glory. She pulled a Barbie Doll out of her pocket and held it tightly to her chest.

"He hurt her, didn't he," said Story taking Joey's hand and putting it over his eyes.

"Is she buried down there?" Joey's words came out in alarm.

Beezer looked apprehensive. "Maybe I shouldn't go on," he said.

"No, you have to," said Glory using her bossy voice.

"Do you all really want me to," Beezer asked.

"Yes, please," said Joey, half hypnotized by the light glinting off Beezer's glasses. He needed to hear more about this Henrietta.

"Okay. But only because you are making me," said Beezer. He leaned toward them and lowered his voice. "Colonel Horsebaum wasn't just mad when he found out. He was *furious*!"

The word rang out in the still afternoon air like the unexpected gong of a great clock. The kids stiffened as they awaited Beezer's next words. Beezer took his time. He looked each child in the eyes before going on.

"He confronted the two collaborators and demanded Applegate give himself up."

"Calibrators?" asked Story.

"Collaborators—the two who were working together," said Beezer.

"Who is Applegate?" asked Joey.

"The fellow who was to take the slaves from Henrietta to the next stop," said Beezer.

"He didn't give up without a fight, did he?" asked Story.

"No. He knew they would just hang him so he tried to get away."

"He only tried? He didn't actually get away?" asked Glory.

"That's right," Beezer said. "Colonel Horsebaum shot him dead right . . ." Beezer walked a few steps toward the tree. "here."

"Wow," said Story.

"What happened to Henrietta," Glory asked. Her voice was anxious. In anticipation of bad news she held her hand over her mouth.

"Oh, she was brave and proud. 'You will have to answer his death before God,' she says." Beezer had changed from telling the story to acting out the parts.

"'I'll have to do nothing of the sort,' answers the Colonel. 'He was nothing but a thief and traitor.'

'You are the thief,' she says, 'for you steal human beings' freedom.'"

Beezer stood as tall as he could when speaking as Miss Henrietta. He screwed his face up and he spoke with a bitter edge as he spoke Colonel Horsebaum's part.

"'I demand that you tell me where you are hiding the slaves,' says the Colonel.

'You may as well shoot me, too. I will never tell,'" Beezer said as Henrietta. He stood with his hand over his heart as he delivered the lines.

"Did he?" asked Story.

"Did he what?" answered Beezer.

"Shoot her."

"I'm a-gettin' there. Don't rush me," said Beezer, his eyebrows coming together. "Colonel Horsebaum, being a reasonably bright man, figured out that the slaves were hidden in the cellar. Dragging Henrietta by her arm they descended into the darkness using a lantern as their only light."

Beezer went through the motions of going down stairs, holding a lantern.

"At first there appeared to be nobody there, but then the Colonel heard a little cry coming from behind a canvas hung on the wall. He tore it down with one hand and there, crouched in fear in a little cave dug in the wall, sat a mother, father, and three young children.

"'Abominable!' shouted the Colonel. 'How could a human being with Horsebaum blood in her veins be involved in such a wicked deed? The Horsebaum name has been ruined forever!' And then he pointed the gun at the father and said, 'We will return these slaves immediately to their rightful owner and say we captured them in the woods behind our house. If you are wise, you will tell no one of what you have done. The Horsebaum name may be saved from dishonor yet.'"

Beezer paused here to prepare for Henrietta's final lines. He put his hand over his heart and straightened his back.

"Henrietta stood up tall, chin in the air, and said, 'The name Horsebaum means nothing to me; but freedom does. For as long as I live I will continue to help these people find their freedom.'"

Beezer stood completely still with his hand over his heart for two or three seconds. It was like he was watching a flag being raised. Then he dropped out of character.

"Colonel Horsebaum was so mad he could hardly speak. When he did finally speak his face was red. Veins bulged at his temples. He told Henrietta that if she was going to take that attitude she would never set foot outside of the house again. He said it would be for her own good and for the sake of their family name."

"That's being grounded for a long time," said Story.

"But she was so good," said Glory. Tears ran down her cheeks. "Someone saved her, didn't they? She got away?"

The children stared at Beezer, eyes wide.

"Actually," Beezer said, "she didn't even think about what was going to happen to her. She was so worried about this family being sent back into slavery. She threw herself on the Colonel and yelled to the family, 'Run! Run for your lives to where I told you. You can find it. Others will be there to help you.'

"Colonel Horsebaum, struggling with Henrietta, yelled for them to stop or he would shoot. He stretched out his arm and aimed his pistol. Henrietta grabbed his arm and pulled the gun down into her own chest. There was an explosion. Henrietta jerked as the bullet entered her heart. Just before she died she looked up into the Colonel's eyes and said, 'Now you must answer to God for two innocent lives.'"

Beezer acted out this last part as he spoke. He grabbed the imaginary arm and gun; jerked as the gun went off. With one arm outstretched and the other across his chest he staggered backward and then fell to the ground dead. For a moment there was silence. No birds sang and no breeze whispered through willow limbs. Tears continued to run down Glory's cheeks. Joey, Glory and Story sat down in the shade of the tree forming a half circle around Beezer. They looked at him thinking of the tragic Henrietta.

"But it wasn't over yet," Beezer said, sitting up.

The kids jumped.

"You mean she didn't die?" asked Glory. There was hope in her voice.

"But you can't live with a bullet in your heart," said Joey.

"Oh, she died, right there in Colonel Horsebaum's arms," said Beezer. "Believe it or not Colonel Horsebaum nearly died with her from grief. She had been like a daughter to him. When he realized he had killed her it was almost more than he could bear. He knew she was right; he had taken two innocent lives. Unfortunately for him his realization didn't bring her back. He buried her in the old Eagle's Flight Cemetery up the road a-piece on the hill."

The kids looked the direction Beezer indicated. They couldn't see it through the trees.

"He got in trouble, didn't he?" asked Joey, bringing his attention back to Beezer.

"He had been trying to stop the escape of slaves, so the law saw his use of force as justified," answered Beezer.

"You mean they didn't put him in jail?" said Glory.

"No, they didn't do anything to him," said Beezer. "They saw him as a kind of tragic hero."

"But that's not fair," said Joey. The anger he felt surprised him.

"Ah, but what did happen was worse than any jail could ever be. In fact it was worse than death itself!"

Beezer paused for full effect. During the pause the world was silent. It was as if the willow tree, the grass, and the entire world were waiting to hear the rest of the story. Joey heard only one sound during the pause—the soft note of a wind chime. It rang and hung softly in the air. Beezer heard it too. Joey saw the recognition in his eyes. Glory and Story showed no sign of hearing anything. They stared unwaveringly at Beezer waiting for him to continue.

"Every night for the rest of his life at eleven o'clock, which was when the Colonel accidentally shot Henrietta, no matter where he was in the house he could hear that shot again. When he looked out that back window right there," he pointed to the kitchen window, "he would see Henrietta's ghost rise through the cellar doors. She would turn and look right at him with burning eyes. Then she would walk into the woods towards the cemetery where she was buried. Some nights he would run out of the house and call to her pleading for forgiveness, but she wouldn't speak to him. She never even looked back. She would float up the hill and disappear at her grave."

They all sat in silence. Slowly, gently, as the magic of the story wore off, the world started turning again. A breeze danced through the willows of the tree. A mocking bird called. A car passed on the highway out front.

"This house is haunted?" Story's eyes were wide. "Cool!"

"You have it all wrong." Beezer said, raising his hand. "The house never was haunted, just Colonel Horsebaum. He was never to forget that he had been wrong in shooting Henrietta and John Applegate. When he died, Henrietta's job of haunting was done."

"You mean she doesn't float around here anymore?" asked Glory. There was disappointment in her voice.

"I didn't say that."

"You're very confusing," she said, folding her arms.

"Not if you'd let me finish," Beezer said. "Henrietta still comes a-visitin' at times—mainly when someone is doing wrong in this house or when someone needs help. These things seem to disturb her and bring her back."

"What do you mean," asked Joey.

"Ten years ago a couple of escaped convicts hid out in the cellar. These men were wanted for some nasty things and had it in mind to harm your aunt. Your Aunt Winocha didn't even know they were there until one night she heard the most horrible screaming. She looked out that there window, the same one Colonel Horsebaum looked out, and saw the cellar doors fly open. Two convicts come running out hollering like they was on fire. It's said they ran straight back to prison screaming all the way."

"So what happened in the cellar?" asked Glory. She sat with her knees up against her chest, squeezing them tightly.

"Henrietta!" said Story, reverently.

"Yes," said Beezer. "Just a few seconds after the convicts came out screaming, Henrietta came floating up the stairs. She got about right here, then turned around and smiled." Beezer got up and acted this out. "And then she disappeared." Beezer snapped his fingers.

"But you said Henrietta always floated off across the fields to the cemetery," said Story. He thought he had caught Beezer in his own words.

"Even a ghost can be in a hurry," answered Beezer.

"Have you ever seen her?" asked Joey. There was something about Beezer—the way he spoke, the way he acted, or maybe it was the look in his eye—that made him believe every word Beezer said.

Beezer leaned forward and whispered, "You gotta promise me you won't tell anyone. A lot of people don't take kindly to people who seen ghosts."

"We promise," the kids whispered.

"I've seen her. One time was about four years ago. It was night. The moon was out. I had been working late on my model train, the one you kids found, and was just coming out of the garage when I heard something."

"Was it scary?" asked Glory, raising her hands to her mouth.

Beezer looked at her and said, "No. It wasn't scary at all. In fact it made me feel good; the way a cool breeze does on a hot day. I heard soft sounds like faraway wind chimes. I couldn't tell where the sound came from. It could have come from any direction. As I looked around I saw her right over there by the lilac bushes. She was meandering along as if she had just come out for a night-time walk to enjoy the summer evening."

"Did she look dead?" asked Story, hopefully.

"Well, she was a little pale," answered Beezer. "But other than that she was beautiful."

Joey felt a warm tingling in his stomach as he listened. He wished he could have been with Beezer that night.

"She was wearing curls all around her head," Beezer said. "Her face was the prettiest you ever saw, and her white dress was flowing and elegant. She glowed."

Joey and Story smiled dreamily as they imagined Henrietta. Glory looked down at her skinny body wondering if she would ever be as pretty as Henrietta.

Beezer got up, went over to the cellar doors and shut them. Looking back at them, he said, "Joey here has good instincts. You best listen to his advice. Now, Joey. I've come to introduce myself to your mother. Where'll I find her?"

Joey got up and led Beezer in through the kitchen and down the long hall to the library. They found Mrs. Johanaby sitting in front of a computer. She stared blankly at some sort of lesson on the screen.

"Ah, a computer," Beezer said. "I've heard of them."

Mrs. Johanaby jumped and whirled around in her chair. "Who are you?" she asked her hand on her chest.

"This is Beezer, Mom."

Mrs. Johanaby stared at him. Her mind seemed to still be on her lesson.

"We told you about him at lunch," said Joey.

"Hello, Mrs. Johanaby," Beezer said, giving an awkward half-bow as he spoke. "Beezer Martin, fix-it-man, at your service. I trust you'll find everything in the house in working order?"

Mrs. Johanaby, finally becoming fully present, asked, "You are the caretaker?"

"That I am," Beezer said with some pride.

Mrs. Johanaby stared at Beezer in silence for several awkward seconds. She had a lot of questions, but all of them would sound rude. As she looked into his magnified eyes she felt her apprehensions evaporate. Looking at him she felt the same peace she felt last night while sitting on Joey's bed.

Finally she found her voice. "It's good to meet you, Mr. Martin—"

"Beezer," he interrupted.

"—Beezer. It's good to meet you, Beezer," she said. "Aunt Winocha's lawyer said there was a helper who stayed here."

Joey noticed his mother's cheeks redden a little as she began speaking again.

"I . . ." She cleared her throat nervously. "I'm afraid we're going through hard times, Beezer. We have no way to pay you for whatever you do around here, but you're welcome to stay as long as you like."

"I should hope so," Beezer said, standing as tall as he could. Joey smiled when he saw that Beezer, even when standing tall, was shorter than his mom. "I kinda come with the house," Beezer looked around for an example, "like the roof does," he said pointing up. "I haven't been paid since long before you were born."

Beezer pushed his thick glasses back up his nose and smiled. "I got a little place out back in the woods—used to be the slave house. If you need anything fixed, just send one of the kids for me. You'll find me very useful." He patted Joey on the shoulder. "I'll be going now. You won't see too much of me unless you call."

He bowed again in his funny way, whirled around, and walked out the library door. Joey and his mother heard his footsteps down the hall followed by the slam of the back door. Suddenly it felt different inside the house—lonelier. Beezer was like sunshine. His leaving was like the sun going behind a cloud. Joey wondered if he were imagining things. Looking up at his mother he saw she felt it too.

"What an interesting man," Mrs. Johanaby said.

"He sure is," answered Joey.

"I think you best leave him alone. Don't go bothering him at his place unless we really need him." Mrs. Johanaby's furrowed her eyebrows as she spoke.

"Okay," said Joey.

"Now you better go keep an eye on the kids and let me get back to my studies." They both glanced at the computer screen. His mom seemed embarrassed. Apparently she wasn't as far along as she would have liked. Joey nodded pretending not to notice whatever it was his mom was embarrassed about. Giving his mother one last smile he turned and ran up the hall, through the kitchen, and out the screen door. He leaped off the back porch as if he were Superman flying in search of his brother and sister.

Chapter 5

As much as he despised the job, Joey took his babysitting responsibilities seriously. He spent almost all of his time watching the twins. Mrs. Johanaby spent every available moment during the day working on her on-line course to be a medical transcriptionist. She had explained to Joey how important it was for her to get the course completed. They were living on the last of their savings. It wasn't going to last very long.

"I have to finish this course and then I can make some pretty good money. Best of all, I can work from home!" she said. "But I have to get it done before the summer is over or . . . ." She trailed off.

"Or what?" Joey asked.

Mrs. Johanaby bit her lower lip nervously. "Or things will get harder," she said.

Joey did his best to keep the twins from interrupting Mrs. Johanaby. It wasn't easy. When the twins got along, which was most of the time, they got along great. There were days, though when they were mortal enemies. On these days their entire goal was to make the other miserable. These were very hard days for Joey. They always ended with everyone—even Mrs. Johanaby—being angry with him. Glory and Story would be angry because he would be forced to take sides with one or the other. There would be an appeal to Mrs. Johanaby. Mrs. Johanaby would be angry at Joey for not keeping the peace better.

At times like these he felt helpless and frustrated. He couldn't control the twins any more than he could control the wind. His mother acted like he should be able to.

On one particularly bad day it all started at breakfast. Glory had on her angry face. There was a hardness to her eyes and her lips were pulled thin. This face always made Joey nervous. Glory was at her meanest when she wore this face.

"What's wrong with you?" Joey asked. He said the words aggressively, trying to show no fear, as a kind of preemptive attack. His attack bounced off of her anger like a bullet off a tank.

"Story wet my bed!" Her words were not loud, but there was a jagged edge to them that told how really angry she was. Story came into the kitchen. His head was down and his pajama bottoms were soggy. "You are never sleeping in my bed again!" Her tone was unmerciful.

"You made me drink the water," Story said. There were tears in his eyes, but his indignation was rising.

"You didn't have to drink it all!" Glory said.

"You gave him water before bed?" Mrs. Johanaby asked as she brought apple sauce for the pancakes to the table.

"You said we don't drink enough water so I gave him a glass last night."

"She bet I couldn't drink it all," Story said. "So I did."

"And you WET MY BED!" Glory yelled.

"Stop it!" Mrs. Johanaby said, losing her patience. "You are in time out young lady. You sit right there and don't say a word. No pancakes, Glory, until I get back." She took a very embarrassed Story to the bathroom to bathe him.

Glory kept mumbling under her breath, "He wet my bed!"

Joey wanted to gloat that he could eat pancakes when she couldn't. The smoldering look in her eyes as she watched him was frightening and ruined the fun of it.

Later that day Glory and Story argued over the banana seat in front of the TV. One had been there and left. The other claimed ownership. Now the fight was on. Their volume rose as they argued. Joey ignored them until Glory angrily whacked Story with a pillow. She was about to do it again when Joey caught the pillow and pushed Glory to the couch.

"And don't get up until I say," he said

"You can't boss me!" Glory said. "Give me my pillow!"

Joey, put out by her behavior, tossed the pillow Frisbee style a little harder than he meant to. It smacked Glory right in the face. Except for shock effect there was no damage done. It was then Joey made his mistake—he apologized.

"I'm sorry . . ." he started to say. Glory, like a shark smelling blood, picked up on his weakness immediately. She was almost smiling as the tears came to her eyes. Then she ran off, crying in feigned pain, to Mrs. Johanaby. Mrs. Johanaby gave him a scolding for using physical force against the children. Joey tried to explain, but she wouldn't listen.

That afternoon, while he was moping outside under the weeping willow, Beezer came out of the garage and joined him.

"You ain't looking too happy," Beezer said.

It didn't take long before Joey blurted out his babysitting troubles. "Mom expects me to control them, but I can't control them any more than I can control the wind." Joey liked that image.

Beezer sat and chewed on a long stem of grass while he thought. Then he said, "It's true, you can't control the wind, but you can direct it. The old sea captains couldn't control the winds, but using their sails they could use it to take them places all over the world. They could even sail against the wind when they had to."

"How did they do that?" Joey asked.

"Tacking," Beezer said, "but the point is the twins are the wind and you have to direct them. If you do it right they won't have any idea what you are up to."

"But how . . ." Joey began.

"I thought you'd never ask," Beezer said. "Hang on." He grunted at the effort of getting up. He went to the garage and came back with a notebook and a pen. He grunted again as he sat down.

"You got to plan activities," he said. "Indoor things and outdoor things along with the best times to do them. Then, when one thing starts to fail you'll have a good idea of what to move on to. This way you can keep them out of your Mom's hair and busy enough so that they don't come after you."

Together they sat and made a list of activities. Joey could see that this might really make a difference. Just as they were finishing Joey heard a rustling sound in the tree limbs above them. He looked up to see a large rocket, parachute deployed, hanging on a limb near the top of the tree. Apparently it had just landed.

"It's about time. That's the longest she's ever been gone," Beezer said.

"Is that your rocket?" Joey said. "The one that . . ."

"That broke my window?" Beezer finished. "Yep. Gonna be hard to get her down isn't it. Do you climb trees?"

"How—?" Joey wanted to know how it was that the rocket, which he had seen shoot up into the sky about three weeks ago came to rest in the tree limbs just now, but he didn't know how to form the question.

"You just grab a hold of the lower limbs and start climbing," Beezer said.

"No," Joey replied. "How did it get there? I mean how was it gone so long?"

"She ain't an ordinary model rocket," Beezer said. "I don't deal in *ordinary*."

Joey wanted to climb that tree to get the rocket. "I bet I could get her," Joey said, longingly, "But—"

"But?" Beezer asked.

"My Mom doesn't want us climbing trees. She says she knows a boy who was impaled on an iron fence when he fell from a tree."

"Oh," said Beezer. He seemed disappointed.

"But I could do it if you wanted me to," Joey said, trying to find a justification.

"What I want is for you to obey your mother," Beezer said. "The wind'll bring'er down sooner or later. It may take some time, but she should have thought of that when she landed up there." Without another word he got up and walked toward the back field and the woods leaving the pen and paper with Joey.

"She?" Joey thought. Beezer spoke of the rocket as if she were alive. She sat, still swinging from her landing, maybe thirty or forty feet above him with her parachute wrapped around a limb. Somehow he was going to get her down.

Late that afternoon Joey took the twins out in the back field. Behind the garage there was a set of wooden steps, more of a double sided ladder, built over the wire. It made getting over the fence a snap. To the twins it was a game.

"I bet Beezer built this," Story said leaping off the top rung. Joey wondered too, but they seemed so ordinary. "Beezer doesn't do ordinary," Joey said.

"It makes me feel like I can jump over the fence," Glory said as she ran up and then down the steps. Joey ran over the steps with them.

Story looked at the windows in the back of the garage as he climbed the steps again. These were the windows to Beezer's magic room.

"Look, the window is fixed," he said.

Sure enough, there was no sign of the broken pane where the rocket had made its dramatic exit.

"Beezer's a good fix-it man," Glory said. "He put the head back on my doll."

Joey remembered the night the doll's head came off. Glory had been brushing her tangled hair and pulled so hard the head popped right off. She didn't think it was funny like her brothers did. Joey failed in his efforts to reattach it.

"I knew you couldn't fix it," Glory said, grabbing the body and head from his hands.

The next day Beezer was the hero. Glory was ecstatic. "Look, no matter how hard I pull it won't come off!" she said, demonstrating.

"Let's go look through the windows," Glory said, an impishness in her voice.

"What if he's in there?" Story asked. Joey said nothing. He looked curiously at the windows. The windows stared back. Something glinted behind them. Glory and Story squealed, leapt off the steps and ran for the field.

Joey turned to follow them. Over his shoulder he looked at the now whole pane. From where he was he could also see the rocket hanging in the tree. It would be easy to forget that the rocket had ever magically taken off. Looking back at the windows

Joey waved in case Beezer was in there watching. He then turned and followed the twins into the field.

The grass in the field was long and green. Summer hadn't had enough time to bake it brown yet. When the kids sat down the grass reached well over their heads. It was the perfect place for a game of hide-and-seek. One of them would kneel down, face to the ground, and count to fifty. The others would run one direction or the other and then just sit down in the grass. If they sat real still they were hard to find.

There were big, puffy clouds floating lazily through the sky trailing their shadows across the ground. Sometimes a shadow would find the kids and lift the weight of the heat. Joey and the twins played for almost two hours before growing tired. There were trails of bent grass zigzagging all over the field. The kids lay down on their backs, their heads together, watching the clouds silently pass by. It wasn't long before they started seeing shapes. There were airplanes and cats and explosions. There was the throw-up pattern in the Thriftway parking lot from when Glory had lost the hamburger and fries she had eaten for lunch. Story pointed out Mrs. Johnson's butt. She was his first grade teacher. Glory and Story giggled over that for some time. For Joey the clouds were a fleet of space battleships moving slowly, but unstoppably, toward their target.

"I love it here," Story said, letting out a sigh of contentment.

Glory sighed, "I love it, too. I bet Dad would have loved it."

Joey's heart beat faster at the mention of his dad. He always had two conflicting pictures of his dad in his mind. One was the silly, but happy grin on his Dad's face when the Pinewood Derby car they had built together hit the stop at the end of the track and the front tires fell off. The other picture was his dad's gaunt face with the sunken eyes. He lay in his hospital bed nearly dead from cancer. Those two pictures fought with each other in his brain until they blurred.

He had photos of his dad. Lots of them. Anymore, when he looked at them, he had trouble remembering what his living dad had looked like. Looking at pictures of his dad instead of seeing him in real life was like eating a picture of a steak—it gave him no comfort.

"If Dad was alive we probably never would have moved here," Glory said.

"Then I wish we had never seen this place," Joey said, bitterly. His words dampened the feeling of contentment like rain at a picnic. Joey could feel the twin's happiness evaporate and float away with the clouds. They grew quiet.

Guilt flooded Joey. It was always the same—anger followed by guilt. Joey had promised a grief counselor and his mother that he was not going to let the hurt from his father's death turn into anger. He learned that sometimes words are empty. The grief counselor had said many nice things. He had made promises in return. And yet all of it meant nothing. His father was still dead and his heart still ached.

The twins had grieved. On top of his own sorrow it broke his heart to see them sob like they did at the funeral. It was only two weeks later when he heard them laughing again. He wondered then how they could find laughter. He wondered now how they could feel such contentment. He suspected it was because they had each other. Joey had no one. He often felt envy of their togetherness.

Glory got up. "C'mon, Story," she said.

Story stretched with his signature moan of relaxation. He got up to follow Glory. Joey stayed where he was trying to push his reawakened grief back into the lower drawer of his heart.

He didn't realize it, but he was drowsy. He was on the edge of sleep when the sound of a chime brought his eyes open. It was a far-away sound, but very distinct. Joey was a long way from the house or any building where chimes might be hanging.

"How far can the sound of a wind chime go?" he wondered. He sat up to look around him. The house and garage were a couple hundred yards away. So were the woods the other direction. He had heard these chimes several times over the past few weeks. Never more than one at a time, and not always the same note. He was determined to find where they were hanging. Every search came up empty or ended early in a distraction. It occurred to him that finding the chimes was another activity to add to his list of things to do with Glory and Story. Thinking of the twins he sat up to look for them. He was just in time to see their heads bobbing in the grass as they slipped out of the field into the woods.

"GLORY! STORY!" he yelled jumping to his feet. They were already gone. He started after them stomping through the grass at a fast walk. He was already mumbling the angry words he was going to say to Glory when he caught up to her. She was there when Mom laid down the rules about staying out of the woods. She knew the rule. She also knew that if she broke the rule it was Joey who was going to get in trouble for letting it happen. Life was so unfair.

Before he got to the woods he found himself on a narrow, well-worn trail through the grass. It was just wide enough for one person. Clearly this is what had gotten the twin's attention. It had to be the path to Beezer's house in the woods. Joey quickened his pace. It was much darker and cooler in the woods. The trees were thick. Joey was soon glad he had a trail to follow. He hoped the twins wouldn't leave it.

In a hundred yards the trees parted into a small clearing. There sat Beezer's house. It was just a little cottage, actually. It couldn't have more than one room. The wood was weatherworn and gray. There were signs that it had been white in years past. On the side facing them a sagging porch led to a door. Next to the door was a window. Blue curtains hung on the inside. An iron fence encircled the house. The fence seemed out of place here in the woods. Joey wondered whose idea it had been.

Then Joey saw the garden. At first it appeared to be nothing more than forest undergrowth. It wasn't like the well-kept gardens he had seen in Oakley. It was wild and unkempt, but still a garden—a beautiful one at that.

Joey, forgetting his anger, joined Glory and Story at the fence next to the iron gate.

"Beezer lives here," said Story, his eyes wide.

"I guess so," Joey answered.

"Oh, he does," Glory said, with authority. "It's just like him."

Surrounding the cottage were tall plants and short plants. Some were delicate and others were bushy. Many wore flowers of red, yellow, pink and purple. Others were just green. There were no paths among these plants. They ran together peacefully. Among them were plants that Joey recognized—vegetables. There were strips of carrots and peas and lettuce. He saw the purple pod of an eggplant sticking above a patch of an herb he knew as Sweet William.

"Wow," Joey said.

"That's what I said," grinned Story.

"Beezer," Glory called out, hoping he was in the cottage.

"What are you doing?" asked Joey.

"I want to go play in his garden," she said. "I bet there are fairies in there."

"He's not there," Joey said. "I'm pretty sure I saw him in his magic room when we went to the field to play."

"Darn!" she said with a little scowl on her face. The scowl left as she thought of something. "Or maybe not," she added. She went to the iron gate and began to open it.

"Where are you going?" asked Joey.

"Where does it look like I'm going," she said. "Come on, Story. Let's go hunt for fairies."

Joey grabbed the gate and shut it. "You can't just go onto someone's property like that. It's trespassing. Mom would be angry."

"I can to. It's only Beezer!" She pulled on the gate, but wasn't strong enough to overcome Joey's hold. "You are such a dweeb!" she yelled. She was determined to go into the garden and nothing was going to stop her. She began to climb the vertical iron bars of the fence. Little arrowheads adorned the top of each bar. The points were blunted in little iron balls so they weren't too dangerous.

"Let's go, Glory," Joey said. "We aren't even supposed to be in the woods let alone trespassing on Beezer's property." Glory slipped down, let out a growl of frustration and started pulling herself up again.

Joey recognized the feeling inside him that told him this was going to end badly no matter what he did. This made him angry. He was only trying to do what was right. He could already hear his Mom yelling at him for whatever was about to happen.

Desperate, he tried a different approach. "Maybe we could ask Beezer. If he and Mom say it's okay we could come back and play in his garden."

Reasoning with Glory was like throwing a rubber ball at a brick wall and expecting the wall to move.

"I'm going in now!" Glory said. "Story, help me!" She tried to swing a leg up on top of the fence. Story didn't move. He just stood calmly, watching her.

When it looked like she was going to be successful Joey pulled her leg down and grabbed her arm to pull her away from the fence. She grabbed an iron bar with her other hand and hung on. Now it was a tug-o-war between Joey and the fence with Glory as the rope.

"Come on!" Joey grunted as he pulled. The fence shook, but Glory did not let go. Keeping a hold of her arm he pulled her thumb free of the iron bar and then was able to pull her hand free. Joey began dragging her down the path toward home.

When Glory realized she was losing she lost her temper. "You idiot," she screamed. "I hate you! I wish you had died instead of Dad."

These words brought tears to Joey's eyes. He wasn't sure why. Did he really care what she thought? The tears made him angry. He grabbed her arm with both his hands and dragged her down the trail. She sat down trying to make it harder and he pulled her backwards over the rusty dirt.

"Ow, ow! You're hurting me," she yelled after they had gone twenty feet this way.

"Then stand up," Joey said, yelling the words.

"I will. I will," she said. She was crying now. "Just stop pulling."

Joey stopped pulling but kept a hold of her arm.

"Let go my arm," she said.

"You'll run," Joey said.

"I won't," Glory yelled. "Let go."

Joey let go ready to tackle her if she tried to run back to the cottage. She didn't. She got up and slapped at the dirt on the bottom of her pink pants. She wiped the tears on her cheeks leaving muddy streaks. She glared through her tears into Joey's face. It was then she noticed Joey's tears. Joey flushed with shame. She had seen his weakness. He waited for her attack. Instead of an

57

attack, he saw her face soften just for a moment. The moment passed and the imp came back into her eyes.

"You are going to be in so much trouble," she said. She stepped around him and ran down the path toward home.

"Race you," Story said. He sprinted past Joey and down the path after Glory.

Joey didn't run. He walked slowly wiping his own tears away. The wood was silent in the late afternoon heat. He stopped and looked around him. Other than leaves and tree trunks he didn't see another living thing—not even a bird or a squirrel. He was alone. He liked the feeling. Glory couldn't torment him now. His mother couldn't yell at him while he was here. He could sit down and think about his father and cry. No one would see.

Not seeing a rock or a log anywhere, he sat down in the middle of the path. He had always felt that if he was alone enough and needful enough his father might come visit him. He desperately wanted it to be that way. He opened his mind to memories of his father unafraid of the tears that would come.

He was at his father's side at a Kiwanis club luncheon. He had come home from school for lunch. His father was just leaving for the luncheon and, on a whim, took Joey. The other men had exclaimed that he was a fine looking boy. His Dad had proudly agreed. He felt so big there; so special with his dad.

The smell of the wood brought him to the morning he woke up in a sleeping bag underneath a pine tree. His dad was standing over him.

He handed Joey a cup of hot chocolate and asked, "You going to sleep all day?" Joey sat in his bag and woke up slowly sipping the sweet, steaming drink. Later that day they had caught three small brook trout and cooked them over a fire in tin foil.

Tears came. He closed his eyes to try to catch every detail of these memories. The memories he had were sweet, but there should be more. There should be lots more. He had spent eleven years with his father and now he had only a few minutes of memories. How could that be? It wasn't right. The thought that he was forgetting his father made the sweet memories turn bitter with grief. People had told him his father would always be with him. They said as long as he carried his father in his heart he would always live.

"Well, guess what?" Joey said with misery. His voice sounded flat in the woods. "I am forgetting. And then what?" He curled up on the ground pulling his knees to his chest. "My dad will really be dead."

Joey sobbed. He felt he could cry for hours, but after a few minutes his tears ran out. He laid there feeling empty. He wondered if the rest of his life was going to be like this.

In the silence after his sobs he heard the chimes. There were two notes at once this time. The chimes were far away, but the notes wended their way through trees to his ears without losing their clarity. Joey sat up to listen more closely. Where were these chimes? He had to find them.

Another sound met his ears—footsteps and a voice. It was Beezer coming up the path. He was talking to someone as he came. Joey stood up just as Beezer came around a bend in the path. Beezer stopped short when he saw Joey. Joey looked behind Beezer to see who he was talking to. There was no one there. Beezer had been talking out loud to himself? With Beezer, this was believable.

Beezer noticed Joey's tears and Joey blushed. Beezer didn't say anything. He just lifted his hand and tousled Joey's hair. Stepping around Joey he continued on his way.

As Joey turned his head to watch Beezer he smelled lilacs. Through the trees he could see Beezer open his gate, walk through his garden and into the house. There were no lilacs at Beezer's cottage. Looking back the other way he half expected to see whoever Beezer had been talking with still standing there. The path was empty. Disappointed he walked slowly towards home.

Dinner consisted of undercooked spaghetti with sauce that had been burned to the bottom of the pan. Mrs. Johanaby's day at the computer had gone badly. She didn't understand computers and her progress in her course was going far slower than expected. What started out as occasional moodiness over the past few weeks had turned into full-time frustration. Everyone knew better than to comment on the dinner—everyone except Story.

"The spaghetti tastes funny," he said.

"Shut up and eat it," Mrs. Johanaby replied, crossly. The silence that followed was deafening. The only sounds were those of forks scraping against plates as they picked at their food.

Glory was reaching for her glass of grape juice when Mrs. Johanaby saw bruises on her forearm and wrist.

"Where did you get those?" she asked. Joey knew things were going from bad to worse. He hadn't seen the bruises until just now, but he knew where they came from. His heart sank. Glory had him now. The proof of his brutality was right there for his mom to see.

Glory glanced at Joey but said nothing. She took her grape juice and began drinking. There had been an uncertainty in her eyes that confused Joey. Where was the impish spark; the malicious grin?

"I asked you where you got those," Mrs. Johanaby said, raising her voice.

"Joey," answered Story. He, too, seemed confused at Glory's hesitation to drop the bomb. There was no maliciousness in his voice when he answered. He just seemed worried about Mrs. Johanaby's building wrath.

"Joey?" Mrs. Johanaby echoed. "Joey what? What is that supposed to mean?"

There was silence around the table as everyone except Mrs. Johanaby stared at their plates to avoid eye contact.

"Someone better tell me where these bruises came from!" yelled Mrs. Johanaby. She was scary when she yelled like this.

Joey sensed that the issue of the bruises had just gone up one level in severity due to the delay in response. Was this why Glory hadn't answered at first—to make it worse for him? He looked at her. She had picked up the doll that had been on her lap while she ate and held it close to her chest. The bruises on her wrist were clear and distinct. He hadn't meant to hurt her. He didn't know he had.

"I grabbed her today when she wouldn't come," Joey said. The words came out fast stumbling over his tongue.

"You grabbed her?" asked Mrs. Johanaby. It wasn't a real question, but the start of an angry lecture. "Those aren't 'just grabbing her,' –those are abuse!"

60

"No, Mom. She was trying to climb the fence into Beezer's garden and wouldn't stop."

"And so you attacked her?" asked Mrs. Johanaby

"I didn't attack her. I had to pull her away from the fence because she wouldn't come." Joey expected Glory to jump into the attack now due to his accusation, but she remained silent. She held the doll in front of her intently studying the doll's face. If she heard what was going on, she showed no sign of it.

"I told you this morning you were never to use physical force on your brother and sister. Why do you ignore me? Do you like aggravating me?"

"No, Mom. I was doing my best. You just don't know Glory."

At this Glory glanced at Joey, but still said nothing.

"I don't' know my own daughter? Is that what you are telling me?"

It did seem ridiculous put like that, Joey had to agree. But it was true that Glory was not the same Glory around Mrs. Johanaby as she was around Joey.

"No . . . yes," Joey said, confused.

"You apologize right now," Mrs. Johanaby said.

"I'm sorry, Mom," he said.

"Not to me, to your sister."

Joey looked at Glory. She glanced at him again before returning her attention to her doll. Joey was confused. Typically she would be eating this up—her big brother was in big trouble. There was no sign of the imp in her brown eyes now. Joey looked at the brownish-bluish finger marks on her wrist. They looked sore.

"Well?" Glory said glancing at him and then at Mrs. Johanaby. There, that was more like it, Joey thought.

"I'm sorry about those," he said. He meant it, too, although his pride kept him from sounding like he meant it.

"Now go to bed," said Mrs. Johanaby.

He didn't move. He wasn't defying her, but she had never punished him like this before.

"Go!" she said, raising her voice. She wasn't looking at him but at her plate.

Joey got up and went to his room, tears of shame brimming in his eyes.

Joey sat on his bed letting the tears run down his cheeks onto his shirt. He forgot all the good things of the day—the sunrise he had seen that morning, his mother's smile when he walked into the kitchen for breakfast, the sweet taste of the popsicle he had eaten after lunch, the clouds he had watched that afternoon. He only remembered that he had to baby sit twins all day, every day; that he had hurt Glory; that he had made his mother angry; that his father was dead.

Joey's eyes were drawn to the cinder block shelves he had built against the wall. Sitting on top were two model ships he had built with his father's help: the frigate with its tall masts, the battleship with its powerful guns. Three cars sat on his desk ready to race: the Corvette, the Porsche, and the souped-up Ford Mustang.

On his dresser were the rockets. The tall one with two stages was painted orange with a black stripe. It was his favorite. He had flown it several times. The first stage took it high and the second stage took it almost out of sight. He often dreamed of making a real rocket and escaping to another planet. Tonight the rocket seemed to mock him. It was only a toy. There would never be any real rocket to take him to freedom. His anger flared suddenly and he picked up his shoe and threw it. It flew straight, hitting the rocket knocking it to the floor. Two fins snapped off and lay at odd angles on either side. Guilt and shame replaced his anger.

Joey was getting up to retrieve the broken rocket when sounds of movement on the stairs distracted him. Joey hurried and got out of his clothes and into bed. He pulled on a string he had rigged up to turn out the light.

Joey was disappointed when no one came up the attic stairs. He half-hoped his mom would check on him. Instead it was Glory and Story going to their room to get ready for bed.

Joey lay there listening to the rhythm of their muffled voices and the sound of running water. Story laughed at something. His laugh sounded like a musical machine gun. It almost made Joey feel better.

The soft sound of his mother's footsteps in the hallway below gave him hope. Joey heard her stop at each bedroom door and say goodnight. He held his breath dreading, and hoping, to hear her steps on the attic stairs. There they were. He counted the twelve steps she took to the attic door.

When he heard the door open he wanted to roll over and call out to her. He wanted to tell her again what had happened that day, how he hadn't meant to hurt Glory. He wanted her to understand that he was doing his best. He wanted her to say, "I know, Joey."

None of this happened. Instead, Joey didn't move. He lay on his side with his back to her. Mrs. Johanaby, thinking Joey was asleep, shut the door gently. Joey's heart fell as the door shut. His father was dead, so he couldn't talk to him. His mother was alive, so how come it wasn't easier to talk to her? The disappointment was sharp in his chest.

It was just a crescent moon tonight, but in its dim light Joey could see the fallen rocket lying on the floor. Slipping out of bed, he picked the broken rocket up and gently laid it on his desk next to the cars.

The window next to the desk was open. He could smell the rich, warm, night air. Crickets in the field formed a community orchestra and chirped a discordant song. Through the tree branches he could see the stars twinkling as happily as ever. They didn't seem to care how he felt. In the dark he could just make out Beezer's rocket hanging on its branch.

A peculiar sound attracted his attention below. It was a soft sound—like when you pull a fingerful of cotton candy off the stick. Joey looked down toward the garage where the sound came from. He caught his breath at what he saw. Colorful lights flickered on the ground behind the garage. They must be coming from Beezer's room. The lights mesmerized Joey. They were—Joey searched for the word—unearthly. It was like firelight, but in so many more colors. Sometimes lights flickered almost as bright as a flashbulb; other lights were soft like a candle.

Joey wondered what Beezer was up to. His mouth dropped open when glowing bubbles of light floated right through the garage roof—pink, red, green, and yellow. There were many other colors he didn't know the names of. They swirled around like soap bubbles in a gusty breeze as they floated into the night sky. Joey watched them until they mixed with the stars.

He looked back down to find it now dark behind the garage. His heart sank. He wanted to see more. He swallowed his disappointment as Beezer stepped out through the garage door. Beezer was just a shadow in the night, but his glasses glinted in the moonlight. He leaned against the garage for a minute as if he were exhausted.

As Joey's eyes adjusted to the darkness he realized Beezer was glowing. A bluish green light surrounded him, lit like fog on the night of a full moon. Beezer bent over and brushed his pants as if they had gotten dusty. With each slap of the hand red, yellow, or green light mushroomed out and slowly dissolved into the darkness. When he finished brushing himself off, Beezer pulled a handkerchief from his pocket. This sent glowing, purple dust swirling away. He wiped his glasses.

Joey lost him for a moment when he walked behind the garage. Beezer reappeared as he climbed the steps over the fence and started across the field toward the woods. With each step there was flash and glow. It reminded Joey of heat lightning on the horizon at night.

Joey knew that no one would believe him when he told them about what he saw. They wouldn't believe him unless they saw it too. Joey turned and ran down the stairs.

Glory, Story," he whispered as he ran into Glory's room.

"Story isn't here," said Glory. "He wet my bed last night."

Ignoring her Joey said, "Quick, look out the window. Beezer is doing strange things."

Glory quickly slipped out of bed and went to the window.

"What is it?" she asked, expectantly.

"See? Right there, going into the woods," Joey said, pointing.

Glory looked just as Beezer disappeared into the trees.

"I don't see anything," Glory said.

"You should have seen it. Glowing bubbles, all a different color, floating up out of Beezer's room in the garage. When Beezer came out of the garage it was like he was a thundercloud with lightning coming off his body."

Glory listened closely as Joey spoke. His excitement intrigued her. She looked out the window again hoping to see something. "Really?" she asked.

"Yes!" Joey said, almost jumping up and down with excitement.

"Well, I didn't see anything!" She sounded disappointed. "Why didn't you get me sooner?" Now she was a little angry.

"It was so amazing that I didn't think soon enough," Joey said. Another thought occurred to him. "So, you believe me?" he asked.

It hadn't occurred to Glory not to believe him until he suggested it. She stood, her skinny form silhouetted in the dim moonlight, and thought. "Maybe," she said. She crawled back in bed, pulled a doll to her chest, and said "Now leave or I'll tell Mom."

Joey's excitement changed to frustration. Seeing something wonderful was no good unless someone else saw it too, or at least believed that you saw it. He stopped in Story's room on the way to the attic stairs, but no one was there. This worried Joey for a moment. He wondered if he should go look for him. He decided Story was probably with Mrs. Johanaby since Glory wouldn't let him sleep in her bed. Story didn't like to sleep alone.

Joey ran into Story in the near blackness of the attic stairway. They both screamed like girls.

"You two better be quiet," yelled Glory.

"What are you doing?" exclaimed Joey, angry at the fright.

"Can I sleep with you?" asked Story, near tears.

"With me?" Joey said. Story never slept with him. He thought a moment. "Have you been drinking water?"

"No," said Story.

"You don't have to pee?"

"No," Story said, becoming more hopeful.

"Okay, then" Joey said. "Come on."

They went up to Joey's room where Story climbed into bed. Joey went to the window and looked out at the garage and then the woods. All was dark and quiet now. Disappointed he climbed into bed making Story move over.

"You know what I saw tonight?" he asked.

"What?" Story answered sleepily.

Not missing any details Joey described the lights and how Beezer flickered and glowed as he walked back to the woods. When he finished the story he stared into the darkness toward the ceiling seeing it all again. Joey desperately wanted to hear Story's opinion of the account. Story didn't respond. He had fallen asleep soon after the story began. He slept on his side facing Joey. His breath smelled of toothpaste. Joey found comfort in the sound of his little brother's breathing. He drifted off to sleep to its gentle rhythm.

Chapter 6

The next morning Joey woke up late. The sun was already high in the sky. He sat up and rubbed his eyes. He felt groggy, like he had gotten too much sleep. Over on the desk he saw the pieces of his broken rocket.

"Oh no," he said.

He slid out of bed and stepped unsteadily to the desk. He picked up the rocket and one of the fins. One had broken off cleanly and would be easy to glue back on. The other fin was ragged at the edge, but if he could get another piece of balsa wood he could make another fin that would work just as well. He was good with his hands. That's what his dad said. For his twelfth birthday his father was going to get him the three stage *Saturn V*, but his father had gotten cancer and died too soon. Joey's birthday was in two weeks.

Outside two quarreling robins zipped by, dodging through the limbs of the tree. Beyond them Joey saw that the day was clear and still. It was going to be hot.

He looked down at the garage. Last night . . . Beezer! He remembered now. The colored bubbles. The way Beezer sparked and glowed. He had seen it, hadn't he? It wasn't just a dream? He turned around and looked for Story. He was already gone.

Joey looked at the clock on his dresser—8:30.

"Oh no!" he said. "Breakfast."

He was late getting the twins down to breakfast. His mother would be even angrier than she was last night. Joey quickly pulled on a T-shirt and his dusty pair of jeans. Not bothering with socks he shoved his feet into his shoes and started for the stairs. He thought of something and stopped. Returning to his bed he felt the sheets with his hand. Finding them dry he smiled.

He ran down the stairs two at a time. Neither Glory nor Story were in their bedrooms. Joey continued down to the kitchen. He was coming through the kitchen door when he tripped over his untied shoestrings. Mouth open and arms outstretched he fell onto his stomach. It would have been enough to fall, but it didn't end there. His momentum carried him under the table and into a chair which fell on top of him.

There was a surprised silence for a moment before the twins burst out laughing. Mrs. Johanaby ran around the table and helped Joey up.

"Are you all right?" she asked, kneeling in front of him with both hands on his shoulders.

Joey nodded. "I tripped," he said.

"Well you sure know how to make an entrance," she responded, beginning to laugh. "You'd better tie up those shoes before you break your neck."

Joey tied his shoes then poured himself a bowl of Corn Flakes. He was relieved to find his mom in a better mood this morning.

After Glory and Story finished their breakfast they rinsed their bowls without being told too.

"What should we play today?" asked Glory. She stood on her tip toes to put her bowl on the shelf. "Steal the Flag?"

"No," answered Story. He stood next to Glory drying his bowl. "I feel like having an adventure today." In a moment he ran through the back door with Glory and her doll right behind him.

"Keep your adventure out of the woods!" Mrs. Johanaby yelled after them.

"Mom *did* hear me last night," Joey thought with satisfaction.

Joey scooped up the last soggy flakes of cereal from his bowl while his mom filled the sink with hot soapy water. She began washing last night's dishes.

"How are you feeling this morning?" she asked, without turning around.

"I feel good. But I slept a little late."

"You must be tired," she said. "Baby sitting is hard work, especially for a twelve-year-old boy who would rather be doing other things."

Mrs. Johanaby was trying to make up for yelling at him last night. It was working. Joey felt better. But the tiredness he felt this morning wasn't from the baby sitting.

"I'm tired too," his mother mumbled to herself. Joey didn't hear.

"Do you believe in magic?" Joey asked. He wondered if Glory had said anything about last night.

"Magic?" she said. She stopped washing the dishes and looked out the window above the sink. "I used to believe in magic," she said. "Your father knew a few card tricks you know."

She didn't know what he was talking about. Glory had apparently said nothing. Joey knew what his mom was talking about. His father could always tell you which card was on top even though he hadn't looked at it.

"But he had other tricks that I think were even better," Mrs. Johanaby went on. "He had magical ways of making me feel good. It was the way he knew when to bring me flowers, the way he made me feel when he played with you kids, the way he made me feel when he kissed me."

Joey saw the red creeping up his mom's neck. She glanced at Joey, embarrassed. Her face was the same color as her neck. "Well, anyway," she said, "I still miss him."

Joey remembered his father brought his mother flowers a lot. Sometimes it was because he forgot their wedding anniversary or Mrs. Johanaby's birthday. Joey didn't remind his mom about that.

"I want you to know that I think you are doing a terrific job with the twins." Mrs. Johanaby's voice was extra sweet. Joey knew she was trying to make up for last night. That was okay with him.

Mrs. Johanaby went on. "Glory and Story came down on time all by themselves today, and did you see the way they washed their bowls?" She turned around so she could look at him while she talked. "It's because of your good example. You'll never know how much influence you have on their lives. That's why—" She paused here.

Joey knew what was coming. He struggled against the anger he felt rising. He could still see the determined look on Glory's face as she tried to climb over that fence even though she knew she wasn't supposed to.

"That's why I'm so concerned about your fight yesterday," she continued. "First of all you disobeyed me. Then you teach Glory and Story that it's okay to use violence to solve problems. Do you understand?"

Joey's hope for a happy morning was gone. He wanted to tell his mom that she was the one who didn't understand. She didn't know what it was like to keep the twins—especially Glory—out of trouble. He wanted to tell her that it wasn't fair how he always got in trouble for what Glory did. He was ready to tell her the whole story again and make her understand. When she turned around she wore her 'forced' happy look. This was her 'I'm not happy, but I'm going to pretend I am' face.

"You understand, right?" she repeated.

Joey swallowed his pride with his cereal and nodded.

"Good," she said. Her relief at getting this talk over with was clear. With a happy sigh she turned around to finish the dishes.

Joey took his bowl to her and watched as she sunk it in the sudsy water.

"So how's the class going?" he asked.

His mother took a deep breath "Oh, okay," she said.

He could feel her force the optimism in her voice.

"Actually, I've been writing a little on the side. I have something I want you to read for me."

She said this sheepishly, but there was hope, too. Joey knew why. She wasn't supposed to be writing. She was supposed to be studying. But she had always wanted to be a writer. She had gotten an English degree about the time she had married his dad. She dabbled in writing ever since Joey could remember.

Joey was pleased his mom wanted him to read what she had written. It made him feel grown-up. He had learned to read when he was five. Mrs. Johanaby complained proudly that he read too much. This had changed since his dad died. He could no longer lose himself in a book.

Joey followed his mother down the hall to the library. The computer was on, but the screen was blank. Mrs. Johanaby grabbed some papers off the printer. She sorted them into order and then handed them to Joey.

Joey sat on the couch and began reading. Their printer was running out of ink and the lines of print faded in and out down the page making it hard to read. What made it even harder for Joey was that his mother sat down on the couch next to him and watched him read. Doing his best to ignore her he read about how families should prepare long before a death in the family for funerals. She had written about how after a death there was so much trauma that the decisions of a funeral were very difficult to make.

It was four pages long. Joey read it very slowly. He glanced at his mother twice to see her watching him read. She watched his eyes move from line to line. He had to read some paragraphs twice because he was more conscious of her watching him than the words he was reading.

"So, what do you think?" she asked, when she saw him finish the last line.

His mother had taught him to be honest, but he knew that to be too honest at the wrong times does more harm than good. The article seemed boring to him. He didn't understand it. "It's good, Mom," Joey said, without looking up. He felt his mother staring at him.

"You don't like it, do you?" she said.

"It's a little boring to me," Joey said slowly. "But that's probably because it's not written for kids." He looked up at his mother anxiously hoping that she thought he was right. He was met by a blank look of someone who's trying not to cry.

"No, it's not written for kids, but you're right—it's boring." Mrs. Johanaby's shoulder's drooped, and she toyed with the wedding ring on her finger.

Joey felt terrible. "Mom, what do I know about writing? You need to have a grown-up read it. Maybe Beezer could read it. Do you want me to go get him? I bet he'll like it." Joey stood up to go.

Mrs. Johanaby let out a long, shuddering sigh as she held the tears in. "No," she said. "It's boring. I knew it even before you read it. I was just hoping that by magic it had become good all by itself." She smiled at Joey. "I just don't know what to write about, Joey. I can't think of anything interesting. What do we know or what have we done that's interesting?"

Joey wondered why she was trying to find something to write about when she was supposed to be studying to be a medical transcriptionist. Her question made him think. He wished his mother had heard what he had heard and seen what he had seen. Joey thought of Beezer and the colored lights; he thought of Beezer's story of Henrietta and her haunting the mansion. "Moving into an old haunted mansion is interesting," Joey said.

"Haunted?" asked his mother.

"You know—Henrietta?" Joey said. The kids had repeated Beezer's stories to Mrs. Johanaby and she had listened with interest and a little alarm. She had worried that Beezer would frighten the kids with such stories.

"Yes, maybe so," Mrs. Johanaby said absentmindedly. She stared out the window for a moment. "I need to stick with the program and let writing go," she said. She looked at Joey and attempted a little smile. Looking back out the window she became lost in her own thoughts again. Joey waited for a few minutes. When it became clear that she had forgotten him he got up and left the room. Looking over his shoulder he saw unshed tears glistening in his mother's eyes.

It was quiet outside. The morning breeze was gone. Nothing moved. The branches on the weeping willow hung limp and lifeless. The long grass in the field stood motionless as if painted on a canvas. He didn't even see the usual flocks of starlings flying about. Out on the highway he heard the whine of truck tires. They sounded far away, in a different world. Where were the twins?

Joey walked over to the fence and searched the field. There was no sign of them moving in the grass. Joey walked under the tree and stared up into the maze of branches. The rocket was still there, hanging motionless. There was no sign of the twins up there. He didn't think there would be. Climbing trees wasn't all that important to them. He wondered why.

There was nothing he wanted to do more than climb the tree as high as he could. The idea of looking out from among the leaves high above the ground excited him. The tree stood there morning, afternoon, and night. It stood unmoved by the blazing sun or the pouring rain. It showed no fear of the world around it. If he climbed the tree maybe he could be strong, too. At the least he could escape his life for a while. No one would know he was up there. He would just disappear. He liked that idea.

He put his hands on the bottom limb to begin his climb when he heard Story call his name. It sounded like Story was on the other side of the house. Leaving the tree Joey followed Story's voice. There was an old, garden patch on this side of the mansion. Skeletons of squash vines lay tangled in the dirt. Unpicked cabbages sat deflated in a row as they decomposed.

"Ugh," Joey said. Glory thought the old garden especially gross. Joey thought it odd that the twins might be over here. He didn't see them.

Annoyed, he continued his circle of the mansion. When he reached the patchy grass in the front yard he heard a loud bang. It sounded like the cellar doors. Breaking into a trot Joey hurried to see what the twins were up to.

The cellar door was open. There was no sign of the twins.

"Glory! Story!" he called looking around. Joey had no doubt it was them who opened the door. The door was heavy. After lifting it up they would have dropped it open. He turned slowly and looked carefully for anything the twins might be hiding behind. There was the tree and the garage. He was sure they were stifling giggles watching him now. He wasn't in the mood to be the butt of a joke today. Joey knew they wouldn't be able to resist the urge to poke their heads out to see the results of their joke. After a minute passed there was still no sign of them.

Annoyed, Joey turned back to the cellar. A frightening idea sent tingles down his spine. Had the twins actually gone down into the cellar? The darkness stared up at him from its lair. In silence it taunted him to come down.

"Glory?" he called into the darkness. He heard the fear in his voice. If Glory was down there she heard it too.

"Story!" he yelled, with a little more conviction. Silence, loud as noise, met his ears.

Glory was stubborn and headstrong. She had a habit of doing exactly what she knew people didn't want her to do. Would her orneriness give her the courage to go down into the darkness? Joey wasn't so sure. All he knew was that if Glory were down there he would have to go down there too. The darkness stared, daring him to come.

Joey reached for the door to close it.

"They can't be down there," he mumbled.

As he lifted the door he heard something. A noise drifted up out of the cellar like a dandelion seed in a soft breeze. Joey froze still bent over with the door in his hands. He couldn't tell what made the noise. Had it been a rustle of movement? A whisper?

Setting the door down he called, "Glory! Don't make me come down there!" Anger and fear mixed in his voice. Glory knew how to prey on his weaknesses. She had gone too far this time.

Joey held back the tears of fear that were ready to fall. Glory was going to force him to go down there. Joey shook his head and said, "No!" He wasn't going down there. It didn't matter if they were lost, or hurt, or starving. They had gone down there willingly. They would have to suffer the consequences.

Joey tried to walk away. He circled around the weeping willow. The thought of them down there in blackness, even if they were playing a joke, was too much for him. If they weren't afraid, they should be. He went back to the cellar doors.

"Glory! Story! Are you all right?" No answer. He was feeling panicked. Someone had to go down there. He couldn't do it. It would have to be his mom.

Joey started for the back door and then stopped. He didn't want to admit his fear to his mother. He didn't want her to see once again that he couldn't handle Glory. Joey changed his course from the back door to the library window.

He approached the window quietly and peered in. Mrs. Johanaby was at her computer. She sat with her head in her hands. Her long fingers passed through her brown hair and curled around the back of her head. She looked lonely and—was it scared? Joey recognized scared when he saw it.

Did she feel as lonely as he did? He wondered how two people who loved each other could be so lonely while living in the same house?

After his dad died Joey felt sorry for himself. He didn't believe anyone could miss his dad more than he did.

Through the window Joey saw Mrs. Johanaby wipe her eyes with her hand and then resume her lonely pose. For the first time since his death Joey wished his dad was alive for somebody else.

If his dad were alive and walked into the room right then Joey knew what his dad would do. He would take his mom by the hand and dance with her. His dad had always cheered his mother up this way. They waltzed together to music only they could hear. Mr. Johanaby would hold Mrs. Johanaby close with a hand around her waist. With her right hand in his left they would stare into each other's eyes as they took two steps and turned again and again. Joey imagined this now. He saw his mother's face brighten with that too-big smile of hers. His own loneliness melted away as the scene played out in his mind.

When the scene faded Mrs. Johanaby reappeared sitting with her head in her hands. Joey stepped back from the window sorry that he had looked in. He knew what he had to do.

Back at the cellar door Joey peered down.

"You are going to be in so much trouble!" he called into the darkness. His heart sank as, again, there was no response. Joey closed his eyes and swallowed. What was he afraid of? The dark never hurt anybody. His dad had told him that. Joey even believed it. But his dad hadn't seen this old mansion. He hadn't felt its strangeness. He didn't know Henrietta had been murdered in that cellar. He didn't know Henrietta still haunted these grounds.

"Just a ghost story," Joey said, weakly. He opened his eyes and took the first step. Then another. He paused at the sixth step. The seventh was in shadow. At nine steps the sunshine no longer touched his body. Lowering his foot from the twelfth step Joey stepped onto the cellar floor. He felt the blackness swirl around him like deep water. He felt dizzy and put his hand against the cellar wall. He jerked his hand back when he felt sticky cobwebs.

The smell was as bad as the darkness. A scent of decay mixed with the odor of damp earth. Slowly his eyes adjusted and dimly he could see a little bit of the large cellar. Wooden supports ran from the earthen floor to the joists that supported the floor above. Rotting cardboard boxes and dirty gunny sacks sat obscurely in the dim light. To his right he could just make out the end of a shelf that stuck out from the wall. Joey thought, but wasn't sure, that there were more shelves behind this one. On the shelf light reflected off a bottle of something prepared long ago. Joey remembered rows of dusty bottles of pickled beets in his Grandma Burton's cellar.

The far side of the cellar was lost in complete darkness. Joey couldn't see a light switch on the walls on either side of the doorway. Places like this usually had a bulb in the middle of the room with a pull string hanging down for a switch. He remembered this from his Grandma Burton's cellar also. There it was. As his eyes adjusted further to the darkness he could just make out a white string hanging ghostlike in the darkness.

Joey wanted to call out again in hope that Glory and Story would reveal themselves. He couldn't utter a sound. He was afraid his voice would squeak from fear. He was even more afraid that his voice would disturb something other than the twins lurking in the darkness.

On shaking legs Joey slowly moved forward, careful to avoid the boxes and sacks he had seen. His heart, already beating fast, leapt when he got close enough to see white fingers sticking through a gunny sack. Joey jumped back and almost cried out before he realized the white fingers were just potato sprouts. This always happened to the potatoes Mrs. Johanaby bought. Joey squeaked a little laugh and tried to steady his breath.

Side-stepping past the potato fingers Joey worked his way to the string. There was a rasping click when he pulled it, but no light.

"Dang," he peeped.

Now that he was in the middle of the darkness he realized that Glory and Story weren't down here. He had come down in vain. The darkness had lured him into its trap.

Mr. Johanaby had often taken Joey stargazing. He had taught Joey that if you want to see a really dim star or star cluster you had to look off to the side of it and it would appear in your peripheral vision. Quite accidentally Joey realized that out of the corner of his eye he was seeing a hole in the back wall of the cellar. He froze when he realized what it was. After all these years it was still there—the hole where escaping slaves had hid. Joey thought he could make out the rotting remnants of the fabric that had hidden the hole on the floor.

The reality of the hole made him think of Henrietta. Beezer was telling the truth. He was standing where Henrietta had died—

where Henrietta still visited. When he looked directly at the hole it disappeared into shadow. In its place Joey imagined movement. It was all he could do to make himself breathe. His legs almost gave out. When he heard the gun shot he fainted.

Joey regained consciousness as soon as his face hit the cold, musty dirt floor. At first he was confused. He thought he had gone blind. Finally his sluggish mind processed the fact that he was in complete darkness. The ambient light from the open cellar door was gone. The gunshot he had heard was the cellar door slamming shut.

"Glory!" he screamed, weakly. Glory may not be down here, but Joey was certain that he wasn't in the cellar alone.

He scrambled to his feet but had no idea which way the entrance was. Out of his mind with fear Joey blindly bolted forward only to run into one of the wooden floor supports. The force of the collision sent him careening to one side where he collided with the shelves. He fell to his back, bottles falling on top of him. One hit the floor beside him with a crash. Sticky liquid splashed onto his face. He smelled something sweet and pungent. Imagining a spirit was throwing things at him he rolled over on his stomach and covered his head.

Joey's fear whispered to him.

You're going to die down here. You will never leave this place.

"Help me!" he cried. "Help me!"

Joey sobbed giving himself up completely to his panic. The sound of a chime cut through his fear. It was a single note with a warmth that betrayed the dark dampness of the cellar. The note hung in the air an extra-long time before fading. Eventually it flickered out like the flame of a faraway candle blown out by the wind. The note seemed to wrap around Joey's panic making it fade and flicker out with it. When the sound of the chime disappeared Joey felt a calm come over him. Slowly Joey sat up on his knees and caught his breath. The coolness of an unbroken bottle rested against his knee. Gently pushing it aside he used the shelf next to him to help him get to his feet.

"The shelves were to my right when I came down the stairs," he thought. "I know where I am."

Moving along the shelves with his hands he found the end, calculated an angle from memory, and stepped out into the dark with his hands in front of him. He breathed deeply with each step. If he just kept going he was going to reach the steps or at least the wall with the entrance. This time, when his hands touched the wall sticky with cobwebs, he didn't pull away. Joey guessed he needed to move to his right. Sure enough, he soon came to the doorway. He felt forward with his foot until it hit something. Raising his foot he was relieved to find it was a step. Looking up he saw a crack of light coming in through the edge of the door. He ran up the steps and pushed against the heavy door with all his might. He threw it open and emerged into the blinding sunlight like a mummy from a tomb.

Glory and Story, who were standing under the weeping willow facing each other as if in consultation, whirled around in fright. They both screamed like girls.

"You scared us," Glory said, clutching a large doll with braided hair to her chest. "What were you doing down there?"

Joey didn't answer for a moment. He soaked in the healing sunshine and caught his breath. He was also trying to determine Glory's sincerity. She sounded like she was really surprised to see him come busting out of the cellar. At the same time, now that her fright was gone, he detected a hint of guilt in her eyes.

"What was I doing down there?" Joey was angry and it showed. Glory and Story backed up a step. "I was looking for you. That's what I was doing down there!"

"But why?" asked Glory.

"I wouldn't go down there. That's where Henrietta lives," said Story with a visible shudder.

At the mention of the ghost Joey turned and slammed the door shut. He didn't think it would stop a ghost, but at least now he couldn't see the darkness below.

Joey turned to face the twins. "You tricked me into going down there!" He spoke with a sharpness that surprised even him. He liked the feeling of power it gave him. Glory's typical boldness wavered under it.

"We never!" Glory said, hesitantly.

"You opened the door and hid knowing I would go down looking for you," Joey yelled.

Glory and Story looked at each other.

"No," said Glory.

"Yes," said Story.

"Okay, yes," agreed Glory. "We opened the door, but I never thought you would go down. I didn't even mean for you to go down." She said this thoughtfully as if wondering why she hadn't thought of that. "We just wanted to see if we could open the door."

"And we did," added Story, "even though it was heavy." He made a muscle man pose.

"Where were you when I got here, then?" Joey asked. "You hid and watched me go down!" Joey was ashamed at how afraid he must have looked.

"We didn't want you yelling at us for opening it," said Glory getting a little of her fight back.

"No!" Story said. "We didn't see you go down. Opening the door made so much noise we knew you would come to see and we didn't want you to yell at us. We ran and hid behind the garage."

"Then why did you shut the door?" Joey asked. It wasn't really a question, but an accusation.

"Because when you didn't come we thought we would close it before you saw it and yelled at us," said Glory.

"But I did come," Joey said, exasperated.

"We didn't know," Glory said. She was almost pleading. "Story found a really big ant hill back there."

"And we destroyed it," Story added proudly.

Glory almost convinced Joey that she was speaking the truth. Story supported her story and he never lied.

"We didn't know," Glory said. "Honest, we didn't!"

With Joey's attack softening Glory had time to see the signs of Joey's panic. There were tear tracks on his cheeks and a shiny spot where the sticky juice had splashed. The knees of his jeans were soiled and there was a smear of dirt on his chin.

"What happened down there?" she asked.

At this question Story looked at Joey and saw what Glory saw.

"Did you see Henrietta?" he asked. Fear and excitement fought for space on his face.

"Did you cry?" said Glory.

Her words, "Did you cry" might have been a sincere question. Whatever their intent they brought back the panic he had felt. His face flushed with shame. Yes, he had cried. Lucky for him she hadn't seen how he had cried. His panic had been spectacular. Running into the support, bouncing into the shelves—he had really thought he was going to die.

"Courage is acting so that you don't have be ashamed after the scary time is over." That is what his father had taught him. Joey had acted shamefully. At least nobody had seen him. Joey hesitated at this thought. Could his father see him from where he was? Joey's shame grew. Somehow Glory seemed to know about his panic. It was too much.

Joey turned and started walking toward the driveway. He wanted to run.

"Where are you going?" called Story

"You have to babysit us," called Glory. "We want to play hide and seek in the field with you."

"She's mocking me," Joey thought. She hates the word *babysit*. "I'm tired of you guys," Joey yelled over his shoulder. "I'm not going to baby sit you anymore. You're ruining my life. From now on you can do what you want—I'm leaving."

Joey sprinted up the lane toward the highway. He had no intention of ever coming back.

Chapter 7

Joey ran so hard he quickly ran out of breath. He reached the highway and wanted to flop down and rest. Knowing Glory, she was already telling Mom about his escape. No, he had to keep going. Joey looked left and then right wondering which way he should go. He turned left and, nursing a stitch in his side, began walking. Turning right would have taken him toward town. Mrs. Johanaby would most likely look for him that direction. He didn't want to be found.

The shame for his panic in the cellar made him walk faster. Joey could still hear his voice crying out, *Help me! Help me!* He blushed at the memory. Fear and shame had been his companions all his life. Even in fourth grade he had been afraid on the first day of school. He was so nervous that he would feel sick. His Mom would have to drive him to school because he would purposefully miss the bus. One year he wouldn't get out of the car. Joey had locked himself in so that Mrs. Johanaby couldn't open the door to make him get out.

Mr. Johanaby had signed Joey up for little league football. He lasted a week. The coaches constant yelling about starting faster, hitting harder, and not being a bunch of sissies made him a nervous wreck. Mr. Johanaby saw how unhappy football practice made Joey. Mercifully he let him quit.

Joey had been in Boy Scouts. He liked working on merit badges. He got to learn things like bicycling, and government.

Building fires and tying knots were fun. Camping wasn't so fun. Camping took him to unfamiliar places with boys he didn't really like. Joey refused to go out in the canoes at summer camp. The lake was deep and the boys would splash each other and ram each other even though they weren't supposed to. The thought of sinking into the dark depths of the lake gave him nightmares.

Joey had learned to swim in spite of his fear of deep water. He had even liked swimming until last year. He had nearly drowned after he had belly flopped off the diving board. He had swallowed water and panicked. While flailing and coughing he had sucked in more water and gone under. The feeling he had at that moment was the same feeling he felt down in the cellar—he was going to die. The life guard had easily pulled him to safety, but Joey hadn't gone swimming since.

Mr. Johanaby took Glory and Story to the local pool every Saturday during the summer. After his belly flop Joey went with them, but he played in the nearby park instead of getting in the pool. From the top of the slide he watched his dad and the twins through the chain link fence. His dad would let them ride on his back as he swam. The sun shimmered on their wet, skinny bodies and they laughed and yelled. Joey always wanted to join them. Then the memory of water in his lungs where air ought to be brought back the fear he couldn't control. He never swam with his dad again.

Joey realized it was people he was afraid of mostly. Other kids enjoyed being in groups at school—clubs or sports. Not Joey. Those situations were painful to him. He always felt that others were expecting something from him, something he couldn't give. They expected him to act a certain way or to say certain things. He could never figure out what those things were.

Mrs. Johanaby told him there was nothing wrong with marching to his own drum. She meant it, too. Still, Joey could tell she wished he could make friends easier. Joey's dad told him that marching to your own drum is a cool thing if you aren't doing it out of fear. Joey didn't know what to make of this.

Mr. Johanaby never yelled at Joey for being afraid, but Joey saw disappointment in his eyes more than once. Joey felt, as the oldest son, he let his parents down. Joey had hoped that one day he would find courage and make Mr. Johanaby proud. Now that his father was dead his opportunity to show him courage was gone. This morning had proved he was still a coward. Joey could taste the shame in the back of his mouth. Perhaps his dad was better off dead than living with such a cowardly son.

Joey gave the soda can he had been kicking an extra hard kick. It bounced and rattled erratically up the highway coming to rest near the yellow line in the middle. Joey angled out into the highway to kick it again. Lost in self-pity Joey didn't hear the semi-truck barreling down the road behind him. The driver saw Joey and pulled hard on the air horn in time to warn him. Taken by surprise Joey took two steps and then dove off the road. He rolled once and sat up in time to see the driver, a bald man with a bushy mustache, laughing as he went by. Turbulent air, mixed with diesel fumes, slapped him in the face.

Joey sat in the grass next to an empty potato chip bag that blew up against him. His heart beat wildly. A woman in a pickup flew up the road the other direction. Their eyes locked as she passed. She had a cigarette in her mouth and a look of puzzlement in her eyes, but she didn't slow down. Joey realized he needed to get off the highway, not just for safety, but because it would be too easy for his mother to find him.

The highway ran through a stand of woods. Joey looked into the cool green of the trees. The trees would hide him from his mom. They would hide him from the world. This is what he wanted; to be anonymous. Mrs. Johanaby didn't want the kids playing in the woods. Joey hesitated, but only for a moment. He was already in trouble so what would it matter? The reasoning was bad, but defiance helped him decide.

Joey got up and walked into the shade of the trees. He didn't go very far before he was out of sight of the highway. If he couldn't see the highway, no one on the highway could see him. For the first time since leaving the house that morning he felt a sense of relief and peace. Joey meandered aimlessly through the woods enjoying the coolness of the shade and the sound of the birds as they did whatever birds do in the leafy canopy above.

The ground was spongy and thick with dead leaves and foliage. Joey felt like he bounced when he walked. This was what it must have been like where Robin Hood lived. Robin Hood was one of Joey's heroes. Story always laughed when Joey brought it up.

"He doesn't have armor. He can't fly. He doesn't have any superpowers at all!"

This is what Joey liked about Robin Hood. Robin Hood didn't need any of those super powers to be a hero. Robin Hood was a natural leader. He could live comfortably in the woods using his own ingenuity. It's true, he was a dead-shot with a bow, but that's hardly a superpower—just skill. What Joey liked best was how Robin Hood freed a kingdom from tyranny using his natural talents and most importantly, courage. Robin Hood could have been killed easily by a sword or an arrow. The possibility of dying didn't stop him. Robin Hood didn't just beat up bad guys, he had a way of changing people's lives for good. He made people want to live better. There was something of real power in this, something more than blades that came out of your knuckles or a suit of impenetrable armor.

Joey picked up a dead limb that made a good pretend bow. Picking out a tree about a hundred feet through the woods he nocked an imaginary arrow, aimed carefully, and let the arrow fly. It flew true and struck the tree with a quivering sound that could be heard all the way to where he stood. Joey's imaginary confidence swelled. He stood taller as he continued walking through the woods. His men, scattered among the trees, looked at him with admiration. They loved their leader.

Were you scared? Did you cry? His little sister's words found him even out here in the woods. Joey's momentary confidence fled like a rabbit from a hawk. His imaginary men frowned and slipped away into the forest. *Help me. Please!* Joey heard his pitiful cries for help in the cellar. Swinging his stick hard he struck a tree. His stick broke in two.

Pushing his sister's words out of his mind Joey started to run through the woods. He liked the feeling of the tree trunks whipping past. The challenge of ducking, dodging and jumping trunks, limbs, and rocks thrilled him. Finally he fell onto his back on the cool earth of the woodland floor. He stared up through the leaves at bits of blue sky and white sunlight. The smell of earth and leaves tickled his nose. He felt better, happy almost.

As Joey lay there his eyes fell on a tree with a split trunk. It looked like it had been hit by lightning a long time ago. The tree was still alive, even the split part that angled sharply away from the rest of the tree. By climbing on the split-off part he could reach the lower limbs of the trunk that were still upright and climb the tree. This wounded maple was no mighty weeping willow, but it still looked fun to climb.

He went to the tree, excitement bubbling up inside him. Joey was afraid of many things, but climbing trees wasn't one of them. In his imagination the limbs above were another world. He envied the birds, so at ease and safe, up in the limbs. They had a different point of view from those who could only see the world from the ground. It was a superior view, one that had to make them wiser. The limbs also promised seclusion. Even with people nearby a person could be alone up there. Too bad Mrs. Johanaby had read that story in the newspaper about the boy falling from a tree and being impaled on an iron fence.

"Like that would happen more than once," Joey muttered. She had banned all tree climbing from that day on. She also thought all those iron fences should be torn down no matter how pretty they were.

Joey got up and walked to the tree. He put his hand on the trunk and felt the texture of the bark. He thought he could feel the life in the tree. He wanted to be part of it. He had run away from home and he was playing in the woods—both things his mother had forbidden. Climbing the tree couldn't make things much worse. Besides, there were no iron fences around. He stepped up on the split trunk, reached a low branch and scrambled up. His heart beat wildly, not from exertion, but from the adventure. He hadn't climbed a tree since his mom had read the article three years ago.

Joey became aware of an something unpleasant niggling in the back of his mind. Was it fear? Or was it his conscience? It didn't matter; he was going to climb this tree! Ignoring the feeling he climbed higher and higher until the limbs were narrow and swayed with his weight. The broad leaves brushed his face and the bark was rough against his hands and cheek. The woody smell of the tree was wildness and freedom.

He stood on one branch his arms wrapped around another. Before his eyes was a world of limbs and leaves and space. Two trees away a red squirrel scampered from limb to limb as easily as Joey could walk down a sidewalk. The squirrel came toward him carelessly transferring from one tree to another. Just before reaching Joey's tree it saw him. It chattered a sharp complaint and scampered back the other way. Joey was delighted at being a part of the squirrel's world.

Almost imperceptibly, the tree swayed under his weight. The feeling was exhilarating. He clung tighter to the branch. He laughed at first, but the exhilaration turned to fear.

"I'm not afraid," Joey said, his eyes closed, his arms wrapped tightly around the branch. He realized he was right; it wasn't fear he was feeling. It was more like conscience. He shouldn't be in the tree.

"It's okay," he said to himself. "I don't have to get down."

The feeling grew stronger. Not only did he feel he should get down, but he felt he should go home.

"No," he said, more loudly. "I won't go home!" he almost yelled these last words. The impression didn't go away. Instead it became stronger. It confused and frightened him. It was the second time that day that he had felt this fear. In the cellar it was the darkness that caused the fear, or something in the darkness with him—an angry ghost of a murdered woman? It wasn't dark here. The sun was out, the woods were green and friendly, and the tree was easy to climb. He had nothing to fear here.

Slowly his confusion and fear turned into understanding—he simply understood that he should get out of the tree and go home. It was as clear to him as the maple leaf in front of his face. Disappointment filled his mind. He had finally gotten away from the twins. He was finally in a tree. He deserved this and didn't want to cut it short.

"No," he said.

He heard wind chimes, softly, but more distinctly than he had ever heard them before. Two high notes struck at once making a tone that was discordant and jarring. There wasn't a breath of a breeze anywhere. If there were a breeze he was too far from home to hear chimes. These chimes weren't natural. Even worse, these chimes were nearby.

Holding on to the tree tighter he tried to conquer his fear with defiance.

"I'm staying here!" he yelled. He was talking to the chimes or whatever they represented. Nothing answered him. The birds had grown silent. All was still—unnaturally so. Joey recognized the stillness. It was a breath before speaking, a calm before the storm, the instant before a tiger leaps. Already holding the limb as tightly as he could Joey wrapped a leg around it also.

The gust of wind hit without warning. It came up from the ground instead of across the tops of the trees. Wind is natural, but this was all wrong. His hair and t-shirt shirt blew upwards as if he were in a tornado. His body tingled like there was lightning in the air. A second gust of wind whirled up from the base of the tree. This time it was stronger, and it didn't stop. Leaves and dirt flew up and stung Joey's back and arms. Joey closed his eyes. He would have screamed if the wind hadn't taken his breath away. The gust began spinning and turned into a whirlwind so strong that Joey thought it was going to rip the tree right out of the ground. It might have if Joey hadn't lost his grip first. Joey realized he was falling. For the second time that day he fainted.

Slowly Joey opened his eyes. He found himself lying on his back at the base of the tree. Everything was still again. It was like nothing had happened; as if he had only fallen asleep and dreamed. Had he? Joey flexed his fingers and then worked his elbows. They didn't hurt. Carefully he sat up. His back was fine. It must have been a dream. He couldn't have fallen from so high up that tree, through all those branches, without a scratch. It was impossible.

"It *was* all just a dream," Joey said.

No sooner had he said it than the leaves around him suddenly shook and rustled in the motionless air. Whatever it was was still there. The feeling that he should go home came flooding into him again.

"Please, leave me alone," he pleaded.

Chimes sounded again. This time multiple notes struck at once. The impression that he should go home became too strong to fight. Getting to his feet he ran toward the road as fast as he could. The feeling got stronger. Something was terribly wrong.

Instead of following the road home, Joey crossed it and ran into the woods to shorten the distance to . . . to where. This wasn't the shortest distance to his house. He didn't know where he was going, yet he knew he was going the right direction. He crashed through branches and limbs that were in his way. They cut his arms and scratched his face but Joey didn't slow down.

He came to a fence made of wooden rails, climbed over it quickly, and then dashed on through a field of tall grass just like the one behind his home. He was in the field neighboring theirs separated only by a drainage pond.

He arrived at the pond suddenly stopping just short of falling down the steep bank into the green, murky water. On the other side of the pond he saw Story acting very strangely. He ran along the pond a few feet then stopped. He put his hands to his face and yelled something. He turned and ran back the other way crying.

Joey's heart almost stopped when he saw what was wrong. Glory's head popped out of the water her arms flailing. He heard a choking cry before she went back under again.

Joey sprinted around the pond to get to the side Glory was nearest to. Story saw Joey and started calling frantically, "Joey! Joey! Help her! Please help her!" He was crying hysterically.

Joey came to a stop next to Story as Glory's face broke the surface, just barely, followed by one hand. She coughed once and there was a gurgle as she went under again. For a moment Joey could still see the yellow of her jumper before she sank too deep in the murky green.

"Save her, Joey! Save her!" Story screamed the words.

Joey couldn't move. He stood on the grassy bank staring at the spot where Glory had disappeared. He didn't want Glory to drown; he wanted to jump in, to save her. In his mind he was on the diving board at the public pool. He was leaping off, feeling the slap of the water against his stomach as it knocked the wind out of him, feeling himself sinking alone to the bottom.

"JOEY!" Story cried. He was pulling on Joey's arm.

"HELP," Joey screamed. He looked across the fields. No one was coming. "Help," he said. This time he said it quietly, without hope. Joey felt an impression, like in the wood. It didn't urge him to run. Instead it was quiet and calming, yet intense like sunlight through a magnifying glass.

"*You know how to swim,*" a voice said to him. It was a voice, but it was like he was speaking to himself. He knew he wasn't.

"I can't," he said. The water was so murky. He didn't know how deep it was.

"If you don't save her she will die," the voice said. There was no threat in the voice, just fact.

"I'm scared," Joey said out loud.

"That's okay," answered the voice. *"Save your sister."*

Joey jumped and slid down the muddy bank into the water. Even by the bank the water was over his head. The water was warm and thick. He panicked and clawed his way to the surface. He had instinctively turned toward the bank, but Story was screaming, "Behind you!" Dog paddling he turned around and saw nothing. How could he find her in this murky water?

His despair changed to sudden hope when his foot touched something. It was Glory. He put his head down and reached blindly with his hands. He felt nothing at first except the soft sliminess of algae. No, it wasn't algae—it was Glory's hair. He grabbed and pulled. To his great relief Glory rose to the surface. The life guard that had saved his life had held him around the chest. With a few strong strokes he had deftly brought Joey to the pool's edge. Joey was no life guard. He struggled to keep Glory's head above water by pulling on her hair as he slapped at the water and kicked his way the three feet to the bank.

Joey's relief at reaching the bank lasted only a moment. It was so steep and muddy he couldn't climb out himself let alone pull Glory out. He managed to get Glory's head and neck against the mud. He had to keep pushing her up to keep her head out of the water. She was unconscious and would slip back under the moment he stopped.

He was having trouble keeping his own head out of the water. *We're both going to drown*, Joey thought. He swallowed the sour water and coughed. Joey looked up to see Story reaching down with a stick, a determined look on his face. The stick was really nothing more than a twig. It was far too short and fragile to help.

Glory was slipping under again. Joey frantically kicked and grabbed at the mud to get her head back up.

I can't keep doing this, he thought, losing hope.

The irony of the situation struck like a blow to the stomach. She was in the pond because he had run away. He had jumped in to save her—now they would both drown. The fact that he had managed to get her to the bank and they would drown anyway seemed especially cruel to him.

"I'm sorry," he said to Glory as they both started to slip under.

The voice came again. *"Try a little longer and you won't have to be sorry."*

Joey heard this voice with his ears. It was a woman's voice. With that encouragement he kicked his heavy legs, pushed on Glory, and clawed at the mud one more time. Looking up Joey half expected to see the voice's owner on the bank above him next to Story. There was no one there. The disappointment was horrible. Joey coughed up water and tried to take a breath before more water came in.

All hope gone, Joey's instinct was to let go of Glory and try to save himself. As he struggled he saw her face. It was smeared with mud. Her eyes were closed. She wasn't breathing. Instead of letting go he pulled her close and began to sink with her.

"They're coming," said the woman. Her voice was calm.

"I can't," Joey said.

"Go up one more time. Don't choose to drown," she answered.

"Choose?" Joey thought. Even with his brain starved of oxygen he felt anger. "I have no choice."

Just then his foot pressed against something solid sticking out of the bank—a concrete culvert. With the last choice of his life Joey pushed. Up they rose for the last time.

There, leaning dangerously far over the edge, was Mrs. Johanaby. The sight strengthened Joey just enough to push Glory a few inches up the bank. Grabbing Glory's hair Mrs. Johanaby was able to pull her up the bank to safety.

Joey felt a great relief as he saw Glory's legs disappear into the grass. "We did it," he said, a feeling of peace coming over him even as he sank beneath the water's surface, exhausted.

"Up you go," said the voice. Joey felt himself float back to the surface just as Beezer's head poked over the bank. With one last effort Joey threw his arm towards Beezer's outstretched hand. It hit the mud with a slap. Beezer reached a little further, grabbed Joey's wrist and with surprising strength pulled Joey onto the grass.

"It ain't your time, either," Beezer said, softly.

Joey closed his eyes as he coughed up foul tasting water. Then he took one deep breath after another of sweet summer air. In it he could taste the dusty grass, the musty pond, and lilacs. It was all so wonderful.

Next to him his mother was giving mouth-to-mouth resuscitation to Glory. His joy at being alive fled as he thought that Glory might actually die even after all he had done.

"Glory," he mumbled and weakly reached out an arm.

"It's okay," said Beezer.

"No, it's not!" said Joey feeling a desperate anger. He had tried so hard and she had died anyway? He struggled to sit up.

"Just watch," Beezer said, letting Joey lean against him.

Glory looked so small lying there in the grass. Mud caked her jumper and the side of her face. Mrs. Johanaby pinched Glory's nose and breathed into her mouth again and again. Her concentration was complete; there was nothing else in the world at that moment. Story was on his knees beside her, crying. He said Glory's name over and over.

Then Glory coughed. Muddy water spilled out of her mouth and she coughed more. Eventually her eyes opened and she groaned. "Mommy!" she whispered.

"A 'Gloryous' sound," said Beezer. He chuckled at his pun. Joey's mind was foggy and slow. Finally, he understood what Beezer had just said. He looked at him. "Sorry," Beezer said. He chuckled again and repeated, "Gloryous." Joey didn't understand what Beezer was laughing at, but the sound of Glory's voice did sound good to him. Glory was alive.

"Oh, thank God!" Mrs. Johanaby cried.

She pulled Glory up into her arms and cradled her like a baby. Then, and only then, did Mrs. Johanaby glance away from Glory's face. Her glance landed on Joey. Their eyes met. Joey saw her freeze just for an instant with a look of horror on her face. There wasn't a word spoken, but he understood immediately what was wrong—she had forgotten about him and had just realized it. She had pulled the unconscious Glory from the pond and forgotten to come back for him. Glory started crying as she coughed up more water and what looked like blood. Mrs. Johanaby looked again with alarm at Glory. Just before she looked away Joey recognized something he knew very well in her eyes—shame.

"I've got to get her to the hospital," Mrs. Johanaby said.

"Go, then. Go," Beezer said. "I'll watch these two. Don't you worry none."

Mrs. Johanaby nodded her gratitude, lifted Glory and ran across the grass toward the house.

Beezer, Joey, and Story sat watching as Mrs. Johanaby climbed the steps over the fence carrying Glory as easily as if she were a kitten. They heard the truck engine start and the crunching of gravel as it left the drive.

"Is she going to be okay?" Joey asked, suddenly feeling the absence of his mother and Glory.

"She's going to be just fine," Beezer said with confidence.

"How do you know that?" Joey wanted it to be true, but he wanted to know how Beezer was so sure.

Beezer gazed for a minute in the direction of the house, then pushed up his glasses with his finger and looked at Joey. "You can know things without knowing them," he said. He wasn't smiling, but it sounded like he was joking.

"Don't tease me," Joey said. "You say Glory is going to be fine. How do you know that?" Joey spoke the words earnestly, almost angrily.

"Joey, I meant what I said. You can know things are true for certain without having any proof to show for it. I know Glory is going to be just fine." He picked a long blade of grass and put it between his lips.

"How can you know something like that? Is it more magic of yours?" Joey was angry now. He felt like he had crossed a line telling Beezer he knew he was magic. Beezer looked at Joey. Joey tried to look away, but found himself drawn in by those blue eyes that were so magnified by the thick lenses. There was a deepness to his eyes—Joey felt like he was looking into the sky on a clear night. There was tenderness there, too, that made Joey feel like crying again.

"Yes, it is a kind of magic, I guess," said Beezer. "But it's not my magic. It's your magic. It's Story's magic." He reached over and tousled Story's hair. There were tear stains in the dust on Story's face. "You will believe and learn how to use it, or maybe you won't; but this magic is the source of everything that's right with the world."

Joey didn't understand this, or maybe he did just a little, because suddenly he knew that there was definitely something right with Beezer.

Story, who had been sitting quietly, scooted on his knees to Beezer's side, but he was staring at Joey. There was something in his dark-brown eyes that made Joey uncomfortable.

"Where were you?" he asked quietly, so quietly that Joey wasn't sure he heard the question.

"What?"

"Where were you?" Story repeated. "We went looking for you. That's how we found the pond. Glory slipped and fell in. You weren't there!"

He started crying again, big tears dropped from his eyelashes directly to his shirt. "I thought she was going to die!"

Story leaned into Beezer. He rubbed his face against Beezer's shirt leaving tear and snot trails there. Beezer patted Story on the back and looked at Joey waiting for an answer to Story's question.

Joey's face burned. He looked down at his hands, empty in his lap, too ashamed to say where he had been; too ashamed to say why he hadn't been there. Finally he found words that were right. They weren't just right—they were true. "I'm sorry, Story. I'm really, really sorry. I won't ever leave you alone again."

He reached out to Story. Story flinched away from Joey. He grabbed Beezer tighter. This sent a pain through Joey's heart so deep he thought he would never find the end of it. Then Story let go of Beezer and nearly leaped into Joey's arms. The pain that went so deep into Joey's heart turned to joy so deep that Joey thought he wouldn't be able to stand it. This had something to do with the magic Beezer had talked about. Joey knew it.

"Come on," Beezer said. "Let's go see what your Mom has in the cupboard for lunch." He grunted to his feet and started through the tall grass toward the house. Story sprang to his feet, ran to Beezer's side and took his hand. Joey got up more slowly. He still felt weak from his struggle in the pond and his struggle with his emotions.

There was the tinkling of chimes—a happy little sound on a playful breeze. Joey looked even though he knew he wouldn't see any chimes.

"Thank you," he said out loud, but softly.

Beezer had heard the chimes, too. He smiled. "Yes, yes, you done well," he muttered.

Chapter 8

Joey followed Beezer and Story into the house. The screen door slammed behind him like it always did. This time it sounded different—hollow. Mrs. Johanaby and Glory weren't there.

"You know, you smell like a muskrat," Beezer said. Maybe you should take a shower and change clothes."

Joey nodded and went upstairs. On the way to the attic stairs he stopped at Glory's room and looked in the door. Her bed was made, although not very neatly. The quilt lay crooked across the mattress. The quilt was special. Mrs. Johanaby had made it out of Glory and Story's old baby clothes. There were frilly dresses, miniature jeans, t-shirts, and even socks. Sitting side-by-side against the pillow at the head of the bed were Glory's dolls. Joey stared at them for a moment. It seemed like one was missing. Had she taken one with her to the pond? On her nightstand was a plastic slinky, three bottles of finger nail polish, an empty box of Nerds, and a framed snapshot of her and Story cheek to cheek mugging for the camera.

After his shower Joey returned to the kitchen to find Beezer in his Mom's yellow apron that said, "I only have a kitchen because it came with the house." It fell at a sloping angle over his pot belly. There was a cookbook open on the counter. Next to it sat an open can of Spaghettios. Joey could smell burning tomato sauce. Beezer stirred frantically at what was in the pan.

"I cook salads a lot better," he said. Turning off the stove he brought the pan to the table.

Joey could see that Story had set the table because he had chosen the right bowls from their mismatched set. Story had the chipped green one that had eyes, nose, and a mouth sticking out on one side. Story had chosen the thrift store bowl for Joey. They had bought it for a nickel. Some child, for an art project, had painted "Papa is great" on the bottom.

Beezer dished out the slightly scorched Spaghettios. Story put a spoonful in his mouth and burned his tongue. They sat in silence for a moment letting them cool. Beezer sat in Mrs. Johanaby's seat. Glory's seat was glaringly empty. Joey tried to ignore the empty chair, but even when he wasn't looking the emptiness tugged at him. Story noticed the emptiness, too. He sat unusually still. Suddenly he got up and pulled his chair around the table next to Joey's chair and sat down. Joey pulled Story's bowl and spoon across the table to his new spot.

This act of companionship wasn't lost on Joey. Story wasn't used to being alone. What touched Joey was that Story had chosen to sit beside him instead of Beezer. It felt strange to have his brother sitting next to him. He didn't often feel like he had a brother. Story had always been one of the twins—Glory's brother.

"I have a brother," Joey mumbled. He glanced at Beezer. Beezer winked one magnified eye.

Story tested his Spaghettios once more. Finding they had cooled he began slurping them hungrily. Beezer hadn't made him wash. His face was still dirty—the tear tracks still there.

Joey felt like he was seeing Story for the first time. Glory got all the attention and pretty much represented both of them. This was odd since Story didn't look like Glory's twin at all. Mrs. Johanaby had explained they were fraternal twins—they didn't come from the same egg even though they came at the same time. Joey pictured Glory and Story hatching from chicken eggs.

Glory had bigger eyes. Story's eyelashes were longer. They were so long they were almost pretty. His hair was sandy yellow and was just a little bit wiry to the touch. Mrs. Johanaby normally buzzed his head so closely he was almost bald. It had been months since she last did this. His hair was unusually long—over his collar and ears. Today it was all tousled and tangled. He was shorter than Glory, but proudly weighed ten pounds more than her. Glory was as skinny as a stick.

Story scraped the bottom of his bowl with his spoon getting the last of the O's. He picked his bowl up and licked the remaining sauce. He set down his bowl and looked in the pan. It was empty. He looked so sad Joey almost laughed.

"Have mine," Beezer said, emptying his bowl into Story's. "I'm not sure why your Mom bought these. They don't seem right. I'll have a green salad with cherry tomatoes when I get home."

When they had finished eating Beezer said, "Well, I guess I had better do the dishes."

"We'll help," Joey said.

After drying a dish Story scratched his cheek with wet fingers creating smeary lines. Beezer noticed and said, "Looks like you are drawing a map on your face."

"Like a tattoo?" Story asked, trying to see his reflection in a wet bowl.

"A tattoo don't hold a candle to what I'm thinking," Beezer said. "Come here."

Story, in his dirty striped shirt and knee length cutoffs stood expectantly, trustingly, in front of Beezer. Beezer turned Story's head to the side and studied the smears closely. He took a fork from the drainer, dipped the tines in the water in the sink and started drawing in the grime on Story's cheek. Story did his best to hold still, but finally a giggle bubbled out.

"Hold still or you are going to change the world," Beezer said.

"Tickles," murmured Story.

"There," said Beezer, proudly, standing back and giving a critical eye to his work.

"What?" Story asked, looking up at Beezer and then over at Joey.

Joey looked at what Beezer had done. It was a map—a very detailed map—drawn in the dirt on the side of Story's face.

"Whoa!" Joey said, getting closer and holding Story's face by the chin. "That's our house, and the garage, and cellar door, and the tree, and the fence, and the field." It was all there on Story's cheek, done as clearly as fine-point pen on paper.

Story could barely contain himself. "I wanna see! I wanna see!" he said bouncing up and down. He slapped Joey's hand aside and ran to the bathroom to look in the mirror. "COOOL," came echoing back down the hall. Then, "What's the 'X'?"

"What 'X'?" Joey yelled. There was the sound of short, running footsteps in the hall. Story came through the kitchen door.

"Right here," he said, touching a spot near his ear.

"Don't touch it or you'll smear it," Joey said. There was an "X", and there was writing too. Neither had been there when he looked the first time. The writing said, "Ten paces." An arrow indicated the direction. It pointed away from the lilac bushes by the garage and pointed toward the bird feeder that stood on a pole. Another arrow pointed from the bird feeder into the yard. "Three paces" was written next to it.

"What's this?" Joey asked, looking at Beezer.

Beezer rolled his eyes and said, "What do you think?"

"TREASURE," Story yelled. "It's a treasure map!"

"Well, sure," Joey began, "but—"

"Let's go get it," Story interrupted.

Joey looked at Beezer asking with his eyes, "How did you—?"

Beezer looked a little ornery. "I'm glad there's one child in the world who knows what to do with a treasure map," he said.

Story was off like a shot. The screen door slammed before Joey had taken two steps.

Outside Joey stood on the steps wondering where Story went. Story came running around the corner with a shovel. The shovel had a long, yellow, fiberglass handle twice as tall as he was.

"Come on," he yelled. "I can't see the map."

Joey checked the map again and then led the way to the far side of the garage where the lilac bushes were. He found the bush on the end and faced away from it. The words said to take ten paces, but how big of paces?

"It itches," Story said.

"Well, don't scratch," Joey said looking over. He saw why it was tickling. More writing had appeared.

"*Your* paces," it said.

It was a real-time map. Joey was tempted to wonder how this could be, then decided not to. He just muttered, "That's a really good map."

Joey counted ten paces towards the bird feeder on the pole. Story dragging the shovel as he hung onto Joey's back pocket. He was afraid of getting left behind. Joey turned 90 degrees and took three more paces. "Right here," he said. There had been lawn here a long time ago. Now it was just dirt and wild grass.

Story did his best to dig a hole. The ground was mainly clay and hard to dig in. After a few minutes he only had a hole three inches deep and no wider than the shovel blade. Panting and impatient he handed the shovel to Joey.

Digging the hole was hard work. Joey had to jump on the shovel to make any progress. After twenty minutes Joey finally had a hole two-feet wide and almost a foot deep.

"There's nothing here," Joey said, breathing hard.

"Ohhh," Story complained, afraid Joey was going to give up. "We have to go deeper."

"But Beezer never even left the house after he drew the map. How would he get treasure here?"

"*Hello*," said Story, sounding just like Glory. "He hid it *before* he drew the map."

"He didn't know he was going to be drawing a map," Joey muttered. He knew none of the usual restrictions applied to Beezer.

"It's itching again," Story said.

Joey looked and saw the message, "Get back to work." He looked around expecting to see Beezer nearby. There was no sign of him.

"Alright already," he said, placing the shovel in the hole. He jumped on it. Little chimes, like laughter, tinkled from somewhere overhead.

Joey stopped and looked up. There was nothing but blue sky. "Do you hear chimes?" Joey asked.

"What chimes?" responded Story, following Joey's eyes up into the sky.

"Never mind," Joey said. He began digging again. He had the distinct impression that someone was laughing at him.

Joey was sweating. The sun was hot and the air was sticky with humidity. Story was sweating too. He paced impatiently on the other side of the hole. Every three minutes he begged for another chance to shovel. Each time Joey gladly gave Story the shovel. It didn't matter that Story knocked more dirt into the hole than he got out; Story's turn gave Joey a chance to rest. Joey worried that Story's sweat would wash away the map, but the map stayed as if it really were a tattoo.

About forty minutes after they started digging, Joey jumped on the shovel and heard a distinct, metallic, "Chink."

His exhaustion fled as a thrill went through his body. They had found the treasure. It wouldn't matter what it was. When someone else buries something and you dig it up, it is treasure.

Story let out a squeal of excitement. "We found it! We found it! Hurry, dig it out."

Story jumped into the hole to start brushing at the square inch of exposed metal with his hands.

"Get out of the way," Joey said.

"But the treasure's here," Story said, brushing harder. Joey had never seen Story so excited.

"It'll take until Christmas that way," Joey said. "Get out of the hole so I can dig."

Story hopped out of the hole. He knelt next to it on his hands and knees to keep a close eye on the work.

It took another ten minutes to find the edges and dig around them. A metal box with an arched lid slowly revealed itself. It was about one foot in diameter and a foot-and-a-half wide. It was a perfect, little pirate treasure chest. There was a decorative skull with a keyhole for a nose.

Joey tried to imagine what might be inside. He had started out with the attitude that this was just a game to amuse Story. If there hadn't been such a fantastic map he wouldn't have participated at all. He had expected to find some rusty bottle caps or a crusty quarter that had dropped from someone's pocket. Finding a treasure chest sparked his imagination. It would be Colonel Horsebaum's gold. Maybe there were rubies or diamonds . . . or . . . or . . . Joey was too excited to think.

"Stop bouncing and help me," Joey said.

"Okay," Story said. He bounced even harder in his excitement.

There wasn't enough room in the hole to stand in it with the chest. They reached down and tried to lift it out by the handles on each side.

Story grunted "It's stuck," he said.

"No, it's just heavy," Joey answered. Joey lifted his side. Story couldn't lift his side even an inch off the ground.

"I can't do it by myself," Joey said, dropping his side with a muffled thump.

"Where's Beezer?" Story asked, panting. "We need his help. I'll get him." Story took off, his arms swinging and his short legs pumping wildly.

Joey lay on his belly on the hot dirt next to the hole. He ran his fingers along the top of the chest. It had been cool when they had first uncovered it, but it was growing hot in the sun. The chest was made entirely of steel. He fingered the keyhole in the skull's nose.

"That is going to be a problem," Joey thought.

He sat up and pulled on the lid. It didn't even wiggle. What if they couldn't find the key? He thought of the time his father had taken him to a lake in Maven State Park. After a day of hiking, rock skipping, and picnicking they had returned to their truck to find they had locked the key inside. Joey had panicked almost to tears. His father patiently held him and said,

"It's going to be okay, Joey. There are always options other than fear. Think, what could we do about this?"

Taking strength from his Dad, Joey thought for a moment. "We could break the window," he said.

"See," his dad said. "That is an option. But I wonder if there is an option where we don't have to break the window."

Joey thought some more. "There's the park ranger station up the road where we came into the park. Maybe he has a phone and we could call for help." Joey's confidence started to grow.

"Yes, an even better option!" His father gave him a high five. "But there is an option that I know about that you don't."

Mr. Johanaby lay down on his back and scooted under the truck a little way. When he came out from under the truck he had a little black box in his hand. He slid the top off and inside was a spare key to the truck.

"I've locked my key in my truck before," he said with a wink. "Preparation is the best option."

Joey was fingering the keyhole remembering his father when Story came skidding around the corner of the garage. Beezer followed at a more leisurely pace.

"It's right here!" Story shouted excitedly.

"Of course it is," Beezer said, proudly. "My maps are never wrong. The only time they can't get you there is if you choose not to see or you quit too soon." He looked at Joey and raised an eyebrow. Joey looked away.

"It's too heavy for us to lift," Story said.

"They don't make them like this anymore," Beezer said. "Joey, you get on that side and I'll take this side."

Together, with a lot of grunting, they lifted the box out of the hole and set it on the ground.

"I have to ask myself why I didn't use a lighter box?" Beezer said, kneeling by the box and breathing hard.

"What does yourself answer?" asked Joey.

"Because I'm a darn fool for authenticity."

"Open it. Open it!" Story said, knocking on the lid.

"Let's put it in the shade first," Beezer said.

Together they pushed and pulled the treasure chest into the shade of the lilacs. After catching his breath Beezer pulled on the lid.

"It's locked," he said. He seemed surprised.

Joey and Story looked at him desperately. If Beezer couldn't open it, who could?

"You don't have a key?" Joey asked.

"There's an idea," Beezer said. He felt his shirt pocket, then his pants pockets. He found no key. He thought for a moment before raising his eyebrows. He plopped down on his behind and unlaced his boot. He pulled his boot off, turned it upside down, and shook it. A big, old-fashioned key fell into the dirt. It looked like the keys Joey had seen in pirate movies. It had a ring on one end and flat metal on the other end that looked like the piece of a jigsaw puzzle. It was far too big to be in Beezer's boot with Beezer's foot. Joey knew better than to ask about that.

Story gasped at the sight of the key. Beezer handed the key to Joey.

"I get to open it?" Joey asked.

"You dug it up," Beezer answered matter-of-factly.

Joey's hand was shaking as he put the key into the keyhole. It wouldn't go in all the way. He thought it was his shaking hand, but after several attempts he realized it didn't fit.

"It's not the right key," Joey said. He was annoyed. How could Beezer pull the wrong key out of his boot?

"Awwww." The anticipation was too much. Story moaned and fell onto his back. A moment later he sat up, an expression of hope back on his face. "What about your other boot?"

Beezer looked at Story and Joey while considering the idea. He shrugged his shoulders and unlaced his other boot. He shook it upside-down like before. Another key fell out.

"Well, wuddayaknow," he said.

"Can I try it?" asked Story.

Beezer looked at Joey. Joey nodded.

"Thanks!" said Story. Using both hands Story carefully put the key in the hole. It fit perfectly. He looked at Joey, then at Beezer. He turned the key. There was a satisfying "click." The lid popped up a little. With visible effort Story lifted the lid to reveal what was inside.

"We're rich," he whispered.

The chest was filled with gold coins. The coins sparkled and danced before Joey's eyes. The chest wasn't very big, but Joey knew that there was enough gold in there to solve his mother's money worries. It was such a beautiful sight that Joey was afraid to touch it. Story wasn't afraid. He pushed both hands in, lifted handfuls of gold and let it drop between his fingers. He giggled hysterically.

Something was wrong. The gold coins landed with a light, tinny sound. Joey slowly reached in and picked up a coin. It was too light to be gold. He looked closer at the design imprinted in the coin. He squeezed the coin between his thumb and forefinger.

Chocolate oozed out the edges. Disappointment nearly suffocated him.

When Story saw the chocolate he grabbed a coin, peeled back the foil, and popped the melting chocolate into his mouth.

"Mmmmm," he said, wiping his fingers on his shorts. "There are so many!" He ate another one. "You can have half and I will share the rest with Glory," he said. Story shoved his hands into the coins again and stirred. He clearly enjoyed the feel.

Story's generosity was not lost on Joey. Glory would have claimed them all to divvy them out as she wished. Joey would have demanded they divide it into thirds. Story was satisfied with half of half. What's more he was satisfied with chocolate instead of gold.

Joey wasn't satisfied. He was angry. The chest was so old and authentic looking. While he sat next to the chest waiting for Story and Beezer hope had sprung up that there really might be treasure inside. The idea of treasure seemed so possible that when Story opened the lid he hadn't been surprised to see gold coins. To find out that they were just chocolate coins in gold-colored tin foil, well—he was disappointed and embarrassed. He was disappointed because he wasn't rich. He was embarrassed because he had expected more than chocolate coins in the first place. Why would it be anything more than chocolate coins? Beezer was just entertaining two boys for the afternoon. Why would he give a chest full of gold to two boys?

"Because Beezer is magic, that's why!" Joey thought.

Joey was certain this chest hadn't been there until Beezer drew the map on Story's cheek. If he could make a chest full of chocolate coins appear why couldn't he make a chest full of gold coins appear?

"Because he's making fun of me," Joey thought.

Joey looked at the coins with disgust. "You take them all," Joey said. "I don't want any. Split them halfway with Glory when she gets back."

Story stared at Joey. "Really?" he asked. "I can't wait 'til she gets back to show her the treasure! I'll get a sack," he said. He got up and scampered off.

Joey and Beezer sat in silence on a patch of grass in the shade of the lilacs. Joey picked blades of grass and carelessly threw them in front of him. Beezer found a longer stem and put it between his lips.

Finally Beezer said, "You don't like chocolate treasure?"

Joey's embarrassment fought with what he knew was his silly anger. He didn't know what to say. Finally he blurted out, "I thought it was real gold." He blushed deep red and turned his head to try to hide it from Beezer.

Beezer considered this revelation. He showed no amusement or judgment. "A chest full of real gold would be exciting, now, wouldn't it," he said.

"I thought it was for Mom. She needs money," Joey explained. "And it's just chocolate." He no longer tried to hide his disappointment.

"It's okay, Joey," Beezer said. "Everyone wants to find a chest full of gold." Beezer changed the stem of grass from one side of his mouth to the other. "Your mother has needs, but a chest full of gold ain't one of them."

Beezer thought a moment, then went on. "Your mother got a greater gift than gold, today."

"You mean Glory," Joey said, unhappily. He wanted gold, not an object lesson, even if he knew the lesson was true.

"No," said Beezer. "It was you."

Me, thought Joey. What did Beezer mean by that? An uneasy feeling came over him as he remembered the look in his mom's eye—she had forgotten him, left him in the pond. What did Beezer mean?

Story returned with a plastic grocery sack. Joey held the sack while Story scooped the golden, chocolate coins out of the chest. He giggled like a greedy old man.

"You better put those in the refrigerator," said Beezer. "They're pretty squishy right now."

Story bounced once in excitement. "Okay," he said. He turned to go, then stopped. Turning back he threw his arms around Joey's neck in an awkward hug. "Thanks for the chocolates," he said. He ran off without waiting for a response.

Joey and Beezer sat in silence until they heard the screen door slam.

"If Mom doesn't need a chest of gold then nobody does," Joey said, still hurt.

"You got that right," Beezer said. He was leaning back on his arms, staring out across the woods to where, far away, high antenna towers reached up into the sky. "If people could foresee what a chest of gold would do to them a chest of gold would be as welcome as a chest of vipers."

Beezer wasn't making any sense to Joey. He wasn't in the mood for puzzles.

"I gotta go," Joey said.

As he got up he saw a bottle in the chest. It was small enough that it could have been hidden under the chocolate coins. Still, he was surprised he had missed it. Something in the bottle sparkled in an enchanting way.

"What's that?" Joey asked.

"Huh?" said Beezer. He had been looking at Joey, but then followed Joey's eyes to the bottle in the chest. "Oh. I forgot I put that there," he said. "That's stardust."

"Stardust?" Joey echoed. Whatever it was it was beautiful. It was more than beautiful; it was mesmerizing. Colors brightened and blended before his eyes. Joey relaxed as the world around him dimmed. All awareness of his problems dissolved.

Joey's trance was broken when Beezer picked up the bottle and hid the contents with his hand.

"Stardust is dangerous," Beezer said.

"H . . . how?" asked Joey as he came back to himself. "It's beautiful. It makes me feel good."

Even as he spoke Joey could feel the dust calling him. It invited him to look again and be happy. Joey had an impulse to grab it from Beezer's hand.

Beezer held the bottle behind his back. With his free hand he took Joey's face by the chin and made him meet his eyes.

"Stardust is so beautiful because it's the dreams of all the good things in the world. It's so dangerous because the dreams overcome reality. It will draw you into the dreams so deeply you will never return to make any of the dreams a reality. Dreams that cannot become reality are the food of despair."

"If it's so dangerous why do you have it," asked Joey, a little bitterly. He was suffering the aftereffect of looking freely at Stardust. It was like an addictive drug.

As Joey woke up a little more he was frightened of how quickly the star dust had drawn him. He realized he would have stood there staring until he died. A shiver went up his spine.

"If used correctly Stardust can help a person realize their dreams," Beezer said. He brought the bottle from behind his back, but kept it hidden in his hands. Joey could see pulsing, glittering lights escaping from between Beezer's fingers. They tugged at his mind and will.

A low chime sounded, like a warning. Beezer jerked.

"Maps," he said, clearing his throat. "Maps are how I use stardust. It's reasonably safe that way."

He reached to the bottom of the chest and pulled out a folded piece of paper. This was not ordinary paper. It was old and thick with a canvas-like texture.

Beezer put the bottle of stardust down on the other side of him. Joey saw the top of the tall, ornate stopper on top sticking up above Beezer's leg. Beezer unfolded the paper on the ground in front of him. It was quite large, maybe two-feet square.

Joey's disappointment of finding nothing but candy in the chest was gone now. Before him were items worthy of an old pirate chest. The blank piece of paper and the bottle of Stardust, whatever that was, excited him much more than his hopes for gold.

"Come closer," Beezer said. He patted the ground beside him. Joey got to his knees and scooted over next to the paper. "I am going to put the bottle of Stardust in your hand. When I do you cover it up so you can't look at it. You already know what it can do."

Joey swallowed hard and nodded. Excitement and fear whirled in his stomach. Beezer transferred the bottle from his own closed hand to Joey's. Joey's hand did not fit around the entire bottle.

"Quick, hold the uncovered part against you," Beezer said.

Joey pressed the bottle against his chest hiding the colors that were escaping. Joey's anxious excitement grew when he realized he could feel the colors touching him. They felt like drops of warm water without the wetness.

"Now, I am going to pull the stopper off and I want you to sprinkle stardust all over the paper. Do it right away, okay?" said Beezer. "Use both hands to hold the bottle. Don't sit staring at what comes out of the bottle, because until they touch the paper they are really the opposite of what they seem to be. Do you understand?" Beezer looked into Joey's eyes for a signal of comprehension.

Joey realized something big was happening. His heart beat faster as Beezer pulled on the stopper. It came out with a "Pop." Immediately bubbles of color came floating out, slowly ascending. The colors shimmered and vibrated with a hypnotizing effect. Joey's will weakened. He just wanted to sit and gaze into the bubbles.

"Pour it! Pour it!" Beezer called from far away. Beezer grabbed Joey's hands to help him turn the bottle over. As the dust reached the paper Joey came back to himself. Joey wasn't so sure the dust was pouring onto the paper as much as the paper was pulling the dust to it. The colors still shimmered and vibrated, but their magical properties were restrained by the paper.

"Now sprinkle it all over the parchment," Beezer commanded gently.

He slowly let go of Joey's hand, ready to grab it again should Joey turn the bottle up.

Using a little shaking motion Joey poured Stardust all over the paper. There was no telling how much stardust would come out of the bottle or how much the paper would absorb. Joey noticed that the stardust wouldn't spill off the paper no matter how close to the edge he got. He poured and poured watching more colors than he knew existed be swallowed by the paper.

The dust sank into the paper like it was absorbed by a sponge. The colors faded, then disappeared completely leaving the paper bare except for a warm glow. Then the glowing slowly diminished until it was gone.

Finally Beezer caught his hand and popped the stopper back into the bottle with a quick move. He took the bottle from Joey's hand, placed it into the chest, shut the lid, and turned the key. "There," he said with a sigh of relief. "It's done."

What had been done Joey wasn't sure. The hand that had held the bottle was tingling like it had gone to sleep. The parchment sat in front of him as blank as ever.

"What . . .?" Joey began, but didn't know how to finish.

"It's a map," Beezer said, leaning back on his arms. He was breathing a little hard as if he had just climbed a hill. "It's *your* map," he corrected himself.

"There's nothing there," Joey said.

"It's still working," Beezer answered. "It has to develop like the film we used to use in cameras. "Stardust and parchment haven't gone digital." He made this last statement with a fully satisfied air.

"What's the—" Joey looked dubiously at the blank piece of paper in front of him "—map for?"

Beezer looked at Joey as if he were trying to figure out what to say. "Well, it's for you," he said, placing another stem of grass between his lips. "The map's for you," he repeated. Beezer turned his gaze back to the distant antenna towers.

He got up. With a mighty groan he lifted the chest. "I'm going to put this away and go check on your brother. He's probably vomiting from eating too much chocolate." He lumbered off around the corner of the garage.

Joey stared at the "map." He was a little bit afraid to touch it. He reached out a hand and took it by the edge. It felt just like thick paper should feel. He picked up the parchment and held it close to his face. He didn't see anything. He held it toward the bright sky. There were no hidden lines or words. He did notice a tingling sensation in his fingertips. It may look blank, but there was something special about this piece of paper.

The creases where it had been folded were still there making it easy to fold again. Even folded it was far too big for his pockets.

"I need to keep this in a safe place in my room," he said.

As he walked under the weeping willow on the way to the screen door he heard the chimes. He looked up into the branches for the source. All he saw was the rocket, still dangling there, waiting for him.

Chapter 9

Joey took the map to his room and put it on his desk. On his way downstairs he stopped to look in Glory's room. His eyes rested on the dolls that lined her pillow. Every day she had one or two of these dolls in her arms. This made Joey wonder. On TV little girls gave their dolls tea parties and dressed them up. Glory didn't do this. She just carried them around pressed to her chest. She wasn't a shy, quiet little girl in need of comfort. Glory was bossy, manipulative, and clever. So why the dolls?

He stared, thinking. It occurred to him that a doll was missing—the skinny, little, Barbie-like doll with bad hair. The doll's hair was done up in dreadlocks. The dreadlocks stuck out in all directions and were tied off with colorful rubber bands. This doll wasn't soft or cuddly, but Glory seemed to favor it. Looking again Joey made sure the doll was missing. She must have had it with her at the pond. It probably fell in with her. What if it hadn't? It could be lying in the grass out there all alone. This possibility bothered Joey.

Downstairs he found Beezer and Story at the kitchen table stacking golden coins.

"I'm rich, I tell you. Rich!" Story said in pirate brogue.

"I'm going out for a few minutes," Joey said.

"Eh? Where you going?" asked Beezer.

Joey wondered what to say. Beezer might not let him go. His Mom wouldn't. Joey wasn't a very good liar. He didn't want to lie, anyway.

"I think Glory dropped her doll. I'm going to go find it for her."

"By the pond?" asked Beezer. He concentrated on his stack of coins as he spoke. It was starting to wobble.

"Yes," said Joey.

"You'll stay out of the pond?" said Beezer. A smile flickered on his lips for an instant as if he were making a joke.

"Yes," said Joey, feeling annoyed.

"Okay. Don't make me come looking for you. I don't like the way that pond smells."

Joey was surprised to be given permission. He wondered how good a baby sitter Beezer was.

Joey climbed over the fence using the fence-steps and made his way toward the pond. He didn't look hard for the doll until he got to the pond. He was sure that if she had dropped the doll it wouldn't have been until she was falling in.

Staying back from the steep bank Joey searched near the pond. He found nothing. The doll must have gone in with her. Joey was tempted to leave it at that. He had done his duty. As he turned to leave Joey felt bad. He realized he wanted to do more than his duty. He wanted to find the doll for his sister.

It occurred to him that the doll might have fallen onto the muddy bank on the slope to the water. To find out he would have to go to the edge of that steep, slippery, slope and look. The thought of getting that close to the pond turned his stomach. A breeze brought a stronger whiff of the sick, musty pond smell to his nose. The memory of the green water closing over his head flashed in his brain. Joey closed his eyes to get a hold of himself. He had to at least look.

Getting down on all fours he crawled to the edge of the bank. There it was, sitting just over the edge. It was face down and pressed into the mud as if Glory had slid over it on her way into the water.

As he reached down to retrieve the doll he glanced at the water—green, still, and deadly. The taste of it rose in his mouth. Grabbing the doll he backed away quickly.

On his way home Joey wiped mud from the doll's face. He used his fingernail to clean its eyes and lips. The dreadlocks were slimy. The doll stank of swamp.

When he walked into the kitchen he found Beezer and Story playing poker with Uno cards and the chocolate golden coins.

"You're bluffing," Story said. "I'll call you a liar and raise you a hundred." Story threw a handful of coins on a big pile in the middle of the table.

"Beat this," Beezer said. "Three green twos, a red seven, a blue three, and . . ." he paused for dramatic effect "Draw Four!"

"Ha! TWO Draw Fours AND a Draw two."

"You cheat!" Beezer bellowed. Story chortled deviously as he reached out with both arms and pulled the pile of coins into his already large stash.

Beezer glanced at Joey and the doll as Joey passed. He gave a satisfied nod. Joey took the doll to the bathroom and put it under running water. The body cleaned up easily, but he couldn't get the slimy mud out of the dreadlocks. Joey took out the rubber bands so he could get water through her hair more easily. He hoped Glory wouldn't mind. Using hand soap he washed her hair and dried it with a towel. Joey tried to wash the slime stains out of the thin fabric the doll had for a dress, but couldn't.

"Sorry, girl," he said to the doll. "My laundry skills aren't too good."

The doll's hair kinked and stuck out in clumps, but at least it was clean. He took a comb breaking it as he forced it through the doll's hair. If the doll were a real girl Joey figured she would take one look in the mirror and shoot herself. Joey glanced in the mirror. He paused at the sight of himself combing the hair of his sister's doll. He almost didn't recognize the boy in the mirror.

Taking the doll to Glory's room he laid it carefully against the pillow in the middle of the other dolls.

"Take care of her," he said to the other dolls. "She nearly died today."

Downstairs he found Story asleep on the couch in front of the T.V. It was playing *The Emperor's New Groove*, a family favorite. A breeze came through the open window and made the curtains dance around Story's feet. The gold coins filled a small box that had "Kraft Macaroni and Cheese" printed on the side. He found Beezer in the kitchen wearing the frilly apron. He had peeled potatoes and was cutting them up into a pot of boiling water.

"Cheesy potato soup," Beezer said without turning around. "You'll like it so much I'll have to teach your mother how to make it."

Joey moved to stand near Beezer. It had been a very eventful day. Fatigue and sadness caught up with him.

"What do you think is taking them so long?" Joey asked.

Beezer was cutting cheddar cheese into cubes. "Hospitals can be very busy places."

"What if Glory . . ." Joey began to say.

"You know she's going to be all right," Beezer interrupted. "When given the gift of faith, don't just throw it away."

When talking with Beezer earlier that day he had felt that Glory was going to be okay. Was that the "faith" Beezer spoke of?

"You don't look so good," Beezer said.

"I don't feel so good," Joey answered.

"Your sister is going to be okay. I'm making you my cheesy potato soup. Story is rich. You should be feeling great."

For once Beezer was wrong.

"I almost killed my sister today." Joey blurted it out. How could he "feel great?" He could barely hold back the tears.

Beezer didn't say anything. He stirred the melting cheese into the soup. After an agonizing twenty seconds he said, "Funny thing is, when I got to the pond I found you saving her life."

Beezer didn't understand. Joey couldn't hold his secret inside him. "If I hadn't run away she wouldn't have fallen in in the first place."

"So you ran off?" Beezer said. He glanced at Joey as if seeing him for the first time. Joey couldn't meet his eyes. Beezer sipped a spoonful of soup. "Mmmm," he said.

Beezer lowered the heat, wiped his hands on his apron, and turned to Joey. "Can you be so sure that if you had been there she wouldn't have fallen in?"

Joey thought about this. No, he couldn't be sure. He didn't have full control over Glory on the best of days. But that wasn't the point.

"I wasn't doing what I was supposed to be doing when she fell in," he said.

"I won't argue with that," Beezer said, offering no consolation.

There was more to Joey's confession. He had a hard time getting it out. "An . . . and then I was too afraid to jump in." Tears slipped from his eyes. He let them roll off his chin.

"So why did I find you in the pond giving your life for your sister?" As he said this Beezer turned and poured a can of evaporated milk into the soup.

Joey didn't answer. It's true, he had jumped in. What Beezer didn't know was that he wouldn't have jumped in if the voice in his head hadn't made him jump. He would have stood there and let Glory die. Joey heard the gurgle she made before she slipped under the last time. Joey closed his eyes and cringed at the memory. He wanted to explain all this to Beezer, but he couldn't find the words.

Beezer turned and looked down at Joey. His big eyes were serious. "Did anyone push you in, or did you slip in, too?"

"No," Joey said. His voice came out raspy. "I jumped in."

Beezer turned to look at Joey. "So you were afraid to jump in, but you jumped in anyway? You know what that's called?"

Joey shook his head.

"That's called courage." He said this gently, proudly. Turning back to the stove he stirred the soup.

Joey heard the muffled sound of crunching gravel and a truck engine. He ran to the front door to see Mrs. Johanaby getting out. His heart skipped a beat. Where was Glory?

Mrs. Johanaby walked to the passenger side, opened the door and lifted Glory out in her arms. Joey watched as she brought Glory up the steps. Glory was awake. Their eyes met as they passed. She looked tired and pale, but was very much alive. Mrs. Johanaby took her straight upstairs and put her to bed.

Joey was setting the table when Mrs. Johanaby came in. She looked pale and tired too.

"The soup is ready," Beezer said. "Sit down and have a bowl."

Mrs. Johanaby looked around the kitchen and slowly took in what Beezer had been doing.

"Oh," she said, looking awkward. She sat down next to a bowl full of steaming potato soup. For an instant Joey caught a glimpse of Mrs. Johanaby as a little girl doing as her mother asked.

As Joey and Mrs. Johanaby ate Beezer cleaned up the counter and then walked to the back door.

"Aren't you going to have some soup?" asked Mrs. Johanaby.

"Nope," said Beezer. "I just made enough for you. My dinner is waiting back at the cottage."

It was then Mrs. Johanaby noticed that Story wasn't there with them. "Where . . . ?" she began.

"He's asleep in the TV room, Mom," Joey said.

"He's probably out for the night," Beezer added. "He found a fortune today. That tends to wear a kid out. Well, g'night." He went out the screen door into the dusk.

"A fortune?" Mrs. Johanaby asked. She asked it tiredly like she didn't have enough energy to hear the answer. She took a sip of soup.

"It was a game." Joey offered.

Mrs. Johanaby looked at Joey not really comprehending. Then looking down at her bowl said, "This soup is really good."

"He says he'll teach you the recipe if you like."

Mrs. Johanaby looked up and managed a weak smile. "Would you like?" she asked.

The question made Joey feel good. For the first time since she had walked in the door she was actually present with him.

"How's Glory?" Joey asked more casually than he felt.

Mrs. Johanaby took her time with a spoonful of soup before answering. "She's going to be fine," she said.

"You were gone so long."

Mrs. Johanaby put her spoon down and rubbed her temples as if the memory gave her a headache.

"It was a madhouse at the emergency room. A nurse looked her over briefly. Then we sat for two hours before a doctor saw her."

Mrs. Johanaby's voice wavered with emotion. "She was coughing and I was so scared. Finally when the doctor did see her he thought it might be good to keep her for observation overnight in the hospital." Mrs. Johanaby stopped and covered her face with her hands.

"But you brought her home," Joey said.

Mrs. Johanaby removed her hands and said rather fiercely, "Because when he found out we didn't have insurance he suddenly decided she was going to be fine!"

They sat in silence and stared at each other. Joey looked down at the last potato in his bowl. "Is she?" he asked quietly.

"Yes, I think she is. She just needs a good rest." Mrs. Johanaby spoke as if trying to convince herself. She went on, stress edging her voice, "It's best she came home. I don't know how we'll even pay for the emergency room visit."

Joey's heart ached at his mother's distress. It ached all the more because he knew his actions had caused it.

"I'm sorry, Mom."

"No! Don't you be sorry for anything. You are a good boy and a good son. I shouldn't be telling you all my problems. *I'm* the sorry one."

"Mom?" Joey said.

"I'm sorry your father died," Mrs. Johanaby went on. "I'm sorry I don't have more job skills so you don't have to babysit. I'm sorry . . ."

"Mom?" Joey spoke a little louder.

"I'm sorry. I'm really, *really* sorry, Joey," she said. She put her spoon down and wiped tears from her eyes, and then tried to go on. "This afternoon, Joey, at the pond. I . . . I didn't . . . Oh, I'm so sorry." She put her hands to her face and sobbed.

Joey felt his heart breaking. He had seen his mother like this once before. It was at Mr. Johanaby's funeral. She hadn't cried about his death until the memorial. As the speakers brought all the memories to the surface her grief overflowed. It looked to Joey like

116

she was suffering that same kind of grief all over again. This time it was his fault.

Joey knew what his mom was going to say. She was thinking of how she had forgotten him in the pond after pulling Glory out.

"Mom!" Joey said. He almost shouted the word to get her attention. Her sobbing continued, but she looked at him. "It's okay. Really it is."

Now Joey began to cry. "I deserved it, Mom."

Mrs. Johanaby reacted as if shocked by an electric current. Her sobs stopped suddenly. "What are you talking about?" Her voice was cold and wary. "Deserved what?" she asked.

"Mom," he said. He stopped while trying to gain courage to say the words. "Mom, I wasn't there when Glory fell in." Joey's voice broke as he sobbed some more.

"You weren't there?" Mrs. Johanaby echoed.

"Glory made me mad this morning and I ran away. I abandoned them."

Joey suddenly felt afraid as he saw understanding growing in his mother's eyes. He shouldn't have told her. What would come next would be too much. He covered his face with his hands.

"You left them alone?" There was bewilderment in her voice with a hint of anger at the edge. "Joey? You left them alone?" The pitch of her voice was rising. "How could you!"

The question ran like a spear through his heart. How could he? He had betrayed his mother, his brother and sister. He was something worse than a coward. What was the word for that?

Joey felt desperate from shame. He would say anything to make his Mom love him again.

"So you see, Mom, it's okay. At the pond this afternoon, when you . . ."

Like his mother Joey couldn't say the words.

"What's okay?" Mrs. Johanaby sounded hysterical. "That your sister almost drowned because you weren't there?"

"NO, Mom. That's not what I meant. That's not wh . . ."

In his guilt his tongue tripped over the words.

"I was bad. I was wrong." Joey's sobs made his words come out slurred and broken. "That's why what happened after, what happened with . . . with you is okay."

117

The weight of the silence that followed crushed the sobs out of him. Joey looked up to see Mrs. Johanaby staring at him with her mouth open, a look of horror on her face. Of all the times Joey had made his mother angry he had never seen her reach this point. He felt fear like a person would feel just before the firing squad pulls the trigger, just before you are caught doing something awful.

"Mom," he whispered.

"NO, JOEY! NO!" Mrs. Johanaby screamed. She pounded the table with each "no." "Nothing today is okay. It's NOT okay that you ran away. It's NOT okay that your sister almost drowned. And it's definitely not . . . it's certainly . . . it's terribly . . ." Mrs. Johanaby struggled for words. She gave up and repeated, "NO, Joey. NO!"

Joey understood. The truth was a horrible monster. He would never be able to hide or outrun it. *No, Joey was not okay. No, Joey was not brave. No, Joey was not loyal. No, Joey did not deserve his mother's love. No, Joey did not deserve to be saved.*

With a wail of despair Joey ran from the kitchen leaving his chair lying on its side on the floor. In the hallway he ran directly into Story who, half asleep, was nonetheless carrying his box of golden coins. Coins hit the roof before landing with Story on the floor. Joey bolted for the stairs. Behind him he heard Story waking up enough to cry. He heard the desperate tone in Mrs. Johanaby's voice as she called his name.

When he ran past Glory's room he thought he heard a little voice call his name. Not slowing down he ran to the attic stairs slamming the door behind him. He was halfway up the stairs before he turned back and locked the door. He wanted to be alone.

The moon was full. Soft light streamed in his windows brightening the room. He threw himself on his bed and buried his face in his pillow. Something hard and irregular was in the way. It was a doll; the same doll Glory had dropped at the pond. The doll was not welcome. He blindly launched the doll across the room. He had meant it to hit the wall. Instead it flew out the window into the branches of the weeping willow. He put his face in his pillow and cried himself to sleep.

Chapter 10

Long after Joey had fallen asleep movement disturbed the stillness of the night. Something gentle, soft, entered Joey's window. A breath of damp, night air brushed Joey's cheek. Joey was so exhausted he could have slept through a thunder storm. But in this almost imperceptible movement of air someone called Joey's name. Pulled unwilling from a deep sleep Joey rolled over and sat up. Groggily, he looked for whoever had spoken to him. There was no one there. Someone had whispered in his ear and awoken him. He was certain. A faint scent of lilacs lingered in the room.

"Who's there?" Joey said. The presence, or the memory of the presence, brought no fear.

In response Joey heard the sound of wind chimes. They were soft and faraway. Joey held his breath. The chimes sounded like crystal goblets tapped by a silver spoon. The sound was beautiful to the ear and the heart. Joey could have sat there forever listening.

The chimes stopped suddenly as if someone had turned off a radio.

"No," Joey said in alarm. Silence filled the space the chimes had taken. Joey went to the window hoping to hear the chimes again. He *needed* to hear them again. There was something soothing and healing in their sound.

The full moon was in the western sky casting long shadows on the ground. The night air was warm and sweet. Joey took a deep breath. He picked out the scents of grass, trees, lilacs, and faintly, the sour smell of the distant pond.

The smell of the pond brought back the memory of his sister and the near tragedy that day.

The doll!

He had accidentally thrown the doll out this window before he went to sleep. He couldn't see it in the shadows below. How had the doll gotten in his room anyway? He had left it on Glory's pillow. Had Glory brought it up? That didn't seem likely. When he saw her she had looked too weak to walk.

Unable to understand how it arrived on his pillow Joey wondered why it was there. That scraggly doll was Glory's favorite. Joey knew that. She would never give that doll to someone she liked let alone someone she hated, like Joey. Giving the doll away would be a sacrifice for her.

A thought came to Joey quietly, clearly, like the sound of the chimes. The doll was Glory's way of telling him "thank you?" The idea moved him deeply. This feeling was immediately pushed aside by guilt. He had almost let her drown. He physically shuddered with shame at the memory. She didn't know or she wouldn't be sacrificing something so important to her.

Another realization slipped into his mind. His mother had not known he had abandoned his brother and sister. She had not known Glory and Story were by themselves when Glory fell into the pond. Glory hadn't told her. Why?

"Why the doll? Why didn't she tell?" The questions repeated in his head until he thought he was going to scream. A thought unfolded in his mind like Morning Glory flowers do in the morning sun.

Glory loves me?

Once again Joey looked down in the shadows for the doll. He had to go get the doll.

Joey crept down the stairs and found the attic door open. He stopped to think. He remembered he had closed it with a bang and then gone back to lock it. His Mom had the key. Had she come up?

He continued down cringing at every creaky step and groaning floorboard. Instead of going through the kitchen to the back door he was distracted by a light in the library. His mother was not one to stay up late. Joey wondered what was going on.

Stepping quietly Joey made his way down the hallway. Peeking carefully into the library Joey saw his mother at the computer typing at a furious rate. After a barrage of clicks she would stop to think. Then she would begin the assault on the keyboard again. The floorboard creaked as he shifted his weight. Joey froze. Mrs. Johanaby was so intent on what she was writing that she didn't hear. Relieved, he backed away and made his way outside.

Joey stepped onto the back step and carefully shut the screen door. The night enveloped him just like the water at the pond that afternoon. The water had been suffocating and frightening; the night felt fresh and welcoming. The crickets near him stopped their song a moment, but those in the distance sang on as merrily as ever.

He looked up at the stars. Sometimes they twinkled and pulsed as if they were happy. Other times they looked like part of something bigger trying to break through the confinement of the night sky. Tonight they just seemed thoughtful.

Joey didn't have to search for the doll. It was lying on the ground in plain sight next to . . . Beezer's rocket? Joey looked up into the branches to make sure it was the same rocket that had been hanging there for so long. It was. It was like they had fallen to the ground together.

"No way!" Joey almost laughed. Sitting down on his knees he folded the parachute into a rectangle, then rolled it up and pushed it into the rocket. He replaced the nosecone. It was far bigger than any of the rockets he and his dad had made. He could almost see his father sitting on the other side of the rocket as they prepared it for launch. He pushed the thought out of his head quickly. Thoughts of his father still made him feel empty.

Leaning the rocket against the tree he picked up the doll. None the worse for the fall she looked up at Joey with happy, unaccusing eyes. Joey ran a finger through her wild hair. He wondered if Glory had given her to him to keep or would she want her back?

A warm breeze, unnatural to the night, made a soft rushing sound through the branches above him. When it stopped the night was still again except for the crickets. It was like the tree had just cleared its throat to get his attention.

Joey looked up into the branches. The leaves glowed pale-green in the moonlight. The branches looked like dark tentacles hanging below a giant jelly fish. Laying his hand on the trunk Joey thought he could feel the tree's pulse. It may have been another breeze, but the tree seemed to sigh with pleasure at his touch.

Joey began to climb by moonlight. As he got higher and the branches became fewer and thinner Joey's breathing quickened. Butterflies danced in his stomach. He had been high on a Ferris wheel once, but it hadn't been near as thrilling as this.

Joey got so high that the thin branches swayed with his weight. Although not at the top of the tree, he knew he was high enough. He sat down on a branch and took in the view. His home looked strange from this perspective. The window to his room was below him. He looked out across the night landscape. The woods and the fields formed soft textures in the shadows.

Joey looked up at the stars. They were beautiful, but they made him sad tonight. As high as he was in the tree, the stars were still so far away. He hadn't really expected them to be any closer; still, he *wanted* them to be. Joey felt that old ache inside him—the ache that had been born when his father died. He was afraid he was going to cry again.

"How many tears do I hold?" He thought. He fought to hold them down.

After his father had died his mother had tried to comfort Joey. She said that Mr. Johanaby was alive just as he had been alive in this world, but now he was in the spirit world.

Looking at the stars he said, "The spirit world is as far away as the stars, so what does it matter if he is there or not?"

The sudden sound of his voice disturbed the darkness. A gentle gust of wind caressed Joey's face and ran fingers through his hair. The tree sighed once more.

Joey felt that speaking out loud had been wrong. "I'm sorry," he whispered to the tree, to the night.

In response Joey heard a single note of the wind chime. He held his breath hoping for more. Two more notes sounded, and then three more. The notes danced in the air like fireflies.

The sounds came from nearby, as if they were in the tree with him. They were more beautiful than all the sounds, feels, and smells of the country night put together.

"Joey."

The voice came from every direction as if the very night had whispered his name.

Joey soundlessly mouthed "Yes?"

"Joey."

This time it was louder, yet still soft and gentle. He recognized it. It was the girl's voice he heard at the pond.

"Joey."

This time it was a laugh. It wasn't a laugh making fun, but a laugh of delight. It came from the direction of the cellar.

Joey looked down and watched a beautiful woman walk through the cellar doors. She glowed in the darkness like a candle. Her dark hair hung in curls around her head. Her blue eyes shone in the dark. The hem of her voluminous hoop skirt dragged lightly on the ground as she moved.

"Henrietta!" Joey whispered.

She must have heard. Her eyes went to the tree and quickly found him. The hairs on his arms and the back of his neck rose. He grew light headed. He wondered what she would do next.

She smiled. It wasn't the ghastly smile of the dead, but a warm and charming smile. She looked happy to see him.

The night started spinning. For an instant he thought he was going to fall out of the tree. He closed his eyes and clung to the branch.

The wind chimes struck a sterner note. *"Don't* do that," Henrietta said.

Her voice stopped the spinning. Joey felt the tree bark cutting into his arms and loosened his hold. Opening his eyes he saw Henrietta walking toward him. She rose higher off the ground with each step as if she were climbing stairs. She walked right through the narrow hanging branches without disturbing them. When she reached the branch Joey was sitting on she turned around and sat down beside him. She had nothing to lean against or hang on to, yet she sat as comfortably as if she were in a chair. Her hoop skirt flowed through the branches. Part of it flowed over Joey's legs like colorful fog. He felt coolness on his legs where the fabric rested.

Joey stared at Henrietta open-mouthed. Here was a ghost—a beautiful ghost—sitting in a tree with him. After Beezer's stories, meeting Henrietta was like unexpectedly meeting your favorite movie star.

After she was settled she looked at Joey. Her face was pale, her lips red, and her eyes glowing blue. Her arched eyebrows lifted and an amused smile rose on her lips. "As a young girl I was taught it isn't nice to stare."

She spoke with a Tennessee accent and with music. Henrietta's voice was the embodiment of all the chimes he had heard since he had arrived at the mansion. The sound of her voice sent shivers of happiness down his spine.

"I'm sorry," Joey said, still unable to take his eyes off her.

Henrietta laughed delightfully. Chimes jingled merrily.

"Actually, I'd be surprised if you didn't stare," she said. "How often does a person get to see a ghost?"

"Especially one as pretty as you," Joey said.

Henrietta's face glowed a little brighter.

"You are a charming young man," Henrietta said. She reached out her hand and tousled his hair. Joey couldn't feel her hand, but the hair on the top of his head blew in a soft breeze.

"I'm afraid I wasn't quite so pretty when I was alive. It's amazing what being dead does for a person." She laughed again, but the chimes didn't sound as happy this time.

Henrietta turned her blue eyes to the stars. Joey continued to gaze at Henrietta. She glowed soft like starlight, but was far more beautiful.

After sitting in silence for a full minute, it dawned on Joey what a strange situation he was in—sitting in a tree with a ghost. This had dream written all over it. Joey pinched himself on his wrist to see if he was really awake.

"Ow," he said, pinching too hard.

Henrietta looked at Joey, curiously. "If you've bruised yourself I suppose in the morning you'll blame it on the evil ghost, won't you?"

"Evil ghost?" Joey asked, rubbing his wrist.

"The one you were so afraid of in the cellar this morning."

Joey remembered his fear in the dark that morning. "Oh," he hung his head. "I don't think it was you I was afraid of. It was just so dark . . . and something bad had happened there once, and my imagination just went nuts."

"Yes," Henrietta said. She was looking down at the cellar doors. She paused a moment in thought. "Something bad happened there, at least for Uncle Orson it did."

"Uncle Orson?"

"Colonel Horsebaum," Henrietta clarified.

"But, it was you who was . . . was," Joey didn't know if it was rude to say it.

"Murdered," Henrietta said. A flat, dull chime sounded. "Yes, it was me that was murdered. But that was only sad—sad for me and those who loved me. It wasn't 'bad.' What was 'bad' was what Uncle Orson did. He did something he could never make right, not in life or in death. Doing something like that is 'bad.' Poor Uncle Orson." The saddest, loneliest chime Joey had ever heard sounded.

"You feel sorry for your uncle?"

"Yes," Henrietta said with a spark. She looked at Joey. Her blue eyes went smoky for a moment. "Having your life taken early is sad, but something even as sad as that can be set right. The act of taking life, if done willfully and with sound mind, cannot be set right. The thought that my uncle might suffer his grief for eternity breaks my heart." Chimes, each out of tune with the next, sounded in dissonance.

Her glow dimmed. She put her face in her hands. The ghostly fabric over Joey's legs grew cold. Joey wanted to put his hand on Henrietta's shoulder to comfort her, but he didn't dare.

"I'm so sorry," Joey said.

"Sorry?" Henrietta slowly moved her hands away from her face. "Sorry for what?"

"Sorry that your Uncle did something that makes you so sad."

Henrietta looked into his face. Her glow returned. He saw translucent lines shining on her pale face. Ghost tears.

"That is a start, Joey Johanaby. Feeling for someone else, it makes you special."

Hearing such kind words from Henrietta's ghostly lips sent a surge of joy through his body. His face burned in such a blush he wondered if it shone like Henrietta's.

Joey wanted to linger in the warmth of her kind words. He wanted to be special. The dark memories of the previous day didn't allow this joy long. They rolled in like dark clouds and snuffed out his joy like sudden gust of wind putting out a candle.

"But I'm not so special," Joey said, hanging his head. It felt important for him to get this out in the open.

"Tell me why," Henrietta said. She didn't stare at him. Instead she gazed across the shadowy nightscape.

"I think you know why," Joey said, staring down into the misty fabric over his legs.

"Tell me," Henrietta said again, her voice soft and compelling.

Joey searched for words. In the year since his father had died this was the first time anyone had asked him how he felt. People had told him how to feel. They had told him that he must feel very sad, that he must feel lost without his father, that he must be very brave to help his mother now that his father was gone, but no one had ever asked him *how* he felt.

"I'm just so afraid all the time," he said. "I'm afraid I'll never see my dad again. I was afraid of things even when he was alive, but he gave me hope that I could learn to be brave. Now I can't even hope anymore." Joey stopped here and wiped tears from his eyes. *I'm also a crybaby*, he thought.

Henrietta, comfortable with silence, sat waiting for Joey to go on.

"Today proved it," Joey said, finally going on. "I was afraid of the dark. I fainted." Joey said the words bitterly seeing no need to try to lessen the truth. He looked over at Henrietta. She still gazed to the west seeing something in the dark Joey could not see.

"I abandoned Glory and Story." Joey wiped his nose on his hand. "Glory drives me crazy," he said, but it was more of an apology than a complaint. "Somehow I always lose to her. I always look bad to Mom because of her."

Joey thought a moment before going on more quietly. "I think Mom loves her—loves her and Story—more than me." Joey paused and looked out where Henrietta looked before going on. "Maybe she should. There's something bold and strong about them."

Henrietta turned her head slowly and looked at Joey with softly lit eyes. Still she said nothing.

"You were at the pond, weren't you," Joey said, his voice quivering with shame. Henrietta nodded slowly.

Joey looked away from her eyes because in them he could see it all again—Glory's pale face breaking the surface of the green water. He heard her cough and choke as she went back under. And he just stood on the bank afraid to help her.

"I saw you save her, Joey," Henrietta said.

"Stop! Just stop saying that," Joey yelled. "That's what Beezer said and it's just not true. I wouldn't have jumped in if you hadn't made me. I would have stood there and watched her drown." The weight of that truth struck him full in the chest. He put his head against the tree and sobbed.

Henrietta gave him a moment before speaking. "I didn't push you into that pond, Joey."

Joey heard her but sobbed on.

"Your sister would have drowned if you had not jumped in and saved her; *and I did not push you into that pond.*"

Her last words were intense, almost angry. Joey could not ignore them. Trying to check his sobbing, Joey said, "Okay, so I jumped in by myself." Joey hiccupped from the crying. "But I wouldn't have jumped in if you hadn't told me to." This was the truth; Joey knew it. If Henrietta refuted it she would be lying.

People always lied to make you feel better. His Uncle Steve had held his Mom just after Mr. Johanaby had died and told her everything was going to be alright. It was a lie. Everything had not been all right.

"Joey."

Joey turned and looked into Henrietta's eyes daring her to tell him he was wrong. Henrietta didn't speak. She leaned in bringing her face closer to his. The light in her eyes went from a candle to a fire. She opened her mouth and exhaled. Her breath was visible like his on a cold morning. It sparkled in the moonlight. When it reached him the night dissolved.

He was standing in the cellar. He recognized the musty potato smell. The room was lit by a lantern sitting on a shelf. Cowering in a little cave dug into the earthen cellar wall was a black man, a woman, and a little baby the woman was holding. A curtain, that had covered the opening, lay on the dirt floor. Facing them and holding a pistol was a tall man in a grey suit. His black tie hung perfectly straight down the center of his white shirt. His mustache covered his upper lip and hung down on either side of his mouth.

"Colonel Horsebaum!" whispered Joey.

Beside him was Henrietta. She *was* just as pretty alive as she was dead. She was wearing the same curls and dress she was wearing now. Joey could see them speaking, but he couldn't hear anything they said. Colonel Horsebaum's face was red and he swung the pistol back and forth as he spoke. Henrietta put her hand on his arm as she pled with him. Colonel Horsebaum shoved her to the ground. The black man moved to help Henrietta. Colonel Horsebaum aimed the pistol at the black man to shoot.

Now Joey could hear. The black woman holding the child cried out, "Miss Henrietta!"

Henrietta, who had raised herself on her arms, threw herself on Colonel Horsebaum. There was a muffled gunshot. Henrietta, her eyes wide in surprise, sank to the floor amid her billowing hoop skirt. A wet, crimson stain blossomed below her left bosom.

Colonel Horsebaum stared down through the gun smoke in horror. The gun slipped out of his hand and he sank to his knees. He gathered Henrietta into his arms and pulled her close. Colonel Horsebaum spoke Henrietta's name softly at first, then more loudly. He looked up at the floorboards and wailed in anguish.

Henrietta's head lay back over his arm. She had died with her eyes open. Surprise and—was it fear?—showed in them.

The fear in her eyes bothered Joey. He tried to look away, but found his eyes locked to hers. He didn't want to see the fear. Then he realized why—it embarrassed him.

Henrietta the ghost was serene and confident. Seeing her like this was wrong. He felt like he had accidentally come upon her half-dressed. He tried to shut his eyes. They wouldn't close.

The cellar faded, but Henrietta did not. Joey found himself back in the tree holding the dead Henrietta in his arms. Her frightened, but lifeless eyes stared into his. Like Colonel Horsebaum Joey called out her name.

"Henrietta!"

The soft blue light flickered back into her eyes. The fear left her face and was replaced by gentle concern. Looking down Joey saw the crimson stain fading away until Henrietta was again whole as a ghost can be. With silent grace she sat up.

Joey wiped his eyes with his free hand. "Why did you show me that?" He heard anger in his voice.

"I didn't want to die," Henrietta said. "I was afraid," She stared down thoughtfully at her skirt.

Joey felt awkward with her admission of fear. To him, fear was a shameful thing. "But you were so brave," Joey said. "You saved that family with your life."

"That's what happened," Henrietta said. "But I didn't mean for it to happen. It wouldn't have happened had not that woman cried out to me for help." Henrietta turned her head and looked at Joey. "Do you see?"

"You . . . you didn't have to leap on your uncle," Joey said.

"And you didn't have to leap into the pond," Henrietta finished.

Joey couldn't argue with this. Her point was made. Why didn't he feel any better? What he had done and what Henrietta had done were similar, but not the same. He couldn't put his finger on the difference. She looked so heroic as she jumped in front of the gun. Had he looked heroic when he jumped in the pond? No. All he could see was the ugly face of his own fear mocking him as he jumped.

Three notes sounded at once in a chord. The lowest of the three notes outlasted the others and floated on the night shadows like a dandelion seed in warm afternoon air.

As Joey listened he wondered. Sometimes Henrietta seemed to control the chimes like a musician. Other times the chimes seemed to live on their own following her like butterflies. These last chimes brought her out of her reverie. The mood changed. Henrietta started swinging her legs with a little more energy.

"Dawn is coming," she said. "Time for all good ghosts to go to bed."

"Bed?" Joey said. "Ghosts go to bed?"

"In a manner of speaking," Henrietta said.

"You go to your grave and rest?" Joey asked. He was thinking of the story of her nightly walk to the grave as Colonel Horsebaum watched in anguish.

"Heavens no," Henrietta said. A ripple of shadow ran across her person at the thought. Joey recognized it as a shiver of disgust. "That's no place for a lady."

Joey was confused. "But Colonel Horsebaum watched you walk from the cellar to the graveyard every night until he died."

"It makes a great ghost story," Henrietta said, showing a little enthusiasm at the idea. "But it never happened."

"Beezer said . . ."

"Beezer," Henrietta said with a smile and slight shake of her head. "Beezer can't resist the romance of a good ghost story." She thought a moment adding, "Although he should."

"Oh," Joey said, not sure if he was hurt or disappointed by this truth.

"No, the last time Colonel Horsebaum and I saw each other was in the cellar on that . . . that night." They both looked down at the cellar door waiting for something to happen.

"So, if you're here, where is Colonel Horsebaum," Joey asked.

Still swinging her legs Henrietta contemplated the answer. "I don't know exactly where Uncle Orson is. I know he's in a place where maybe, just maybe, he might learn something about himself."

Joey sensed Henrietta's pending departure. He still wasn't certain if this was all a dream. If it was a dream he knew it would never happen twice. He wanted to know more, and dream or not here was the one person who might actually know the answers.

"Henrietta?" Joey said.

"Mmmm?"

Joey spoke nervously. "Why are you wandering around this house? You don't seem like the type for haunting."

"I'm glad to hear that," Henrietta said with a light laugh that danced with the tiniest chimes. "The truth is I'm not really a ghost at all, at least not the haunting kind. My interests don't really lie in this world anymore. I've just been sent back to accomplish a task."

"A task?" said Joey. "Who sent you? What task?"

"There, you see! I've said too much already," Henrietta said, chiding herself.

"My dad," Joey said quickly. He was so afraid Henrietta was going to disappear before he could ask the question. "My dad died of cancer just last year. Have you seen him?"

"No, Joey. I haven't seen your father." She spread her arms like she was presenting herself, "But I know he's there, just like I'm here," she said.

"How can you know he's there if you haven't seen him?" Joey said, angrily.

"You know how I know," Henrietta said. "Beezer has talked to you about this."

Yes, this "knowing without knowing" business. Joey wanted something more.

"If you can be here talking to me right now, then why can't he?"

"Joey," Henrietta said, softly. Joey wasn't listening.

"I need to talk to my dad." Joey reached for Henrietta's shoulder. He touched nothing but cold mist.

"Joey," Henrietta said again, trying to get his attention.

"Please! If I could just talk to him once."

"Joey!" there was a dissonant clash of chimes. The sound hit Joey's ears like slap on the face.

"I came to help you understand how brave you are. I came to help you understand how much you love your family." More softly, as if speaking to herself she added, "This was supposed to be a happy visit." Henrietta looked troubled.

"I have to go, Joey." She hesitated, giving Joey time to respond. He didn't. Instead he looked away, ignoring her.

"I think you are brave and patient and thoughtful and wonderful in every way," Henrietta said. She put her pale hand through Joey's hair. His hair lifted in a breath of air. She stood and then descended to the ground becoming more transparent as she went. By the time she reached the ground she was gone.

The moment after she disappeared a double bitterness hit Joey. He missed his father more deeply than ever. Added to that was the knowledge he had acted badly toward an extraordinary person.

"Henrietta?" He desperately wanted to apologize. "I'm sorry," he said. He listened carefully. No chime answered. Joey put his head against the tree and moaned in pain and shame.

Joey sat in the tree until his legs started going numb. Depressed and dead tired Joey made his way toward his attic loft. As he passed Glory's room her little voice called out startling him.

"Joey?"

Joey could just make out the edge of her bed by the light of the setting moon. "Yes, it's me," he whispered.

"I thought I heard something outside," she said.

"You did?" he asked.

"I thought I heard music," she whispered. "It was pretty, like wind chimes."

Joey stood there for a moment looking into the darkness where Glory's voice came from. Finally he said, "Wind chimes? Yes, I've heard them, too."

"Goodnight, Joey," she said.

Joey heard her turn over in her bed. "Goodnight," he whispered.

Slowly, Joey climbed the attic stairs and fell across his bed into sleep.

Chapter 11

Joey awoke late the next morning feeling stiff and used up. He had slept in his clothes. They were wrinkled and twisted around his body. As he sat up he noticed that his shoes were sitting neatly side-by-side next to his bed. He didn't remember taking them off.

He stumbled over to the window looking out on the weeping willow. The late morning sky was overcast with heavy, dark clouds. Looking up he found the branch he had sat on the night before with Henrietta. Last night it had been magical. This morning it looked so ordinary.

Henrietta had been lovely; her musical voice so pleasant. He stared up at the branch remembering how she looked. Her glow. Her blue eyes lit from inside like Chinese lanterns. He brushed his thigh with his hand remembering the coolness of her dress on his leg. More than how she looked it was how she was that Joey remembered—graceful, strong, kind.

He remembered the way their talk had ended. She had been loving and supportive. He had been depressing. The shame of it hit him again. He hung his head. How could he ever make that right? Joey raised his head and listened. More than anything he wanted to hear chimes. A single note would do. There were no chimes that morning. There were no usual morning sounds at all. It was like the world had stopped.

A big drop of rain fell against the window sill with a *plop*. It splashed onto his hands. Another drop hit the window pane over his head. It sounded like a small stone against the glass. He heard two more drops land against the limbs of the weeping willow. Guessing what was coming, Joey shut the windows.

On his way downstairs Joey stopped at Glory's room. He found it empty. Her dolls lay shoulder to shoulder on her pillow. That made him think—had he brought in the doll he had gone out to fetch last night? No, he forgot to pick up the doll when he had finally come down from the tree.

He hurried downstairs to the back porch. The rain was coming down steadily now. Everything was already wet and dripping. Joey was surprised and dismayed when he saw there was nothing at the base of the tree—not Glory's doll or Beezer's rocket. Had Glory seen it and already retrieved it? The possibility worried him. What would she think of him?

He went back through the kitchen to the family room where he heard the TV blaring. Glory lay on the couch propped up by pillows. She was dressed in her pink robe and eating butterscotch pudding. Mrs. Johanaby always fed them butterscotch pudding when they were recuperating. Glory's leg hung over the edge of the couch. She swung it restlessly. Story lay on the floor stacking his treasure coins into columns that looked like the ruins of ancient Greek buildings.

Joey entered the room quietly. He wanted to see if Glory had the doll before Glory saw him. She was engrossed in a show on TV featuring slime. He got close enough to see she had her arm wrapped around one of her nicer dolls—one in a long blue dress. It had a porcelain head with green eyes.

Joey felt relieved it wasn't the doll he threw out the window. He was beginning to back out of the room when he noticed Glory's swinging leg change directions. He watched as Glory's restless leg swung a little farther each swing until her big toe made contact with the nearest column of coins. Story sucked in a breath as the column of coins rocked. The column teetered over knocking down several other columns with it.

"Glory!" he yelled. He scooped the golden coins together and then pushed them out of her reach. "You did that on purpose."

"I didn't," she lied. Then she grinned and giggled.

"I'm going to tell Mom," Story threatened.

A look of pain crossed Glory's face and she sank deeper into her pillows.

"I don't feel good," she moaned.

Story was considering Glory's sincerity when he noticed Joey.

"Hi, Joey," he said.

Joey nodded a "good morning" and headed for the door. He didn't want to talk to Glory until he found the doll. Glory's head popped up over the back of the couch. Joey glanced over his shoulder as he went out the door and their eyes met. Her dark-brown eyes were pretty. He had never noticed that before.

Down the hall he could hear rapid tapping. Peeking into the library he found his mother much as she was the night before—sitting in front of that giant, old monitor typing furiously. Her hair was mussed. She was wearing her ragged, cut-off sweat pants and her old Scooby Doo t-shirt.

He backed away from her door. The house felt strange this morning. Something had changed since yesterday. The dark clouds and rain had something to do with it. It hadn't rained since they got there. But it was more than that. Mrs. Johanaby was usually so structured. The daily routines were not in effect today. What happened last night between him and his mom still hung in the air.

Joey went to the kitchen and made two pieces of toast. The toaster was set on high, the way Story liked it. The toast came out extra crunchy. Joey tried to counter the crunch with extra butter, but crumbs fell with each bite. Joey brushed the crumbs from the table onto the floor and then climbed to his attic room to look for Glory's doll. Maybe he had brought it up and forgotten. It wasn't there.

Joey stood by his bed in the middle of his room and thought. The rain pounded steadily on the roof in a hypnotic way. The house felt wounded by yesterday's events. A blueness settled deep in his chest. Joey sat down on the bed and wondered how he was going to get through this day. The dark clouds outside sucked the goldness from his room. The walls looked grey this morning.

Like a match flaring to life a little patch of goldness flickered against the wall. Joey noticed it out of the corner of his eye. It was coming from his desk. Joey got up to investigate. At the back of his desk was the map that Beezer had made for him the day before.

It had been folded in half two times with the free edges facing the wall. The source of the light was inside the map.

Joey picked up the map and carefully unfolded it. As he did so the darkness of the day melted in a bright, warm light. What had been a blank piece of paper the day before was now a map. The map wasn't just ink on paper; it was a window into another world. On the paper Joey saw ships, islands, and a vast country with low lands rising to high, snowcapped mountains. Joey smelled ocean and trees. He heard crashing waves and singing birds. The ships dipped and rose on the swells. Birds sailed on warm air currents.

The dark day disappeared as Joey stared into the map. The sights, sounds, and smells enchanted him. He would have stood staring all day had not words appeared at the bottom. Light flared like a flame as each letter appeared in a flowing script.

The adventure starts in Beezer's room.

The adventure ends in your heart.

Joey didn't know what the last part meant, but he understood the first part clearly enough. The power of the map was strong. It took great effort to fold it. As he did the darkness of the day swept back into the room making Joey feel weak. He reached out and steadied himself on the desk.

The adventure starts in Beezer's room.

Joey could see the words in his mind. They excited and frightened him at the same time. Despite his fear there was no question he would go and meet this adventure. He would do anything to escape the darkness of the mansion today. As his strength came back Joey turned and left his room. He stopped and looked back over his shoulder. Deep down he had a feeling that he might never come back.

Joey hesitated on the back porch before running out into the torrential rain. He put the map inside his shirt and leaned forward as he ran to try to keep it dry. The rain was warm as it ran down his neck. He was soaked after three steps. When he got to the garage he found the doors shut and latched from the outside. It didn't matter. He knew that Beezer was in there. Joey unlatched the doors and pulled hard to slide one side open. He wondered if Mrs. Johanaby could hear the screeching of the rusty wheels through the sound of the pounding rain.

The garage was dark inside on a sunny day. Today the shadows were almost impenetrable. Joey walked slowly up the narrow corridor between the piles of junk. He imagined he could see the glowing, red eyes of rats and hear the fluttering of giant bat wings. He would have been afraid if it weren't for the colorful lights escaping from under Beezer's dream room door.

As he reached the door he heard strange, soft sounds coming from the other side. He had heard them before—the sound of tufts of cotton candy being pulled from the stick. Joey took a deep breath and knocked lightly on the door.

"Come in." Beezer's voice was low and solemn. It sounded far away.

Joey didn't move. He was suddenly afraid of what he might find on the other side. What was making the lights? The rushing sound? What adventure was he walking into? He was fairly certain he wouldn't be digging chocolate coins up out in the yard.

Struggling with his fear he forced his hand to turn the doorknob. It wouldn't turn.

"It's locked," Joey called.

"Only to those who don't *really* want to come in," answered Beezer. "Maybe you should just go back to the house."

Joey thought of the darkness in the house that day. He saw Glory's questioning eyes looking at him over the top of the couch. He saw Mrs. Johanaby typing furiously at her computer as if she were trying to drive thoughts of him from her mind. A mean, little voice Joey kept suppressed broke through.

She forgot to come back for you!

With that Joey knew he didn't belong in that house. He wasn't really a part of the family. He was going to go wherever this adventure would take him. Joey tried the door handle again. It turned. The door swung open by itself.

Joey's jaw dropped at what he saw—Beezer sat on the far side of the room next to a fire that burned brightly in what looked like a wok, the kind of pan his mom made stir-fry in. The pan was empty of any fuel, yet colorful flames leapt and danced energetically. Instead of smoke and sparks, glowing, colored bubbles rose out of the fire. The bubbles circled and dipped as they floated upward. When they reached the roof some of them popped raining a fine, radiant dust onto the fire and Beezer. The bubbles that didn't pop floated through the roof.

"Is your jaw broken?" Beezer asked. He wasn't smiling, but he seemed amused.

Joey closed his mouth.

"Come in," said Beezer. "You can't turn back now. Come, sit by the fire."

Joey sat cross-legged on the opposite side of the fire. He didn't notice the puddle of water forming around him. His jaw dropped again as he got a closer look at the bubbles. Each one had a scene inside it. Each scene centered on a person. There was a boy his own age wearing a tunic and breeches. He saw an Indian girl, older than himself, out in a desert that could have been in Utah or Arizona. There was a man at the bow of a ship next to a carved dragon's head. He was a big man dressed in animal skins. The picture panned back and Joey saw a whole row of oars and shields.

"That's a Viking ship," Joey said.

"And that man you see is a Viking," added Beezer.

"What are these pictures?" asked Joey.

"These are friends of mine," answered Beezer.

"Friends of yours? But the Vikings lived a thousand years ago."

"Perhaps I am very old," said Beezer. "Or maybe time and space is not what it at first seems. These are friends who need help, like you. Sometimes I like to see how they are doing."

In another bubble Joey saw a knight engaged in battle. Four enemies pressed in on him. He fought with great strength and skill. Even so Joey could tell he was losing—his battle was nearly over. The bubble popped before they could see what happened.

"Some of my friends never learn. It's almost more than I can bear."

Beezer looked across the fire at Joey. His eyes were sad. "You will learn, won't you, Joey?" Three more bubbles burst and glowing dust floated down on both of them.

"What do you mean?"

"The map. You brought it didn't you?"

Joey reached into his sodden shirt and pulled out the map. "It got wet," Joey said, as he carefully unfolded it.

"It would take a lot more than a little rainwater to destroy that map. Can I see it?" Beezer reached through the flames and took the map from Joey. He studied it carefully.

"You made the map," Joey said. "Don't you know what's on it?"

"I didn't make the map," Beezer said, not looking up. "You did."

"But I didn't draw anything." Joey was confused.

"Maybe not with your hands, but you drew the map," Beezer said. "The star dust reacted to the dreams and needs of your soul. This is what it came up with. I see pirates. I see a land of birds." He hesitated a moment and then added, "Big, scary birds."

Beezer quieted as his eyes shifted to another part of the map. Finally he spoke.

"I see a beautiful, uninhabited land." Beezer looked troubled as he studied this last land. He looked as if he wanted to say something more. Thinking better of it he handed the map back to Joey. "You have your adventure cut out for you."

Joey looked at the map. Once again he felt he was looking through an open window. He could feel the wind, taste salt on his lips, and smell the smells of unknown lands. The pirate ship he had seen earlier was there. Now it was doing battle with another ship. He could see cannon flashes and drifting smoke.

There was an island dense with jungle. Birds of varying sizes darted back and forth. A larger bird—much larger—flew alone. That must have been the "scary" bird Beezer referred to.

Joey turned his eyes to the larger land that looked like a continent. There was seashore followed by lowlands, lakes, and forests. Eventually, the land rose to snowcapped mountains then to sparsely detailed lands beyond.

Beezer must have been following his eyes, because as Joey looked at the uninhabited continent he nodded and said, "There will be your greatest test."

Joey didn't understand. The continent looked beautiful and far less dangerous than the other two places. Before he could ask, Beezer went on.

"What you are holding is not a toy, Joey. It's a doorway into another world. The map is a wonderful tool if used wisely, but it doesn't come without dangers."

"Dangers?" asked Joey.

"The world this map will take you to is real, not a dream. If you fell off a cliff there you would . . ."

". . . really die?" Joey finished.

Beezer nodded. "Just like in this world. I am allowed to give you some protection." He rubbed his fingers together while mumbling something and then flicked his fingers at Joey. A white dust puffed out over Joey's face. For a moment he glowed like Henrietta did, but then the glow disappeared.

"Now, every time you use the map to travel to a different land, you will be invisible to that land's inhabitants. While you are invisible, you cannot be hurt."

Beezer leaned forward. "Now listen closely, Joey. The moment you *purposefully* do something to interfere with what is going on in the land, you will lose your invisibility and your protection until you use the map again."

Joey's stomach tingled with excitement. Beezer's warning would have frightened him except for the protection. He would have to interfere to be in real danger. Why would he interfere?

"There's one more thing," Beezer said, interrupting Joey's thoughts. "When you decide to come home you must touch the home heart."

Joey looked at the map. Down in the right hand corner was a big red heart with the word HOME written across it.

"That is the only way back. If you lose the map you lose your way home. Although I will be watching you from here, there will be little I can do for you."

Beezer's warning made Joey uneasy for a moment. What could go wrong? He would keep the map inside his shirt where it wouldn't get lost. That mean, little voice inside escaped Joey's efforts to suppress it and spoke again.

Maybe you won't want to go home.

"Can I go now?" Joey asked.

Beezer met his eyes. There was tenderness in them. He nodded.

Joey didn't hesitate. He pressed his finger against the pirate ship. All the shapes in the room became distorted and lost their color. He heard Beezer's voice, now sounding quite distant, "Remember Joey, there's always a way back to the ones you love."

Joey wanted to ask Beezer what he meant by that, but he couldn't speak—he felt like he was being squished into a quart jar. The shapes mashed together into a white haze. Suddenly the white haze shattered like an egg shell. The smell of salt water washed over him. Bright sunlight made him close his eyes.

Chapter 12

Joey became aware of the sound of creaking wood. He felt the wind on his face and the heat of sun beating down on him. Squinting against the light he found himself sitting on the deck of a ship surrounded by pirates—very smelly pirates. Joey wrinkled his nose at the stench. He was unprepared for the difference between reading about pirates on paper and suddenly finding himself amid their hot, sweaty bodies.

It would have been one thing to come among them while they swabbed the deck and ran up the rigging. Joey had arrived at a special moment for the pirates. They were gathered together in a crush at the side of the ship. They brandished swords and knives above their heads. The profanities and insults they shouted made him sick to his stomach.

Joey was terrified. Surely one would look down and see him any moment. He panicked and reached for the Home Heart. Before he touched it one of the pirates stepped right through him. Then he remembered Beezer had told him he could not be seen nor touched unless he interfered in their world.

Joey relaxed a little and dared look up at the shouting jeering faces around him. They were ugly faces, not so much from scars as from meanness. He had met mean kids at school and thought he knew what mean was. Looking at these faces he realized he had never met a truly mean person in his life before.

Feeling shaky, but with a little confidence, Joey got to his feet. He kept his map at the ready just in case. When no one noticed him he relaxed even more. He thought this might even be fun.

Joey folded his map and considered where to put it. It was too big for his pockets. He dropped the map down his t-shirt. His shirt was tucked in and held the map securely. The feel of the thick parchment next to his skin gave him comfort.

All set for his adventure Joey made his way through the pirates. He walked between some and through others until he reached the railing. From there he could see what had their attention. What he saw turned his adventure into a nightmare. His knees went weak and he nearly vomited.

"Beezer, where have you put me?" he said in a weak voice.

He thought he was looking at a monster. A tall, slim man stood on a plank facing the ship. His hands were tied behind his back. The man's face was made monstrous because his ears and nose had been cut off. Blood flowed freely. Joey could hardly recognize the face as a man's. The man had been wounded in the stomach also. His white shirt and tan breeches were soaked in scarlet.

In spite of his horrible condition and impending doom the man stood straight and proud. The man's eyes, the only things not bloody on the man's face, were dark and unafraid. It was this man's courageous demeanor that kept Joey looking in spite of the dizzying sickness he felt.

A caustic, commanding voice rose above the rest. "Go ahead and jump, ya coward. You call yourself a Captain?"

Joey turned his eyes to the speaker and saw what had to be the ugliest pirate in the world. He was dressed better than the others with black breeches and a red jacket. His hair was long and stringy; his nose made a sharp turn to the left just below the bridge, and none of his rotting teeth seemed to be growing the same direction. He was missing the little finger on his right hand.

"Why don't *you* come out and make me," the man on the plank called back with a calmness that belied his situation.

His reply was unexpected and the jeering quieted. The pirates were confused. They looked at each other, then their captain, to see what he would do.

The captain roared in anger, but made no move to come down and face the man. Joey saw the sea below, red with blood and frothing from the churning bodies of numerous sharks. He understood why the pirate captain didn't want to meet the challenge in spite of the wounded condition of the prisoner.

"Twenty pieces of gold to the man who cuts out his tongue and then pushes him in," shouted the pirate captain.

It seemed to Joey that only a fool would take up such an offer considering the precarious position where the prisoner stood. Two fools, apparently overcome by the thought of the gold, rushed to the plank. There they scuffled briefly before one took the lead. The loser, not willing to give up, brazenly pushed the leading pirate off the plank to the sharks below and started out on the plank himself. He was either drunk or too much in a hurry—on his second step he lost his balance and followed the first pirate into the water with a cry.

Joey was horrified. The water below boiled higher as the sharks fought for a bite. The rest of the crew thought it funny. They roared with laughter.

"Shut up! All of ye! Or I'll lower ye down slow and ye can watch yoursel's be eaten."

The crew quieted immediately.

"As for ye, coward, join your crew and let's be done with it."

The pirate captain pulled out his musket, aimed at the prisoner, and fired. There was a dull boom and a puff of black smoke. The prisoner flinched, but did not fall.

"I do believe you missed," said the prisoner calmly. "I think you couldn't hit a wall with your fist if your nose were pressed against it."

"JUST KILL HIM!" the pirate captain screamed.

Another pirate with a knife leaped onto the plank. Ignoring the feeding frenzy below, the pirate kept his eyes on the prisoner as he deftly slid one foot in front of the other. When he was within range he smiled vilely and prepared to jab with his knife.

The prisoner acted instantaneously. Instead of resisting as the pirate expected, he ignored the knife thrust and stepped into the pirate. It was his last act of battle. The pirate cursed as he lost his balance—they both fell into the churning water below.

The pirates were silent as they watched the sharks feast on their mate and their enemy. Then the pirate captain drew his sword and held it high in the air. The crew erupted into cheers and celebration. They gave each other bear hugs and danced in a rhythmless mass.

Joey sank to the deck with his back to the railing. He vomited on the deck between his legs. He read about such things in books and had even seen such scenes in the movies. They hadn't prepared him for the reality of it. He pulled his knees up to his chest and buried his face against them.

One thing stopped his descent into shock. It was the wounded prisoner's face. The pirates had made it ugly and monstrous, but they had left his eyes. The prisoner's eyes had been proud and uncowed. He had stood there straight and calm in spite of what was happening to him. How could that be? This man was gone now, yet something about him remained. Joey could feel it.

The pirates continued their celebration. They drank and danced around Joey, sometimes right through him. Joey kept his hands over his face and ignored them hoping that he would find enough strength to pull the map from his shirt and leave.

Pirate ships had fascinated him his whole life. Here he was living his dream. This wasn't a restored ship at a maritime museum with informative plaques, but a real pirate ship in action. What he had just seen was horrific. "Enough of pirate ships and pirates," he thought. The ship was of no more interest to him now. It was a dark, ugly place and he wanted to leave. As soon as he got his stomach under control he would leave.

"Excuse me."

A gentlemanly voice made its way through the confusion in Joey's mind. It stood out from the raucous voices of the sailors.

"You don't appear to be a part of the crew?"

Joey raised his eyes. In front of him stood a tall man in fine dress. He wore tan breeches and a white shirt with a fine blue jacket. A captain's hat sat on his head. His face was very pleasant even if his nose and ears were on the large side. He certainly was not one of the pirate crew. There was none of their meanness or ugliness about him. When two pirates carrying cups of rum, their arms around each other, staggered right through him Joey realized who this man was.

"You . . . you just died!"

"Oh my, does it show?" the man asked looking down at himself.

When the man smiled Joey realized he was teasing him.

"You appear to be dead, too," said the man. "But you were not on my crew."

"I . . . I'm not dead," Joey said. "I'm . . . ," he thought for a moment and then finished, "just visiting."

The man wrinkled his brow as he thought about this. He turned to watch the pirates celebrate. Finally he spoke again. "I must say, you picked an ugly place to visit, or, maybe you just came to see my execution? Is that it? Did you come to mock me?"

Joey didn't understand. "I just wanted to see a pirate ship. I didn't want to see anyone killed. I just happened to get here when you were out on the plank." Tears spilled out of Joey's eyes. "It was horrible."

The man stared at Joey, the hard look on his face slowly softening. He turned and sat down next to Joey.

"I'm sorry," he said. "I can see now that you are of far higher quality than these savages."

They sat in silence for a few minutes while Joey got control of himself. With this man near him the darkness of the ship lessened somewhat.

"Tell me, what is your age?" asked the man.

"I'm twelve." Joey voice was weak.

"My sister has a son your age. A fine boy."

"He's probably braver than me," said Joey, trying to wipe the last of the tears from his face.

"If by brave you mean he wouldn't have been horrified by what he just saw, no, I hope not. I am Richard Call, by the way," said the man. More quietly he repeated, "Captain Richard Call." He seemed to be thinking about those words. Then he turned to Joey and asked, "To whom do I have the pleasure of speaking?"

"Joey Johanaby," Joey said, reaching out to take the captain's offered hand. Their hands moved through each other disconcerting them both.

"This will take some getting used to," said the captain. "How came you to visit here?"

Joey wondered where to begin. He reached into his shirt and pulled out the map. He heard the captain take in a breath as he unfolded it and its magical properties became apparent.

"Where would a boy like yourself get such a powerful item?" asked the captain.

"Beezer," Joey said. "Beezer gave it to me."

"This Beezer is a witch?" asked the captain suspiciously.

"No, no, Beezer is good. He helps people." Joey wanted to make sure the captain understood this.

"This Beezer is helping you by sending you to a ship of such horror and tragedy?" The captain's voice shook with emotion.

"I don't understand either," Joey said. "Actually, Beezer didn't make the map." Joey didn't want Captain Call thinking badly of Beezer. "I can't really explain it, but Beezer said it was me who made the map; something about my dreams and desires. Whatever it is I don't like it. I just want to leave now."

When the captain didn't answer Joey looked up at him. He was staring intently at the map. "What is this?" He pointed to a second ship that had just appeared on the map coming toward the pirate ship.

"I don't know," Joey said. "I know just before I came here I saw two ships fighting. This ship looks different than those two."

"This ship here," the captain pointed to the new ship, "is a sloop. The other is the ship we are on. It is an armed merchant ship. The fighting ships must have been this ship and mine." Now it was the captain's turn to rest his face in his hands. "Ohhhh," he moaned. He sounded so pitiful that Joey almost moaned with him.

"What is it, Captain?" Joey liked the way it felt to say "captain."

"Ohhhh," the captain moaned again, "How will I ever be forgiven? I fear I cannot be. I am guilty of the murder of my men."

"No," Joey said, not believing it.

"YES," shouted the captain. He sprang to his feet the way only a ghost could and swung his fists at one pirate than another. His fists passed through as if the pirates were fog. Pacing the deck he said, "I fed my men to these vermin like a boy feeds baby mice to a pet snake."

Joey got to his feet and followed the captain at a distance.

"Ragulet, the pirate captain, is smarter than he looks." Captain Call motioned toward the place they had last seen him. He was gone now. "This is not the ship he was last seen on. This must be one he captured. He lured me in with a distress signal. Look how his sails are ripped and hanging. See how the ship leans to one side. It is all a ruse. He has good sails ready to be hoisted. The ship lists only because he has shifted all the cargo to one side. And he had men dressed as women and dwarf pirates like children."

The captain turned to face Joey and looked him right in the eye for his final confession. "I sailed my ship right up next to this one in complete confidence that I was helping a merchant ship in distress."

The captain walked past Joey stopping at the railing where he looked into the water. A red tint remained.

"My men were fine, fighting men. They didn't have a chance when caught so off-guard. I watched Ragulet feed each of them to the sharks." The captain closed his eyes as he relived the scene.

"My only consolation was that not one of them begged for mercy or took up Ragulet's offer to join him.

They both stood in silence for several minutes while the drunken celebration continued behind them. The captain visibly fought with his emotions. Joey was uncomfortable. He felt he shouldn't be seeing the captain's private distress.

"You were very brave," Joey said quietly.

"What's that?" asked the captain.

"You were very brave," Joey said louder. "On the plank."

The captain thought about this and finally said, "Perhaps, but what did it matter. My bravery did not save my men."

"It mattered to me," Joey said. A thought occurred to him. He looked up at the captain and said, "I think seeing your courage was the reason for my visit."

Captain Call looked down at Joey, doubt and despair on his face. Joey met his eyes. No matter the reason Captain Call had lost his ship, the man who had displayed so much courage on the plank was an honorable man. Joey could see the captain's courage and strength even now as he looked into his sorrowful eyes. The captain's face softened a little as he saw the way Joey looked at him.

148

"SHIP AHOY," a hoarse voice cried out. "Off the port stern."

The pirate captain came bursting out of his cabin door.

"My eyeglass!" he yelled. The first mate handed it to him. He studied the area off the port stern for some time. "She looks to be a sloop. Aye, easy pickin's. Rich pickin's," he said. "What a day fer pirates! We'll get her the same way we go the last'un. Men, you know what to do. If any of you are too drunk to fight I'll have your guts for garters."

Several men, already drunk, put sober looks on their faces and tried to stand straighter. The sailors cleared off the deck in an instant. Eventually a tall sailor came onto the deck dressed like the captain of a merchant ship. He was followed by two sailors dressed like women. They were younger sailors and either had no beard or were clean shaven. Even this close these sailors made passable women. One carried a parasol; the other wore a bonnet and carried a fan. They seemed to enjoy the part they played in this deception. They walked with little, mincing steps and practiced turning about gracefully.

A moment later a dwarf pirate came running onto deck. He was dressed as a boy about Joey's age. He was clean shaven, but not as young as the sailors playing the women. Joey didn't think he made a very good boy. When this "boy" stood next to one of the "women" at the railing and didn't move Joey could see how the size difference and the boys clothing would easily deceive the unsuspecting eye.

There were eight barrels by the railings. Joey saw the "acting" captain lift out a grappling hook, adjust its position and place it back in. He could hear men below deck running about. From the few words he caught they were preparing the cannons for firing.

Joey looked about in sudden fear. Captain Call was nowhere to be seen. Even though he couldn't be seen or hurt, now that he had met the captain he didn't want to be alone on this ship. He noticed a movement above him and saw Captain Call sliding down a rigging rope at a pace that would have burned the skin off the hands of a living man. He hit the deck without a sound and turned to Joey with a desperate look on his face.

"It is my brother's ship," he said. "I feared so when I saw it on the map. I could tell plainly from the crow's nest." The captain paced anxiously back and forth. "It is his first command. He is intelligent and efficient. Still, he is a man with a heart and will surely fall for this deception as I did."

The captain ran to the railing crying out, "I must warn him."

He attempted to get up on the railing as if he wanted to jump over to swim or somehow travel to his brother's ship. The captain found he could not leave the deck. Joey joined him at the railing. He could just make out the sails on the horizon.

"I am in Hell," said Captain Call. "Why else am I trapped on this ship? I am to pay for the murder of my men by being forced to watch the murder of my brother and the men and women on his ship." The captain groaned painfully. "I cannot bear it," he said.

Joey's heart nearly broke to see him like this.

"He has women on his ship?" Joey asked.

"His is a merchant ship and his cargo will undoubtedly include women and children. What they will do to them will make it all the more unbearable. Oh, God in Heaven have mercy on me; on them!" he cried.

Joey felt Captain Call's pain. He wanted to help him; to help the people on the other ship. He couldn't bear to watch the horror that he had just seen—and with women and children. It occurred to him that he didn't have to watch. He had the map. He could leave. But Captain Call couldn't leave. He would be left to suffer here by himself. Captain Call, who was so brave, didn't deserve this punishment.

An intuition grew in Joey's mind. This coming horror didn't have to happen. He knew as certainly as the sun was in the sky that there was something he could do. But what was it?

"Captain!" he yelled. "Maybe you can't warn them, but I know that somehow I can."

The captain knelt in front of Joey with a desperate hope in his eyes. He tried to grab Joey's shoulders, but could not. "How, Joey?"

Joey didn't know how. He felt sheepish then and looked down at his map thinking hard.

"Is it your magic map, Joey? Can you travel to that other ship as you travelled here and warn them somehow?"

Maybe that was it. Joey touched the other ship, which was much closer now. Nothing happened. The look of disappointment in the captain's face was heartbreaking.

"What's going to happen if I can't warn them," Joey asked.

"They will lure them in with the distress flag that is already flying. The ship looks like it is in distress, so it will fool them into thinking there is nothing to fear. When they get close the pirates will open all their gun doors and shoot grapeshot and cannon. It will shred the sails and destroy the masts. Then they will use the grappling hooks to board the vessel and overwhelm the crew. They are quite vicious." The captain said all this with eyes closed and in a steady voice that betrayed all hope. He was recounting what happened to him.

Joey looked up at the flag flying in the wind. He noticed at the bottom of the mast lay the black flag with the skull and crossbones. It was attached to the rope already so that when the distress flag was lowered it would be raised.

"Captain, look," he said. "If we raised that it would warn them of danger, wouldn't it?"

"If they saw it in time it would, certainly," said Captain Call.

"If we waited until they got close enough to see it could they still get away?" Joey asked.

"They are in a sloop. With good sailors sloops are very fast. Faster than this ship. Yes, I believe they could get away easily. If they got away they could get the warning out about the deception." The captain had forgotten his hopelessness for a moment. It returned in an instant. "But neither you nor I can raise that flag," he said despondently.

"I can," Joey said, quietly.

"What do you mean?" asked the captain. "You are like me."

"Except that I'm not dead, yet. Beezer said I could interfere if I chose to. It's just that my protections would be gone."

"You mean if you wanted to you could touch the rope and raise that flag?"

"Yes," said Joey. He didn't know how this worked, but he believed what Beezer had told him.

"What do you mean your protection will be gone?"

"I think it means the pirates will be able to see me. I will actually be on the ship."

"If this is true the pirates will kill you." The captain stated the fact bluntly. A look of hope and fear came into his eyes. "Would you give your life for those on that ship?"

The captain asked this question as if it were really possible that Joey might do this. A panic rose inside Joey at what he had started. Captain Call would sacrifice his life in a heartbeat if he could. He actually believed Joey would be willing, too.

The thought of facing death by these pirates made Joey feel sick. He couldn't face death, not even to save all those people. He felt the feeling of defeat rise within him. It was the same feeling he had while watching Glory drown. Captain Call saw the look in his eyes and knew what it meant.

"It's okay. It is too much to ask. Why should you die for my mistake?" Captain Call resigned himself to his personal hell.

Joey's heart broke as he saw defeat register on the captain's face. The impression that there was something he could do remained. Glory's rescue required him to risk his life. His life hadn't been taken as a result. A flame of hope flared up in him now that gave him courage. Joey had an idea. He might not have to die while helping the captain.

"Captain!" Hearing hope in Joey's voice Captain Call gave Joey his full attention. "If I can raise the flag and then use my map in time, I could escape," Joey said.

Hope brightened Captain Call's eyes for an instant before it left. "But it didn't work when you touched it," said Captain Call.

"I'm pretty sure that's because I am already here," said Joey. I would have to touch one of the other lands."

The captain stared into Joey's eyes for a long moment. Joey saw the captain was conflicted.

"A man cannot honorably ask a boy to risk his life like this."

"You are not asking. I am offering." When Joey spoke these words tingles ran up his spine. He had never felt the meaning of words strike so deeply in his life.

"Joey, you are courageous."

The captain's words thrilled Joey. As he looked up into the dark brown eyes of the captain, he knew the captain could see the fear in his eyes. Still, the captain had said those wonderful words.

"I am proud to know you, Joey," said the captain. He raised his arm in a salute. "I cannot be in Hell, because Hell cannot hold people like you."

These words filled Joey with strength and warmth. Joey wanted to throw his arms around the captain's neck, but knew better than to try.

"You will have to work quickly. As soon as the pirates notice they will be upon you. I will do everything I can to help you, Joey." The captain said the words with determination, but without much hope. They both knew there was little he could do.

Joey and the captain went to the flag mast. Joey studied the loops that held the rope fast. He hoped they weren't as tight as they looked. The dressed-up pirates were on the main deck down a set of steps. The steps partially obscured Joey.

Fear swarmed like angry bees in Joey's stomach. "It's okay to be afraid," Joey said, repeating Beezer's words, "as long as you do what you have to do anyway."

Joey looked over at the captain who was standing by the railing watching the approach of the sloop. He found comfort in the sight of that tall, brave man. Then he focused on the rope and pictured in his mind what he was going to do. He had stuck the map in the top of his pants so that most of it hung out and he could grab it quickly. He wondered if he could do it quickly enough.

"Okay, Joey," said the captain, coming over. "The *Rebecca* is close enough." He gave Joey a tender smile and nodded his head. He then positioned himself at the top of the steps between Joey and the pirates as if on guard.

Joey reached out to the rope and felt nothing. His fear was replaced by despair. If he couldn't touch the ropes, all those people would die! How was he supposed to be able to interfere in this world?

Filled with determination Joey said out loud, "I will touch these ropes!" In an instant Joey felt his weight on the deck, the wind on his face, and the rope in his hands. His protection was gone. His fear came flooding back. Ignoring it, Joey began undoing the looped rope from its stanchion. His hands shook. The rope was heavier than it looked and was looped many times. It felt like minutes before he got it unwound although it was only a few seconds.

"'Ay, 'oo's that'? said the dwarf pirate.

Joey's hair stood on end. He had been seen. Swallowing panic he pulled on the rope to raise the pirate flag. Tug as he would, the rope wouldn't move.

"Stop 'im!" yelled the fake captain. The dwarf pulled a knife from behind his back and ran to the stairs.

"No, no, no," thought Joey. "This has to work!" In that moment Joey was more worried about failing than dying.

Panicked tears stung his eyes when he realized he was pulling the wrong way. He was trying to raise the distress flag higher when he needed to lower it to raise the pirate flag. He switched directions, but knew it was too late. The pirate was at the top of the stairs and only a few steps away. Joey wouldn't get the flag high enough to be seen.

Captain Call, who still stood guard between Joey and the Dwarf pirate, cried out, "You shall not touch him!" and made as if to push the dwarf pirate in the chest.

The pirate, stopped in his tracks, raised his arms as if to protect himself and then tumbled backwards down the steps. The pirate had seen the captain. Joey stopped pulling in amazement.

"Pull, Joey. PULL!" yelled Captain Call.

"What in the blazes . . ." yelled the fake captain, and he came running for the stairs.

Joey pulled as hard as he could. The Skull and Crossbones ascended the mast and unfurled in all its grim glory.

"Run, Joey. RUN!" yelled Captain Call. The fake captain leapt onto the deck. He couldn't see Captain Call. The pirate came at Joey with sword drawn.

Joey didn't have time to use his map. He ran to the rigging that went up the mast and started climbing. The pirate stopped to lower the skull and crossbones before continuing the chase. Joey discovered that climbing the rigging was not as easy as the pirates made it look. His feet slipped through the ropes and his legs became tangled. He was still in easy striking distance of the pirate's sword. He struggled frantically to free himself.

"The map, Joey. Use the map!" Captain Call was standing near him now looking afraid. The pirate, having lowered the flag, took two leaps and raised his sword. Joey grabbed his map and desperately tried to unfold it. As the blade came down Joey's fingers slipped inside the open end of the map. The sword passed right through him. Instead of a blow from the sword Joey felt the squishing pressure of the map at work. Everything began to blur. As the ship faded away Joey faintly heard Captain Call's voice, "They saw, Joey . . ."

Chapter 13

The heavy scent of green vegetation met Joey's nose; a horrible screeching filled his ears. Joey was lying on his back. He opened his eyes to see a thick canopy of leaves above him. It was so thick he could scarcely catch a glimpse of the sky. The canopy glowed green, lit from bright sunlight on the other side. Waves of little yellow birds with black beaks moved from tree to tree eating tiny berries that grew among the leaves. The small birds made a big noise as they cried out ownership of the berries.

In spite of the new scene in front of him Joey still saw the pirate's blade arcing down towards his head. His heart still beat wildly and he struggled to catch his breath.

"Beezer, why didn't you tell me how it would be?" he thought. Mrs. Johanaby would be furious at Beezer if she knew the danger he had put Joey in.

With thoughts of the danger Captain Call's last words drifted in.

"They saw, Joey!"

The memory of these words calmed his heart and filled him with joy. He had saved the captain's brother and all the people on the ship. He had been afraid to do what he did, yet he did it anyway. That was courage, wasn't it? The captain had said it was.

He remembered Captain Call standing wounded and disfigured on the plank. Captain Call stood there in great pain facing a horrible death. Even so he stood straight and proud betraying no fear. Joey realized that the captain had been afraid; he had just chosen not to show it.

Joey knew he had looked afraid when he was struggling to raise the flag, but that didn't matter. He had done what he had to do anyway. He was just a little bit like Captain Call. He wondered if Beezer had seen him in one of those colored bubbles. He hoped so.

Joey would have laid there longer enjoying the realization of his courage if birds above hadn't gone crazy. Where they had been flying in a pattern of waves from tree to tree and making a constant din, suddenly they were flying in all directions at once and their calls increased in volume. The panic he sensed among them was so overwhelming that he had to fight the urge to run.

The noise was so loud—the birds' movement so erratic—that Joey covered his ears with his hands. He wanted to scream. A large shadow passed ominously over the canopy above him. It was gone in an instant. With its passing the birds quieted. Eventually they returned to their patterned waves and regular raucous din.

Joey stared up at the canopy wondering what it was that had passed overhead. He vaguely remembered Beezer saying something about big birds when he was looking at the map. But that shadow was too big for any bird. Still, he was glad the canopy had been between him and whatever it was.

Joey sat up to take a look around. He was sitting in ferny undergrowth that rose higher than his head. He couldn't see much at all, so he got to his feet. There was an explosion of flapping wings just behind him. A covey of quail-like birds, startled by something, took to flight. In his fright Joey felt the map slip from his fingers. He had forgotten about the map until that moment. He dived down after it fearing something might steal it from him.

Clutching the map, Joey stood trying to catch his breath as he waited for the next surprise. When nothing else unexpected happened he looked around. The trees weren't overly dense. Still, he couldn't see very far in any direction. The tree trunks were slender, the bark smooth. The feathery leaves of the undergrowth came to his waist. Joey moved through the plants as if they were nothing more than a green ground fog.

When Joey felt safe enough he made sure his shirt was tucked in, then folded the map and put it back in his shirt. He meandered through the undergrowth dragging his fingers through the soft leaves. The forest was anything but quiet and tranquil. Different kinds of birds operated at every level of the forest. There were those high up in the canopy that did more leaping and running from branch to branch than flying. Then there were robin-sized birds that flew among the thinning branches below the canopy. Joey watched other birds, with pointy crests on top of their heads. They clutched the tree trunks with their feet and searched for food among the little flowers that grew on the bark. A wave of tiny, little black birds with white wings swept over Joey as they flew down among the undergrowth searching for seeds. This cloud of birds swarmed around him momentarily and then quickly disappeared.

For some time Joey walked through this forest fascinated by the color and movement around him. He wondered how big the forest was. No matter how far he walked, everything seemed to stay the same. He could be walking in circles for all he knew. In any case there didn't seem to be too much adventure in this land.

Joey heard a growling and froze. An animal was hiding just ahead of him in the undergrowth. He was afraid he was about to meet the first non-bird creature in this land. He heard the growling again and tensed up wishing he had a weapon. When he heard the growling the third time he was embarrassed—it was only his stomach. He was hungry.

The reality of the situation stopped Joey in his tracks. His first adventure had happened so fast. The idea that he needed to eat and sleep while using the map hadn't occurred to him. How was he supposed to eat if he couldn't touch anything? Well, he could touch things, but then he would lose his protection. It also occurred to him that even if he could touch things he didn't see anything around him he could eat anyway. There were birds, but how would he catch them?

"Beezer, this isn't fair," Joey said.

Maybe it was fair. He understood now that these challenges were part of every adventure. Columbus spent long days of routine sailing before making his exciting discovery. Lewis and Clarke's adventure consisted mainly of hiking and trying not to starve to death.

The leaves in the canopy weren't glowing as brightly now and he realized night was coming. His heart sank a little bit. The thought of sleeping on the ground in this forest didn't appeal to him. He thought of his bed in his attic room and of the sloppy, Sloppy Joes his mother made.

Joey patted the map underneath his shirt. He could go home. It was as simple as touching the Home Heart. Joey took out the map and looked at it. He was thrilled to see the sloop a long distance from the pirate ship. He had done that. A sense of pride and joy returned to him. Joey noticed that the ships and the ocean they were in were a different color than the rest of the map now. He also realized he couldn't smell the sea like before. Cautiously he touched the sloop. Nothing happened. It was as he thought. Once he used the map, he couldn't go back.

Looking at the Home Heart Joey had the sensation once he used it the power of the map would be broken. The journey would be over. He thought of his home when he left. How long had it been—just a few hours? It was dark and raining there. A gloom pervaded the house. His mother didn't want him; Glory and Story didn't need him. Joey didn't want to go back to that. He wasn't ready yet. Maybe he would never be ready. Joey's determination to stay grew within him. He would spend the night here. He would find a way to survive. His stomach growled again telling him it wouldn't be easy. Folding the map he put it back inside his shirt.

Joey heard a sound coming from the undergrowth that wasn't his stomach. It was a thrumming, like someone beating on a little tom-tom. Up ahead of him, about twenty feet, the undergrowth moved. There was the *thrum thrum* again. The movement in the undergrowth came towards him. Joey froze in place wondering if this creature could be his dinner or if it would be the other way around.

Suddenly a head popped up out of the undergrowth and tilted left and then right. It rose a bit higher on a long bald neck. It reminded Joey of an ostrich except it was shorter. The head turned backwards and seemed to be studying the forest behind it. Then it disappeared down into the undergrowth as quickly as it had appeared. Joey watched as the disturbance in the undergrowth came toward him stopping just in front of him.

As if it were the top of a periscope the head shot up in front of Joey's face. Joey flinched and yelled. The bird didn't react. Joey remembered the bird couldn't see or touch him. He was glad. The bird had a strong beak that wasn't far from his eyes. The bird turned its head and looked behind it again.

Joey had gone pheasant hunting with his dad in the fields around Oakley, Idaho. He had felt the adrenaline rush when a pheasant had burst into the air in an explosion of flapping wings. It was a colorful rooster with red and green on its face and a white ring around its neck. His father had shot and missed. They watched in bitter disappointment as it escaped.

This bird stood so close in front of him that Joey could reach out and grab it by the neck. It wouldn't get away. A vague thought relating to food entered his mind. This thought, along with the opportunity the bird presented was a temptation Joey couldn't resist.

While the bird studied the forest behind it Joey reached out with both hands and, fully committed, grabbed it. In an instant the bird stood to its full height—two feet taller than Joey. Joey realized his mistake. The bird flapped its stubby, but strong wings and rose three feet into the air carrying Joey with it before dropping back to the ground. Joey hung on tightly. He was afraid of what the bird might do if he let go. The bird squawked and danced about on its surprisingly strong legs. It pecked him viciously on the top of his head. "Peck" was the wrong word—it felt like golf balls were landing on his head. Flapping its wings it rose into the air again and tried to disembowel Joey with the large, but thankfully dull claws on its feet.

Joey had had enough. He let go of the bird and fell to the ground. He covered his head and waited for the bird's attack to continue. Now free, the bird had no desire to keep up the fight and ran swiftly off through the forest.

Joey lay for a minute stunned by the ferocity of the bird. He would never look at a chicken the same again. He slowly got to his feet and looked at the damage. His shirt was ripped, his left arm was bloody with a nasty cut, and there were lumps on his head.

"Beaten by a chicken," he mumbled.

When he looked up Joey froze. A boy four or five years older than Joey stood in front of him with a spear at the ready. Joey stared in shock. The boy appeared so suddenly that Joey wondered if he were a ghost. Then he remembered how the bird had been looking behind it. It knew something was following.

The boy stared at Joey with hunter's eyes. He was ready to launch his spear. Joey raised his hands slowly in surrender. The boy was wearing a leather skirt with a knife sheathed in his belt at his waist. A large bag hung under his arm from a strap around his neck. His skin and eyes were brown, but his hair was blond. There was a greenish tint to it.

Joey was certain the young man was going to throw the spear. He thought of the captain and tried to find courage as he waited to die. Instead of feeling pain as a spear pierced his heart, Joey heard the young man chuckle. Joey's fear changed to indignation as the chuckle grew into a rolling laugh. The young man laughed so hard he bent over and slapped his leg. Joey lowered his arms and frowned.

"What's so funny," he demanded. A moment ago he had been trying to find the courage to die. Now he was being mocked.

The young man caught his breath for a moment and spoke in another language. Joey didn't understand his words, but he understood the young man's pantomime. He pointed at Joey and, still laughing reached out and grabbed his spear with both hands as if it were the bird's neck. He hopped wildly about. He let go of his spear and fell to the ground. The young man laughed even louder.

Joey marched over and stood over the young man.

"I don't think it's funny. That bird could have killed me." The young man ignored him and continued to laugh.

Joey waited until the boy's laughter eventually wore itself out. It was a long time. The young man, wiping tears from his eyes, got to his feet and took a closer look at Joey.

He walked around Joey eyeing his shirt and pants with interest. He even reached out and touched Joey's shirt. Fearing for the map, which Joey was relieved to feel was still there, Joey swatted his hand away. The boy said something in his language. Joey guessed that it was a question.

"I don't think we speak the same language," Joey said.

The young man and Joey stared at each other a moment. Then the young man placed his hand on his chest and said what sounded to Joey like "Tahee" except there would have been more letters in it for sounds Joey couldn't make.

Joey understood and put his hand on his own chest. The paper of the map made a crinkling sound as he touched it. He froze fearing Tahee might have heard it. Tahee gave no sign. So Joey went on. "Joey," he said.

Tahee wrinkled his brow as if those sounds were hard for him to make. "Juwee," he said.

Tahee took a closer look at Joey's arm and then motioned for him to follow. He led Joey through the forest with the confidence of a person walking around his own neighborhood. Soon they came to a stream of clear water. There Tahee helped Joey clean the cut. Joey did his best not to wince or show any fear. He was proud of himself. Joey was pretty sure he would be crying over this cut if he were home.

After cleaning the cut Tahee took a little ointment bag out of the bigger bag and applied a cream to the cut. It burned at first, but then became cool and soothing.

"Thanks," Joey mumbled in appreciation. Tahee pursed his lips and nodded.

Tahee sat and stared at Joey. Joey tried to ignore him, but felt uncomfortable. He watched as green birds with narrow wings swooped down over the water snapping up water bugs that floated by. Tahee paid them no mind. Finally Tahee said several things in his strange language and pointed different directions.

Joey understood that Tahee was probably asking him where he lived. How could he tell him? Joey thought of showing him the map, but decided against it. Tahee would not understand and might think Joey an evil sorcerer or something. Joey just shook his head and shrugged. Tahee seemed a little frustrated at this. Eventually he indicated that Joey was to stay where he was. Tahee trotted off into the forest.

Joey grew nervous after Tahee left. Now that Joey had met someone here in this land of birds Joey didn't want to be alone. He wasn't sure he was going to get through the night without using his map to end his adventure and go home. He got up to up to walk in the direction he had seen Tahee leave. He hadn't gone far when he realized if he left the spot where Tahee had told him to stay Tahee might never find him again. He returned to the creek and sat down. Taking off his shoes he soaked his feet in the cool water. He spotted bugs like water skippers in an eddy behind a rock. Taking a stick he teased them. He looked for fish, but didn't see any.

Eventually he laid back and stared up into the canopy. The sky was growing dimmer. The on-coming night worried him.

It was almost dark when Tahee, in his silent way, suddenly appeared beside him. Joey tried not to show his relief. Now that Tahee had returned he knew he would be okay. Tahee brought a dead turkey-sized bird in one hand. Taking a small ball of shredded bark out of his bag, and using something like a flint and steel, Tahee soon had a fire going. Plucking the big bird was hard. The skin was ripped and ugly by the time they got done. Still, it smelled good once it was impaled on a stick over the fire. The fire hissed and popped as grease dropped into it. Joey was so hungry that as he ate a partially burned drumstick he thought his mom had never cooked anything that tasted so good.

Tahee showed Joey how to gather the ferny undergrowth and make a mattress that would keep him off the damp ground. Tahee appeared to go to sleep as soon as he lay down. Joey stayed awake a little longer and stared into the embers of the dying fire. The constant noise of the birds that had pressed his ears all day stopped as soon as the sun set. The forest was eerily quiet now except for the warbling call of a night bird.

This was a little like camping with his father. He wished his father could see him now. Joey thought of his family and was surprised to realize he didn't miss them. He liked how he felt right then. He had helped save a ship from pirates. He had fought a monster bird. The bird had kicked his butt, yet he had survived. Now he was sleeping in a forest with a forest warrior.

"I'm not even afraid, Dad," he murmured before slipping off to sleep.

The birds were making their noise long before Joey awakened. Their raucous calls and songs worked their way into his head slowly drawing him from fragmented dreams. Eventually the noise overcame his sleep and he opened his eyes. The canopy overhead was glowing green again. The air above him was busy with movement. Joey looked over at Tahee's ferny mattress. Tahee was nowhere to be seen. A pang of anxiety shot through Joey's stomach. Maybe Tahee had moved on and left Joey on his own.

Joey got up and walked over to the creek. He had just reached the edge when he was surrounded by a flock of little, green birds with long, slender beaks. Their wings hummed loudly as the birds hovered around him checking him out. They appeared so quickly and made such a buzzing noise that Joey was startled. He swung his arms about as if they were bees. The motion caused him to slip on the muddy bank and fall into the creek. He sat there up to his chest in water and caught his breath. The birds, all facing him, hovered to one side as if considering why he had done that. Then, on some unseen signal, they darted up the creek and disappeared around the bend.

It was then that Joey recognized Tahee's laughter among the other noises. Looking over his shoulder he saw Tahee downstream, spear in one hand and a willow with two fish strung on it in the other. Joey was glad to see Tahee, but he wished Tahee didn't find him so amusing.

It didn't take Tahee long to fillet the fish and broil them over a small fire. Joey didn't like fish, but the meal tasted delicious anyway. After the meal Tahee sat and stared at Joey as if he were wondering what to do with him. He looked uneasy. This made Joey uneasy. Finally Tahee began to speak. He seemed to be giving Joey a lecture. Twice he pointed at the sky and said the same thing. Joey wished he could understand.

Tahee got up and began to trot through the trees. He stopped when Joey didn't move and motioned impatiently with his arm. Joey understood he was to go with Tahee.

"Yes!" Joey said. Tahee started off at a trot again and Joey happily followed.

As they ran Joey wondered where they might be going. Tahee had to have family somewhere. Maybe they were going to his home. On the other hand maybe Tahee was on a hunting trip. Joey hoped that Tahee would teach him how to use a spear. He could learn so much from Tahee.

After ten minutes went by he stopped wondering where they were going and focused on keeping the pace. After twenty minutes he could no longer keep up the pace and started to fall behind. Soon Tahee disappeared in the trees and undergrowth. Joey half-heartedly called out for Tahee to wait. He didn't want to lose Tahee, but he was embarrassed that he couldn't keep up.

Joey leaned over with his hands on his knees and gasped for air. The courage he had felt the night before quickly left him now that Tahee was gone. He couldn't build a fire or spear fish. He had no idea where to go in this forest. It seemed that the whole island was covered by it. As he got his breath back he called out, "TAHEEEE."

It was hopeless. Tahee was gone. It was just him and the birds again. He patted his chest. The map was still there. He took a little comfort in this. It was a two-edged comfort. With the map he could go home. But going home too soon would be quitting. He wondered how he would know when he could use the map to go home without quitting. Joey realized that Beezer might be watching. He straightened up and decided he would go on even without Tahee. Looking around the forest his main problem was figuring out where to go and why.

Joey stiffened when he felt a pointed object pressed against his back. A familiar voice said, "Juhweee." He whirled around to see a grinning Tahee leaning against his spear. He wasn't at all winded and stood as if he had been there all morning.

Joey blushed with embarrassment. How long had Tahee been standing there? There was no sound of his approach.

"I'm sorry, Tahee. I can't run like that," Joey said.

Tahee bent over, put his hands on his knees, and began breathing heavy, mimicking Joey. "TAHEEE!" he yelled, and then raised his hand as if to signal "just wait a minute," then lowered his hand and began catching his breath again.

Joey rolled his eyes in annoyance. This brought more laughter from Tahee. Despite the laughter, Tahee came over to Joey and patted him on the back. He said a few words and motioned Joey to follow. This time he walked for a while before jogging. After jogging for a few minutes he walked again. Joey still struggled and never fully caught his breath, but with determination he was able to keep up.

After several hours of running and walking Joey noticed a difference in the light up ahead. It was more yellow than green. After all the hours of greenness the change in color stood out. It wasn't until Tahee stopped that Joey realized what was causing it— they had reached the edge of the forest. The sudden end of the forest made Joey catch his breath. The trees stopped the way grass does at the edge of a sidewalk. Beyond the forest for as far as he could see was grassland. The grass was waist high and golden-green in color. A breeze rolled through the grass changing it from more golden to more green as it bent and swayed. It had an almost hypnotic effect.

Joey moved to step out of the forest into the grassland. He wanted to walk with the breeze in the sunshine. Tahee grabbed his arm with a suddenness that startled him. He pointed at the sky and gave a stern warning. Joey looked up and saw nothing but blue sky. There wasn't even a cloud to break the blueness. What was Tahee so afraid of? Then he smelled smoke in the breeze and caught the sound of faraway voices. Tahee heard them too and crouched, pulling Joey down with him. Tahee put his finger to his lips.

The voices came and went with the breeze. Tahee listened carefully. When it was clear the source of the voices were not getting any closer Tahee got up and slowly made his way through the forest toward the voices. Tahee's walking crouch and his tighter grip on his spear worried Joey. His heart rate sped up even without the running. He wondered what was drawing Tahee toward danger. Then he wondered why he was following.

The smell of smoke got stronger and the voices got louder. Joey smelled something else also—horse manure. He looked down. Sure enough he had stepped right in some. Looking up ahead he could see horses in a makeshift corral in the forest. They were munching on a pile of grass that someone had put there for them. That seemed strange to him. The horses belonged in the grasslands where they could get grass for themselves. Beyond the horses Joey spotted tents of skins. The voices came from behind the tents. There were many voices, a gathering of some sort. Someone started a rhythm on a drum. A flute-like instrument joined it. Several voices started singing.

Tahee got as close has he dared. He knelt down behind a tree right at the edge of the forest. He seemed startled when Joey knelt down at his side. Tahee had forgotten Joey was there. He gave another stern signal for silence. There was no laughter in his face now. He seemed to be listening intently trying to catch what the voices were saying. His expression went from stern to angry. Joey felt uneasy. If Tahee had met him in the forest with this expression he would have run for his life. Tahee mumbled angry words and glanced at Joey as if he could understand.

"What is it?" asked Joey. "What's this about?"

Tahee bared his teeth, jabbed at the sky, and whispered more angry words.

Joey's nervousness turned into outright fear. He sensed something bad was going to happen. He had been taught in school that when you sense that you are in a bad situation, like with friends who are using drugs, you need to leave immediately. That advice didn't work here. Where would he go? Even in danger he would rather be with Tahee than alone.

Activity in the grassland caught his attention. Some distance past the tents people stepped out of the forest. Joey had expected people who looked like Tahee, but they were much more spectacular. They were tall and dark-haired. Instead of the leather skirt that Tahee wore these people were dressed in colorful robes that shimmered in the sunlight billowing lightly in the breeze.

"Feathers," Joey said. Their robes were made of colorful bird feathers. They were grand and beautiful. Joey quickly realized this was a procession of some sort. A man wearing the most ornate robe of them all led the group. He had a feather crown on his head and an amazing scepter of feathers in his hand.

Following the leader was a man leading a horse. Sitting on the horse was a young woman not too many years older than Joey. Even from this distance Joey was struck by her beauty. Long black hair fell over her shoulders and down her back. The blackness was broken by small, downy feathers that had been interspersed throughout. Her shoulders and arms were bare, but a feather gown covered the rest of her down to her thighs.

The only thing that marred her beauty was an aura of unhappiness that hung about her. She sat straight and proud on the horse, but her discomfort was apparent. Her face looked grim. She grasped the rope in an unnatural manner.

Joey looked again and realized she wasn't holding on to the rope—her hands were bound to it. She was surrounded by six men carrying spears. No, they weren't spears, Joey decided, but pikes. They were much longer than spears. Unlike the first two men who were walking confidently in the front, these six men were watching the sky closely. Every so often they would turn around to check the sky behind them.

When Tahee saw the girl he forgot his own warnings for silence and cried out. The expression on his face went from anger to despair. Joey recognized fear and a hint of panic. Tahee's cry had not been loud, but the leader of the procession must have heard. His demeanor changed and he looked their direction. Tahee and Joey were relieved when they continued on.

"What is it? What's going on?" Joey whispered. Tahee threw Joey a dark almost vicious look. It was clear that Joey was not to speak another word.

The girl on the horse, as uncomfortable as she looked, tried to keep her head high with defiance. As they got further away from the forest and more exposed in the grassland she seemed to lose her courage. Her head drooped towards her chest. Joey could see sunlight glint off tears on her cheek.

It wasn't until the procession almost reached it that Joey saw the post. It stood a foot taller than the grass with an iron loop attached at the top. Not wasting any time the leader attached the horse to the post. He tied it so that the horse's nose almost touched post. The horse couldn't move anything but its hind quarters.

The six pike bearers stationed themselves around the horse at regular intervals and planted their pikes against the ground before kneeling next to them. They kept close watch on the sky. The man with the feathered scepter raised both hands to the sky and sang out a dreadful sounding chant. The girl, head bowed, sat motionless on the horse. She had resigned herself to whatever fate awaited her.

Tahee could barely control himself. He crouched ready to spring. He loosened and then tightened his grip on his spear repeatedly. His eyes focused intently on the girl. Joey got the feeling Tahee knew her. Joey wondered how. Tahee didn't seem to be from this tribe. From the way Tahee was hiding he clearly wasn't welcome here.

Joey understood that the girl on the horse was in trouble and that Tahee wanted to help her. It was also clear to Joey how hopeless the situation was. There were six armed men between Tahee and the girl. All of them were older and bigger than Tahee. They were very alert.

In the books Joey read the hero would sneak out low in the grass. One at a time each man would silently disappear into the grass as the hero took them down. For some reason the other men wouldn't notice. After the last guard was gone the hero would cut the horse free and ride away into the sunset with the girl.

Joey saw how in reality this wouldn't work. First there would be an obvious trail of moving grass. He would be spotted long before he got close. Second, the guards were too close to each other not to see an attack on one of their members. One would cry out and the others would quickly capture and kill Tahee.

"What would the captain do?" Joey wondered. The experience on the pirate ship had given him confidence. Even so, try as he might, Joey could think of nothing to help the girl. He felt helpless and weak again. Joey wasn't sure even Captain Call would try something. Captain Call had been courageous on the plank in the face of certain death. Death for Tahee wasn't certain here, unless he chose to help. If Tahee chose to try to save the girl he would certainly die. Would that make trying to save the girl courageous, or stupid?

Out at the post the men were preparing to leave. Whatever fate awaited the girl didn't involve the men hanging around. The guards surrounded the leader and the horse bearer in a protective circle. They kept their watchfulness on the sky as they made their way back toward the forest. They walked much faster going back than coming out. This time even the leader of the procession was watching the sky.

Tahee watched the group of men closely as they got farther away from the girl. His eyes would leap regularly up to the sky, too. Joey sensed that Tahee was about to take action.

A cry rang out from two of the guards. Their arms pointed to the sky above the forest where Joey could not see. Then the others cried out and pointed also. The procession, forgetting its dignity, began running toward the forest. The guards sped ahead of the more portly leader leaving him behind. He screamed some sort of threat. The guards, looking very unhappy, stopped to let him catch up.

Joey sensed that Tahee was restraining himself from bolting out into the grassland. He looked desperate to get to the girl and yet continued to wait on his knee beside Joey. Did he have a plan?

Was he just afraid? Joey wanted to scream out his frustration at not being able to communicate.

The procession was almost to the trees, trailing feathers behind them, when Joey spotted what everyone was afraid of. Flying into his field of vision out over the grassland was a single bird.

"Really?" thought Joey. "Could that really be it?"

Joey saw Tahee watching the bird. For the first time Joey saw fear on Tahee's face.

"It's just a bird," mumbled Joey, looking again. The bird was very high. Even so he could see its wings clearly outlined against the blue. Its wings never moved. The bird sailed by as if it were an airplane. The bird looked like it was going to continue straight to another destination when it suddenly banked to begin a broad circle over the girl. As Joey watched the bird circle he began to realize that this was a very large bird flying very high. Still, he wondered how afraid a man with a pike should be of a bird?

When the last man in the procession entered the forest Tahee said something and sprang into action. He leaped up and started a sprint toward the girl. Joey was caught by surprise. He stood up confused. Was he supposed to follow or had Tahee just told him to stay there? And what was the big deal anyway? Why had Tahee chosen that moment to run to the girl? The guards would surely see him. Wouldn't it have been smarter to try crawling slowly through the grass? Tahee might have gotten a lot closer to the girl before the guards noticed him.

It was a quarter-mile to where the girl was. Tahee hadn't gone fifty yards before Joey heard a cry of alarm from the villagers. In a moment the six guards were racing out after him. Tahee was fast. He reminded Joey of a cheetah the way he flew through the grass. If the guards chased Tahee they would never catch him. But they weren't running toward Tahee. They were running toward the girl. As fast as Tahee was he was starting from a point farther away from the girl than the guards. The guards would arrive at the girl at the same time.

Joey saw Tahee glance in the direction of the guards. He must have seen as clearly as Joey that he wouldn't get to the girl in time. It didn't seem to matter. Tahee didn't slow down.

"He's crazy," Joey said.

The guards and Tahee glanced up at the sky at the same time. Joey followed their glance. The bird had dropped in altitude while it circled. Joey cried out when he suddenly perceived how big this bird really was. Joey spent an afternoon at the little Oakley airport and watched a man in a Cessna 172 practice his landings and take-offs. This bird was as big as that plane. Joey decided this must be an eagle of some sort.

The eagle made a magnificent sight in the sky. It was still quite high, but Joey could see it clearly now. It was brown with blood-red streaks that shimmered when the sun hit them. Joey could see the individual feathers at the ends of its wings vibrate in the wind. He knew they would be as long as he was. He saw the tail feathers, spread wide, angle one way and then another as it steadied the bird in flight.

The eagle was magnificent until it began its dive. As it grew bigger the eagle went from magnificent to dreadful. A man fighting the eagle with a pike would be like a man hunting a grizzly bear with a pellet gun. Joey realized that the girl was a sacrifice to the eagle. Not just the girl, but the horse, too.

Joey saw that the guards were no longer a threat to Tahee. Even if he reached the girl the eagle would snatch them up in its enormous talons.

As the eagle dove the guards stopped the chase and stared up in dismay. Even Tahee slowed down at the terror of the sight. The guards yelled instructions to each other and formed a circle. They knelt down, bracing their pikes against the ground with the points up in the air. The eagle wasn't diving toward the girl and horse—it was diving for them.

In a flash Joey understood Tahee's plan. He was playing a dangerous game of timing. Tahee knew the guards would chase him. He knew that he couldn't beat them to the girl. Tahee also knew the eagle was coming. He must have hoped for this exact scenario. He just might have a chance at rescuing the girl if the eagle was distracted long enough by the guards. How Tahee knew the eagle would go for the guards first Joey didn't know.

The eagle never made a sound as it dove. Had the guards kept their eyes open they might have used their pikes a little more effectively. As it was the pikes were aimed too high. The eagle in its silent horror angled out of its dive below the points of the pikes and hit the group of men from the side. Pikes and men flew through the air as if there had been an explosion. It was then the eagle screamed its horrible cry. It seemed clear to Joey the eagle held something against the forest people.

Most of the men lay still, dark heaps in the tall grass. One, dazed and injured, staggered to his feet. He began limping toward the forest crying out as he moved.

The eagle pumped its massive wings flattening the grass below it with gusts of wind. Tahee, frozen in terror as the eagle struck the men, regained enough sense to fall to the ground as the eagle passed over his head. He was still some distance from the girl. Luck was on his side. The eagle gained altitude and circled back for the remaining guard. Tahee saw his opportunity and continued his run for the girl.

"Come back, Tahee!" Joey yelled. Tahee might reach the girl, but they still couldn't get to the forest in time. The eagle would kill them before they reached safety. Joey didn't want Tahee to die. Why would he do something so futile?

For a moment it looked as if the wounded guard just might make it to the safety of the forest. He was close enough to hope. No one in the village came out to help the limping guard. Instead, as he got closer they melted back further into the forest. The eagle came down at a steep angle. There was a whistling in its wings as it pulled out of its dive. It hit the guard so hard the man flew two hundred yards through the air landing not far from where Joey stood in shock. The poor man had died so close to safety and yet he had died all alone.

Joey started to understand what Tahee was doing. He wanted to save the girl, but if he couldn't, at least she wouldn't die alone. Somehow Tahee knew this girl and loved her. He didn't want to live without trying to help her even if it cost him his life.

Tahee reached the post as the guard's body landed in the grass. The eagle circled and gained altitude. Tahee, in his rush, was struggling with the knot in the rope. As he pulled out his knife to cut the rope the eagle prepared to dive.

Joey didn't think. If he had he wouldn't have done what he did. He knew Tahee needed more time. Sprinting from the forest he waved his arms and yelled at the top of his lungs. For a moment he thought it would work. He saw the eagle cock its head to one side and focus its terrible, yellow eye on him. In that moment Tahee cut the rope and leaped onto the horse behind the girl. The eagle, forced to circle one more time, directed its attention back to Tahee.

"No," Joey thought. He was still running toward Tahee when he tripped over a pike that had stuck at a low angle in the ground. Joey yanked it free and brandished it at the eagle in a last desperate attempt to distract the eagle. It worked.

The eagle had just begun its dive when it spotted Joey with the pike. The pike made all the difference. The eagle had a hatred for humans bearing pikes. It changed the course of its dive for Joey.

Joey stopped in his tracks. The eagle's wingspan was thirty feet. Its eyes were as big as his face. Its talons were far thicker than the pike he held. These facts, along with the malevolence the eagle focused on him, made him fall to his knees. Joey knew he ought to be running back toward the forest, but his legs wouldn't work. Transfixed by the horrible majesty of the approaching eagle Joey waited for the end.

The last working part of his brain directed him to point the pike at the eagle. The butt of the pike was resting against the earth. Joey froze in horror as the eagle filled the sky above him. One large set of talons opened wide and dropped down around him. His pike slipped between the talons and sunk deep into the eagle's upper leg. This and the fact that Joey was falling backward saved his life. The pain distracted the eagle. Its talons didn't impale Joey, but merely closed around him. The eagle crash-landed on top of Joey. A crush of feathers absorbed the weight of the eagle. The eagle righted itself on its good foot, reached under with its powerful beak and snapped what was left of the pike shaft. Then it leaped off its good foot, and with powerful strokes of its wings rose into the air carrying Joey with it.

Joey was almost delirious with fear as he saw the ground, upside-down, dropping away below him.

"JUWEEEEE!" Tahee screamed. Joey saw Tahee and the girl riding directly below him. Tahee and the girl looked up at him helplessly.

Tahee's scream brought Joey back to his senses. He was in pain from the deadly tightness around his waist. He was gripped in one set of the eagle's talons, his back to the ground. One arm had escaped the eagle's grasp and hung free.

Joey felt the eagle change course to follow Tahee and the girl. As the eagle maneuvered a shaft of wood pressed against Joey's shoulder. In spite of his pain Joey looked and saw the broken end of the pike sticking out of the eagle's leg. Joey, in agony, grabbed the spear with his free hand and pushed. The eagle lurched in the air. It momentarily forgot the horse and its riders below. Pushing once more on the pike shaft he eagle screamed and released Joey. With the sudden easing of pressure Joey lost consciousness.

"The map, Joey."

The words with their familiar chimes woke Joey. The map was coming out of his shirt. The ground was rising fast. Joey grabbed desperately at the map as the wind caught at it. His fingers slipped between the folds and the world started to fade. As they entered the safety of the forest Tahee and the girl saw Joey disappear twenty feet above the ground.

Chapter 14

Instead of the hard shock of the ground Joey felt gentle pressure as he moved to another world. He came back to his senses knowing something was wrong—he was still falling. In a panic he began flailing his arms and clawing at the air. His horror was made worse when the map slapped against his face as it was whipped away by the wind.

"The map didn't work," he thought. "I'm dead."

An instant later it wasn't ground he hit, but water. The water closed around his body cold and silent. The sudden weightlessness made him dizzy. He didn't know which way was up. His nightmares about water came flooding back—the pool he nearly drowned in; the pond where his mom had forgotten him. As he flailed about he felt his foot strike air. He struggled to right himself and finally brought his head above water. He coughed and gasped and splashed.

"Help!" he coughed. "Help me."

In the other two lands there had been someone to help him, to guide him. Where was the person in this land? While struggling to keep his head above water Joey realized he was in a lake. He saw no signs of human life on the forested shores around him.

"Beezer," he yelled. "BEEZER!" Beezer had given chocolate coins to Story; to Joey he had given a map that was going to kill him.

Joey swallowed more water and coughed. He realized that the reality of drowning was very near. His panic increased.

"BEEZER!" he cried.

Thoughts flashed through his desperate brain. "Pirates, blood-winged eagles, and then I drown in a lake." In spite of his panic he almost laughed at the irony.

A thought came to him quietly. *"You don't have to drown. There is another choice."*

Joey looked about him again. The lake was large. It seemed nearly a mile to shore on one side. The other side—it was only 100 feet to shore. He was just 100 feet from life.

"You're not going to get to watch me die here, Beezer," he said. With angry determination Joey began dog-paddling toward the shore. He made painfully slow progress. He was tired and could barely keep his mouth and nose out of the water. He remembered his swimming lessons from what seemed to be another life.

"When you are tired you can just float on your back for a bit," his swimming teacher had said. He could still see her chubby, smiling face as she said it.

Joey rolled over onto his back and filled his lungs with air. His legs started to sink, but when he kicked them they stayed near the surface. It worked. He got his breath back. Joey rolled back onto his stomach and continued with his half-dog paddle, half-breast stroke. The bank was getting closer.

"I'm going to make it," he said. He felt the sweetness of confidence. With the confidence came an awareness of life in place of the death that had been so near a moment ago. He was aware of the cold water on his body. He was aware of each labored breath of air. There were smooth stones along the shore that he wanted to touch. He could smell the pines further up the shore.

"Yes," Joey said. "I choose to live."

Joey had to rest on his back twice more. The cold water sank into him and he shivered violently. In spite of his determination to live he grew tired. He realized choosing to live had a price.

Rolling back over to his stomach the third time he was startled when his hand struck a rock. Then he was elated—he was in shallow water. His legs were too weak to carry him so he dragged himself onto the warm, dry rocks of the shore. Exhausted he lay on his stomach on the rounded stones. The solid earth beneath him and the warm sun on his back brought him a comfort so deep that even spotting his map slowly sinking into the water 150 feet out bothered him only a little.

As he warmed in the sun Joey dozed off. While he dozed he dreamed about the captain and Tahee. He saw the captain calmly defying the pirates from his perch of death. He saw Tahee running like the wind to save the girl even though he knew he would die trying. He felt such pride as he saw them—pride that turned into joy. He wondered at how he felt until he realized it was because, when given the chance, he had acted like them. He was one of them; he was brave.

Suddenly the giant eagle was overhead; its fierce, yellow eye focused on him. A horrible cry sounded from its deadly sharp beak. Talons tightened around his waist and he was lifted high above the Earth where the eagle dropped him. He knew he would be all right. This had happened to him before—he had the map. As he fell he pulled the map from inside his shirt and began unfolding it. The wind whipped it violently and to his horror ripped it from his hands. He watched, breathless, as the map disappeared above him. He tumbled over to see the ground rising fast. Just before he hit Joey awoke with a jerk.

The rounded stones no longer felt comfortable. They pressed painfully against his body. Joey slowly sat up feeling sore and bruised. With the dream fresh in his mind his hand went to his chest. The map really was gone. Looking wildly around he didn't see it anywhere. He touched his face remembering it had slapped against him. His eyes turned suddenly to the lake. What had he seen as he had fallen asleep? The wind had torn the map from his hands as he had fallen. It had fallen in the lake.

"Oh no," he said fighting panic. He realized he had watched the map sink into the lake.

"Why didn't I go get it?" Joey said in a shaky voice. He answered his own question. "Because I had just nearly drowned." He shivered at the memory. Map or no map, he wasn't going back into that lake, ever.

Joey knew losing the map was serious. How serious it was hadn't sunk in yet. He pushed the matter to the back of his mind and slowly got to his feet. He wanted to have a look around. The lake was large. It might take a full day to walk around it. On this side of the lake the shoreline was rocky. On the other side pine trees came right down to the water's edge.

As he walked along the shoreline Joey found a round, flat stone perfect for skipping. Forcing his sore body to obey him he threw the stone giving it good spin with his finger. The stone skipped five times on the lake's mirror-like surface. His dad would have liked that. One of their favorite walks in Oakley passed by a small pond. His dad was an avid rock skipper. Joey skipped more rocks, each time watching the line of circles from each skip spread until they were no longer discernible.

He heard the sound of the wind in the pines and realized how silent this world was. There were no jeering pirates or flocks of chattering birds. Nearby flies buzzed around a dead fish that had washed up on shore. Other than them there was only the breeze in the pine boughs sounding like distant rushing water. It was a lonely sound.

Joey looked behind him and saw a rock-strewn meadow with tall grass. Red wildflowers punctuated the green. Large bushy shrubs grew on the far side toward the tree-line. The pine trees started where a steep hill began. It wasn't a mountain—more of a tall hill with a bald spot on top. Joey decided that from up there he could get a good look around.

Remembering how Tahee travelled Joey started off at a run. Soreness in his hips quickly slowed him. Joey pulled his waistband down a little and looked at his hips. There was a large, purple bruise there about the size of his hand. He remembered the crushing pressure of the eagle's talons.

He stared at the bruise proudly for a moment before carefully covering it back up. He liked what it represented. He had been brave. He imagined showing it to Glory and Story and telling them the story. The sound of the lonely wind in the pine boughs brought the troubling fact about the lost map back to mind. How would he get back to tell them his stories? He pushed the problem out of mind by thinking of Beezer. Beezer might have seen him in his magic bubbles.

"Did you see that, Beezer?" Joey said. "I did good." He punched the air at an imaginary foe and then raised his arms in victory.

It took a long time to climb the hill. Joey guessed maybe two or three hours. He was sweating and breathing hard when he came out of the trees onto the bald spot at the top.

"Oh, wow," he said, as he caught sight of the magnificent view.

The lake lay in a wide, forested valley. The dark waters of the lake harmonized with the dark green of the pine trees. Joey could see the rushing waters of a creek winding its way through the forest into the lake.

The forest of pines filled the valley and the hills beyond. The pines thinned when they reached the mountains far away. The mountains rose sharply. Cliffs and rocks filled its slopes. Snow glistened in the crevasses. Scattered here and there in the forest were meadows that stood out as spots of light green. Joey could make out the white trunks of quaking aspens at the edges of the meadows.

Looking behind him Joey saw more hills. The hills got progressively taller and rockier until they were mountains. The mountains were much closer this direction. The air was clear and he could make out the details of a jagged ridgeline with the scree on a steep slope below. Large patches of snow lay on shaded slopes.

This land was big and beautiful. As far as Joey could tell he was the only human being there. A feeling of smallness and loneliness came over him. He felt uneasy as the issue of the lost map came to mind again. Joey picked up a stone and threw it off the face of the hill. It arced out and downward before being lost in the trees below.

Beezer had made it clear that he needed the map to return home. He had lost the map. Could it be true that he might be in this land forever?

"This will be your greatest test," Beezer had said of the world he was now in. Joey understood now. There were no pirates. There were no giant eagles. There was just him and no magic map. He couldn't go home.

Joey's knees went weak. He sat down hard on the hilltop.

"Beezer? Henrietta?" he said weakly. All he heard in response was the wind in the pines.

The next word that came to mind was too much.

"Mom?"

His new found courage gave out and he began to cry. He lay on his back and looked up at the wide, blue sky and let the tears run back into his ears. The empty sky was too lonely. He rolled over onto his stomach and cried into his arms.

Joey had been crying his entire life. A sense of shame always accompanied his tears. The shame was born out of the fear behind his tears. Today as he cried he felt no shame. After a few minutes Joey became aware of this. His tears slowed.

"Why?" he thought. "Why am I not ashamed to cry? Is it because I'm not afraid?" Oh, but he was afraid. He was afraid of dying here slowly, all alone. He was afraid he would never see his family again.

"So, if I'm afraid why am I not ashamed?" Joey's tears stopped now. He rolled over and sat up. Below him he saw a hawk. It flew in wide circles sailing on unmoving wings. As it circled it rose slowly on warm updrafts from the valley. Around and around it went ascending each time without a flap of its wings. The hawk continued its silent circling until it was high above Joey's head. It had a nobility and control in its flight that reminded Joey of Captain Call and Tahee. The bird didn't seem to be hunting. Instead it seemed to be flying for the sheer joy of it.

"I'm afraid, but I'm not afraid," Joey said. He wasn't sure what that meant. He knew it represented a change in him. Standing Joey picked up another stone and threw it. It flew much farther than the first stone before getting lost in the trees below. Then he turned and started down the hill.

His stomach growled. He wished Tahee were here now. He would know how to get some food. Joey wended his way through the pines kicking large pinecones that had fallen. One fell just in front of him and rolled across the dry needles that cushioned the ground. Another fell and bounced off his head. He picked up the pinecone and studied it.

In cub scouts his den mother had shown them how she was harvesting pine nuts that year. The pine nuts were hard to get out of the cone unless you heated them. She put them in the oven for a while on low heat. It wasn't long before he and the other scouts were able to free the nuts from the warm cones, remove the shells, and eat the chewy, pungent nuts.

These freshly fallen cones had nuts in them, but how would he get them out? He wished he had his Swiss Army knife. His dad had given it to him on his eighth birthday. He never carried that knife for fear of losing it. He kept it on his desk in his room.

Joey's hand went instinctively to his pocket. He caught his breath. Reaching into his pocket he pulled the knife out. He stared at it disbelieving. He didn't remember grabbing it before he left. He opened the main blade. It was still shiny and sharp. He hardly ever used it. He closed the blade and turned the fat, little knife over. From a receptacle on the other side he pulled out a narrow little flint and steel. He struck them together. Sparks flew.

At the bottom of the hill where the slope leveled off Joey cleared a spot and prepared to build a fire. He had seen demonstrations of fire building using a flint and steel in scouts. Just last night he had watched Tahee do this. Joey knew he could do this. He had to. Tahee had pulled a little ball of shredded bark out of his bag and used a bit of it to start the fire. Joey set about gathering pine needles and small pieces of bark.

Tahee had his fire going in two minutes. Joey worked for forty-five minutes. Three times he gave up in frustration. Each time his growling stomach made him try again. Finally he saw a tiny flame spring to life. Joey's excitement over the first flame was quickly snuffed out when he realized he didn't have any wood ready to keep the starter flame going. The second fire started easier simply because he knew he could do it. He had dry pine boughs ready this time. The fire began to crackle and pop. Joey got up and strutted around the fire.

"I did it! I built a fire!" He shouted to the trees, to the lake, and the mountains. "If Dad could see this," he said feeling more confident than he had ever felt before. "Beezer, do you see this?" He looked in the fire half hoping to see Beezer's face in there looking back. There was no Beezer and no answer. There was just the crackling of the fire.

Joey fought back a feeling of disappointment in not having anyone to show what he had done. He began gathering pine cones and placing them by the fire. It wasn't as simple as putting them in an oven with controlled heat like his den mother had. Several pine cones burned in the fire. Eventually he succeeded in breaking out some pine nuts. He put the nuts into his mouth one at a time and cracked the shells with his teeth. Then he peeled the nuts out with his fingers. They were fat, sweet, and piney.

"Who would've known pine trees could taste so good?" he thought. It got easier as he kept at it, but like eating sunflower seeds, it was a lot of work with little reward.

By the time his fingers were too sore to pick out any more pine nuts the growling in his stomach quieted. Still, he was hungry for something else. Joey walked to the edge of the lake. He wondered if there were fish in there. In answer he saw a tiny ripple form in a perfect circle when a fish touched the surface of the water. Farther out another circle formed.

"I wish I had a fishing pole," he said.

He walked along the edge of the lake toward the stream he had seen from the mountainside. After an hour he could hear the sound of water rushing over rocks. It wasn't hard to find after that. The creek was twenty feet across where it entered the lake and not too deep. Joey was able to hop across the creek on rocks.

From a large rock in the middle of the creek he leaned down and drank the cool, clear water. While he drank he saw a fish dart by no more than a foot away. It was so close he could have reached out and touched it. He didn't like fish, but he was so hungry it looked good. How could he catch one? Tahee had a spear with a sharp, stone spearhead on the end.

Joey hopped back to the shore and looked for spear-making materials. He was disappointed when he didn't find anything that would work. The dead pine boughs were all bent. If he got lucky and found a good stick would he get lucky again and find a sharp rock? In the movies the natives had always just had spears—he had never seen them make one.

Joey wandered along the stream watching for fish. It wasn't long before he hit the jackpot. He came to a large rock that sat in the stream by the bank. Behind it was a quiet pool that was six or seven feet deep. In it Joey saw several fish rising and sinking. They waited patiently for food to float into the pool from the water flowing past. Joey sat down and hungrily watched them for several minutes. They moved so slowly that he could catch them with a net . . . if he had a net.

Joey sat up with a sudden thought. He had passed under a dead pine tree just a little ways back. One of the bottom branches had a dense growth of what looked like dead twigs on the end. His dad had told him it was called mistletoe. This wasn't the kind that people kiss under at Christmas. It was a kind of parasite that eventually kills pine trees. Joey ran back and found it. The growth was dense enough to stand against the water and the weight of a fish, but loose enough to let the water through. It wasn't a very good net, but it might work.

Joey broke the branch off. It had a good four foot reach. He ran back to the pool and put the tangled end in. It wanted to float, but with effort he was able to keep the end under a few feet. The fish scattered at first. Joey stood very still like he had seen Tahee do when spearing fish. Slowly the fish calmed down and slowly returned to where they had gathered to wait for food to drift into their pool.

Joey wanted to scream as he watched the fish swim *under* his makeshift net and hide there. Eventually his patience paid off. A fish that had darted out into the edge of the moving water swam back above the tangle. Joey pulled with all his might. He watched in disbelieving joy as a fish sailed through the air above his head and landed, flopping, in the dirt under the trees behind him.

Joey whooped for joy and ran to the fish to make sure it wouldn't find its way back to the water. He banged its head on a rock until it quit flopping. It was a big fish, maybe a foot long, with black spots on its side.

"I caught a fish. I caught a fish. I caught a fish!" he sang as he danced around holding the fish above his head. For a moment he pictured Story and Glory dancing with him. They would be so excited if they were there. The thought of them made him stop his dance, his joy suddenly gone.

Joey noticed the sun had gone behind the hill. He was in deep shade. Holding his slippery fish in both hands he began the hike back to his camp.

His fire was still smoldering when he got there. Adding twigs and pine needles while blowing softly he was able to build flames again. Using his knife he gutted the fish. Compared to Tahee he made a mess of it. Tahee cooked the fish evenly over coals he had prepared. Joey pretty much burned his fish over a fire that was too hot. He ate most of the fish hungrily anyway.

Just above the mountains a strip of sky burned red. Directly overhead the sky was black. An early star was out. It was getting cool. Joey felt uneasy at the pending night. He wished for the protective walls of his attic room. Looking out across the lake he could feel the open miles surrounding him. It was going to get cold.

Joey fought back fear that wanted to take over. He thought of Captain Call and Tahee. They had been so strong in the face of death. He wasn't facing death; not yet anyway. He could get through the night.

Remembering what Tahee had taught him Joey went to the meadow and gathered armloads of the tall grasses and wild flowers. It took several trips. He had quite a nest built when he was finished. Joey gathered more wood and added some to the fire before nestling down into the grasses. He could smell the green. Joey lay facing the fire. The forest, though pleasant enough in the daytime, turned sinister in the dark.

Joey found comfort staring into the embers of the fire. He had lived an unbelievable day. He could feel a low throb in his hips from the bruising. He had faced the Blood-winged Eagle and helped Tahee rescue the girl. A feeling of happiness swept over him. Where had that brave Joey come from?

His mind went to the lake and the panic he had felt struggling in the water. From courage to panic in just two minutes. Was it just him or did this happen to everyone who sought courage? At least his panic hadn't won—he had survived the water. Then he had built a fire without matches and caught a fish without a fishing pole.

"Yes, what a day," Joey mumbled. He imagined sitting under the weeping willow telling Glory and Story all about it. In the back of his mind, where he worked to keep it, was the fact he had lost the map. With a mixture of happiness and anxiety Joey drifted off to sleep.

Sometime during the night Joey woke up needing to relieve himself. It took him a long moment to remember where he was. The moon was out and bathed the landscape in a soft, white glow.

The forest sat silent in deep shadow. Joey turned his back to it and took a few steps toward the lake to take care of business. As he stood there his sleepy mind cleared a little. He tried to pretend that this was a dream. He wasn't really alone by this lake with no way to get home. Once again fear tried to rise and take over. Joey, with sleepy determination pushed it back down. Shivering in the cold night air he hurried to get back to the small comfort his grass bed gave him.

He was in such a hurry that he almost missed it. Far across the lake he saw a light. It was small and soft like a flashlight or lantern. The light dimmed and brightened as it moved slowly through the trees. Joey watched, confused. The land was uninhabited. Beezer had said so. Who was over there? *What* was over there? Did he really want to meet the owner of the light? Yes. The light was the only hope he had.

As he raised his arm to wave and shout, the light disappeared for good. He stared at the spot where it disappeared for several minutes praying that it would come back. It didn't.

"Oh please, PLEASE!" he mumbled. He started walking quickly on the lakeshore. He couldn't wait for morning to follow the light. The landscape dimmed to near blackness. Joey looked up to see that the moon was setting. Soon it would be too dark to find his bed again let alone walk around the lake. Shivering from cold and excitement he stepped back into his camp. He added wood to the fire before crawling back into his earthen bed and pulling grass over him.

Excitement and longing, as well as the cold, kept him awake for a long time. Eventually, with only the stars piercing the darkness in the valley, Joey finally fell asleep. He dreamed of his golden room in the attic. He was watching himself sleep on his bed. He still had his clothes on. His door slowly opened. Glory and Story tip-toed in giving each other the "shush" sign with a finger to their lips. They took turns at each window, pointing at things they saw. They gravitated to his shelves where his models sat. They picked them up one at a time to look closer. They were told to never touch his models, but as Joey watched he didn't care. It made him happy to see their delight in the ships, rockets, and airplanes.

Mrs. Johanaby came in. Glory and Story turned with a guilty jerk when they heard her. She gave them the "You know you're in trouble look. Joey knew that look. It sent a thrill of happiness through him to see it now. Glory and Story quickly put the models down. The landing gear broke off one of the airplanes. Glory gave a horrified little laugh in her usual style and rushed out of the room with Story.

Mrs. Johanaby came over to the sleeping Joey and ran her fingers gently through his hair. She took his shoes off his feet and placed them neatly by his bed. Even though he was only watching her do this, Joey could fee her warm touch. He tried desperately to wake as she walked out of the room, but couldn't.

Chapter 15

The sun was shining down fully upon Joey when he opened his eyes.

"Oh," he said, sitting up stiffly.

He looked at his fire. It was only cold ashes.

"Dang," he thought.

The thrill of building a fire was gone. It was only a lot of work now. The air was chilly, but the sun was warm on his back. Joey was content just to sit for a while and wake up. He had seen vultures in trees sit with their back to the sun and wings spread as they warmed up. He spread his arms, but quickly folded them again. The vulture trick didn't work for him. He noticed grass and bits of leaves stuck to his shirt and pants. As he brushed at them he noticed how dirty his hands were.

"I'm a mess," he mumbled. Looking at the lake he thought of washing up. In spite of the sunshine the air was chilly. The thought of splashing cold lake water on himself didn't motivate him. "Later, when it's warmer," he promised himself.

Joey had spent a night out all by himself; and he had done it with no supplies.

"Well, would you look at me," he said, standing up. "I'm a regular mountain man like Grizzly Adams."

Even with the brave words he couldn't fool himself. He wasn't looking forward to another day alone here. This day alone would be followed by another day alone, followed by another. His courage was failing fast.

"Oh, Beezer. I need help." He blinked back tears.

Joey looked through his tears at the lake. His map home sat at the bottom. He hated the lake.

He lifted his eyes to the forest on the other side. He remembered bits of dreams—of being asleep in his room, of Glory and Story, of his Mom. He remembered a moonlit night and a light moving through trees.

"Wait," Joey said. "the light wasn't a dream." Excitement grew within him. He stood up and studied the edge of the forest on the other side of the lake. The forest was still in shadow. Joey saw no light or any sign of life. Something had been over there last night. He had to go see what it was.

It was a long hike around the lake. He was ready to leave except for his empty stomach. Joey reached down and picked up a clump of large leaves sitting a rock. He unrolled the stiffened leaves and uncovered what was left of his fish from the night before. The fish was cold and stiff. It didn't look appetizing, but there were two or three bites left. The thought of eating it made him gag. After the first nibble he ate it hungrily. His stomach was growling for more when he set out.

It wasn't a difficult hike. He wound his way between the pines and through clumps of undergrowth. He kept the lake in sight on his left at all times.

The sun was high in the sky when he finally reached the opposite shore. He had taken a break when he came upon some wild currant bushes with ripe clusters of fruit. He picked and ate currents until he was sick of them. His hands and shirt were stained with red juice.

Now that he was over here he couldn't tell exactly where along the shore he had seen the light the night before. Across the lake he could see the rocky meadow with the hill behind it. He could just make out where he was camped. The light had been here somewhere.

The forest floor was thick and springy with pine needles. Pine cones lay strewn about. He made a sport of kicking them as high and far as he could. There were fallen trees, some fresh with bark and branches still intact; others old and rotting. Joey kicked off chunks of rotting wood with the toe of his tennis shoe.

It was so quiet that he wished for sound, any sound other than wind. He longed for the irritating, impromptu knock-knock jokes that Glory and Story always made up.

"Knock knock?"

"Who's there?"

"Pokey."

"Pokey who?"

"Pokey Porcupine!"

Joey could hear Story's intense little laugh at the end of this. Joey smiled at the memory.

He stopped and looked around. Pine trees, logs, pine needles, the lake seen through the trees—there was nothing more; no sign of anything that would have made that light.

A breeze hushed through the pine boughs above him. Joey stopped to listen. He felt no air movement and looked up to see if the pine boughs were moving. They weren't. It sounded like the trees were sighing. Joey wondered how he could stand the days of loneliness to come.

Another breeze moved. Joey saw this one. It touched the surface of the lake out in the middle travelling toward him. Shimmering ripples appeared in the water. The pine boughs sighed again as the breeze reached them. This time the breeze reached through the trees and touched Joey. It was fresh with the expected hint of pine. Joey smelled something else, something familiar, but not of this world. It was . . . lilacs.

The smell of home brought a lump to Joey's throat. The breeze passed as quickly as it came. Joey longed for more. Out on the lake the breeze touched the surface once again and skipped toward shore. This time the breeze would come ashore ahead of him. Joey ran through the forest like a deer. He dodged trees and jumped logs. More than anything he wanted to smell the lilacs again. The breeze had passed by the time he arrived. The lake was smooth as glass.

Joey fell to his knees and leaned forward on his hands to catch his breath. Once more the lump rose in his throat, this time for lack of the scent of home. He dug his fingers into the thick layer of pine needles on the forest floor. He put his forehead against his hands.

"Oh, please, I want to go home," he prayed.

He lifted his head and froze. He was staring into the eyes of the little, wild-haired doll Glory had given him. The doll was sitting on the ground leaning against a fallen log about twenty-five feet away. She was sitting in the same position Joey had sat her at the bottom of the weeping willow. Her thin, white dress stood out against the browns and greens of the forest.

Joey stared for a full minute. He was afraid to move, afraid to blink, for fear the doll would disappear like the light in the night, like the smell of home. When his back began to ache he stood and walked over to the doll. It didn't disappear. Joey carefully picked it up. He felt the hard plastic body in his hands. He looked into the unblinking blue eyes.

"No," Joey said, speaking to the doll, "Your hair couldn't look nicer today." He put her to his nose and smelled. Amid the plastic and fake hair there was Glory.

Joey pulled the doll close to his chest and snuggled her. He sat down on the log and smoothed the doll's hair with his stained fingers. How had she gotten here? The light had something to do with it, he was sure. Joey sat where he was as the sun moved across the tops of the pines. This is where he saw the light. This is where he smelled home. This is where he found the doll. If there was any hope for him in this world, he figured it would be right here. He wasn't going to move until he found that hope. His bottom was beginning to ache, but he remained resolute. The sun passed overhead and started angling toward the hill on the other side of the lake. Still he stayed.

Joey's thoughts drifted through time and space to his home and his past. Memories came in fragments. A chilly, autumn day in Idaho; sitting on the sidewalk with Glory helping her get her pants free from between the chain and sprocket of her bike. Sitting in his sixth grade class and seeing his Dad at the door. He brought Joey's clarinet for after-school band practice. Story lying next to him in bed and sobbing the night after Mr. Johanaby died. The look in Mrs. Johanaby's eyes when she realized she had forgotten him in the pond.

The trees sighed once more bringing Joey back to the present. The high, clear note of the crystal chime floated in the sigh like a dandelion seed in a breeze. Joey stiffened and then closed his eyes concentrating on that beautiful sound. As the chime died away he heard a voice that seemed to float among the pine boughs with the breeze.

"You have an entire world to explore and you just sit there, Joey Johanaby?" The melodic voice was framed with a Tennessee accent.

"Henrietta?" Joey asked softly, holding back tears of relief and hope.

"How can you be so sad in such a beautiful place?" Her voice hushed from the trees on his right to the trees on his left as she spoke.

"But there's nobody here," Joey said.

"Yes, why is that?" Henrietta asked. *"Why would you create such a beautiful, yet lonely world?"*

Joey remembered Beezer telling him the map had been created from the dreams and desires of his heart. He thought of the day he had run away from his family. He'd had enough of his family. He wanted to be left alone. Joey started to understand how this world was created.

"It is beautiful," Joey said, opening his eyes. Sunlight glistened on the water. Graceful pine boughs reached out to him on every side. "It's just that I can't leave. I lost the map."

"Oh, that could change a person's perspective," Henrietta said. *"Where is it you want to go?"*

"Home," Joey said. "I want to go home."

"You've had such wonderful adventures and you just want to go home?" Her voice came from the direction of the lake now, as if she were walking along the shore while talking to him.

It was true. His adventures with the map had been wonderful. He thought of Captain Call and Tahee. They had inspired him to be courageous. He missed them. It wasn't danger that was the adventure, but helping them in their troubles. He didn't have anyone in this world to help. It occurred to him this world was rather meaningless. Home wasn't meaningless. He thought of Mrs. Johanaby, struggling and alone. He thought of the twins, how they really did need him. There were no pirates or giant eagles, but there was adventure just the same.

"Yes, Joey said. "I really, really want to go home

"Then why are you staying here?" The question came from right beside him in a voice more solid. Joey looked. She was sitting next to him. Even in the daylight her blue eyes glowed softly. The soft folds of her expansive dress were cool where they enveloped his legs. Her smile radiated warmth like the sun.

"It is so good to see you," Joey said, restraining himself from hugging her.

"I feel the same pleasure," she beamed. They sat smiling at each other for a moment, taking pleasure in each other's company. Eventually Henrietta went on.

"Joey, you have done well."

"I have, haven't I." Joey said, feeling the warmth of pride.

"You are brave, and what's more important, you are full of love! Do you still doubt it?"

Joey looked down at the doll in his lap. "No," he said. "I don't doubt it anymore, but I'm not sure I understand. Is love greater than courage?"

"Love is the living soul of courage. There is no courage without love. You didn't jump in the pond to save Glory because you were brave . . ."

"I jumped in because I love her," Joey finished.

Henrietta pulled an imaginary rope. A bright sounding bell rang once. "Yes," Henrietta said. "I think you have arrived. Love grows courage."

They sat for a minute looking at the lake together and listening to the breeze. Suddenly a hawk flew into view. Joey thought it might be the same hawk he saw yesterday soaring so high. This time it swooped down to the water and snatched a fish from just under the surface.

Thrilled by the sight Joey said, "I caught a fish yesterday."

"Yes, Beezer told me," Henrietta said, nodding her approval.

"Beezer *was* watching," Joey said.

"Oh, yes. Beezer takes his responsibilities very seriously."

Joey pictured Beezer in his room watching the bubbles. He thought of the hole he had dug with Story just outside of Beezer's room and the treasure they had found. All those golden chocolate coins—he suddenly wanted to stack them with Story. He wanted to argue with Glory. He wanted to hug his mother.

"Can you take me home now?" Joey asked.

"No," Henrietta answered.

Her answer was soft, but it sounded like thunder in his ears. "What?" Joey said.

"There is only one way to go home. I believe Beezer explained it to you."

Henrietta grew more reserved suddenly. Joey was confused. He had assumed that Henrietta had come to take him home.

"But, I lost the map," Joey said, a feeling of desperation beginning to rise.

"If that is true you may be here a long time," Henrietta said, laughing as if she had just made a joke.

Joey shot her a hurt glance which she saw.

"Forgive me, Joey," she said. "I sometimes put things badly when I was alive, and I still haven't learned. Let me restate that. By lost you mean you don't know where the map is?"

"It's in the lake," Joey said weakly. "I watched it sink."

"Oh, then it's not really lost," she said. "Lost treasure is lost only if no one knows where it is."

"But how will I get it?" Joey asked.

"It seems to me that your adventure isn't over in this world. Just remember, Joey, you are brave. Don't forget why you are brave." Then, without any goodbyes she was gone.

Joey sat with his mouth hanging open. He felt betrayed. Feelings of anger followed. Henrietta had appeared as if in answer to his prayer. She left and nothing had changed.

"Why'd she even come," he thought, fighting tears of anger. "What was that all about?" he yelled. "What am I supposed to do now? 'You are brave,' she said. So what? Am I supposed bravely live here alone all the rest of my life?"

Joey was yelling. He hoped Beezer was watching. Then he was embarrassed because Beezer might be watching. He wasn't acting very courageous. He was hurt and confused. Henrietta spoke of courage and love. How would that help him now? He was still trapped in this land. The map was still at the bottom of the lake.

Joey kicked a pinecone. It flew between the tree trunks and landed in the water near the shore. It bobbed and floated in its new resting place. Joey kicked another and then another into the lake. Walking closer to the lake he raised his arm to throw the doll into the lake. He stopped when he realized what he was doing.

"No," he said. "No, I won't do that. I would never do that to you." He stared at the doll's unblinking eyes; he was seeing Glory in his mind. He held the doll close to his chest again.

"*Remember why you are brave,*" Henrietta had said.

"For love," Joey mumbled. "For love of my family." Joey's anger faded.

"*Seems to me like your adventure here isn't over.*" Joey could still hear the words as she spoke them.

Then it hit him—the adventure of this world would be finding a way to go home. In the other two worlds he was saving someone else. This time he was saving himself. He looked out across the lake. The only way home was through the map. The map was at the bottom of the lake. He was a bad swimmer and scared of the water.

"Oh, boy," he said anxiously, when he realized what he was going to have to do. Fear, familiar like an old enemy, started buzzing in his stomach again. How would he ever swim down to where the map was? It was impossible. That's why he hadn't already tried it. "There must be a way," he said. Henrietta wouldn't have come and given him hope if there wasn't. He was sure of that. Warm confidence grew in him even though he didn't have the answer yet. He began to think.

On this side of the lake the bank fell away sharply into deep, dark water. On the far side, the side his camp was on, the water color was lighter.

"It's not so deep over there," Joey thought.

He looked about where he had seen the map sinking. Yes, the water was lighter there, shallower. Still, anything over his head was too deep. He could never swim out that far without drowning. He had barely made it to shore from where he had landed in the water. The map was another fifty feet out. Feelings of despair fought with feelings of hope as he paced back and forth. This was just too much. His eyes fell on the pinecones floating in the water. Before he had taken swimming lessons his dad had put him in the pool with a life vest. He had floated like these pine cones. An idea formed in his head.

Joey started back around the lake. It was late afternoon when he got back to his campsite. He had come up with a plan and already put it into action. Taking off his t-shirt he stuffed it full of pinecones, so full he worried it might rip. He tied the top and bottom of the shirt closed with his shoelaces. What he ended up with was something like a poky, lumpy beach ball.

Fear gripped Joey as he stood at the edge of the water. He did not want to go out into the lake again. He remembered the feel of water closing in over his head. Fear whispered, *"You will drown."*

Before his first near drowning experience he decided to jump off the high dive at the city pool. He had gotten to the edge and looked down. He couldn't do it. He turned around and went back down enduring the jeers of the other kids. Joey turned and looked at what he would be "going back down to" here. There were forests and meadows; hills and mountains. But there was no family. All this beauty was meaningless without someone to share it with. Without the map this land was just a big, beautiful prison. He looked down at the doll he had sat on a rock facing the lake. She stared across the water with untroubled eyes, totally content.

"I can't be content here, like you," Joey said. "I need to go home." He leaned over toward the doll and whispered, "I miss Glory." The doll listened quietly. Joey knew she would keep his secret.

Joey stared at the lake again. It was a simple choice: risk death for the opportunity to be among those he loved, or live here alone forever. Pushing against an icy fear Joey chose. He waded out into the lake, stumbling over the rocky bottom as he went. He stopped when the water was waist deep. It was cold. He sat his pinecone beach ball in the water. It floated.

"Yes," he said pumping his fist.

That was as far as his victory went. When he lay across the lumpy pine cone ball it sank under his weight. It hardly pushed back. And like a beach ball it didn't want to stay under him. It continually tried to float up on either side of him. He tried to hang on to it with one arm and paddle with the other. That didn't work either. Fighting with it made him more tired than just swimming. As he struggled with it he swallowed water and coughed. Frantically he reached for the bottom. He was grateful when his foot touched a rock and he was just able to keep his head above water.

Shivering, Joey made his way back to shore where he rested on the warm rocks. His pine cone ball bobbed low in the water out where he abandoned it. The bitter taste of disappointment rose in the back of his throat. When he had the pinecone idea he was so sure it was the answer. If the flotation device wasn't the answer, what was? Joey's anxiety grew as he sat thinking. Perhaps he *was* stuck here forever?

"No!" He just knew there was a way to get the map.

Standing up he addressed the lake.

"I *can* swim," he said. "I'm not very good at it, but I *can* swim."

With sheer determination Joey waded back into the lake. He forced himself to keep going until the water was up to his neck. Then he lifted his legs and swam. His head immediately went under and he swallowed water. He rolled over onto his back to float. His legs and rear end sank. Water splashed over his face. Panicking he thrashed and splashed his way back to where he could touch bottom. Defeated, he made his way back to shore.

Salty tears mixed with the fresh lake water on his face.

"What am I supposed to do?" he yelled. He wiped his nose on his hand. "WHAT?"

The doll sat silently on its rock nearby. The serene look on its face annoyed him.

"You're a big help," Joey said. He wiped the tears from his face with his hands. Wet and without his shirt he was cold. The sun was nearing the mountaintops behind him. He didn't want to spend another night here.

Joey lay back on the warm rocks and stared at the sky. The map was just 150 feet away. His family was so close and yet so far away. If he could just float long enough to get over the map just maybe he could swim down and get it. In water "down" was a direction he seemed good at.

His wet jeans stuck to his legs. They were heavy and made his attempts at swimming harder. Would taking them off make the difference he needed? He didn't think so.

The thought of his jeans triggered a memory. Joey sat up. If the doll could have, it would have laughed at the look on his face. In Cub Scouts he had gone to a lifesaving demonstration put on by a local scout troop. During part of the demonstration they had turned their jeans into life preservers. They tied the leg ends together, zipped the zipper and buttoned them up. They filled them with air by blowing in them underwater. It was as clear in his mind as if he had just watched it yesterday.

Joey got up and began to peel himself out of his wet jeans.

"Don't look," he said to the doll. She didn't turn her head, but he wasn't so sure she wasn't peeking out of the corner of her eyes.

He zipped and buttoned the jeans and tied the ends of the legs together as tightly as he could. Shivering, but full of hope, he waded back out into the lake. Steeling himself against the cold he put his face under the water and blew air into the pants. The legs began to inflate.

"Yes!" he cried.

With the legs filled with air the pants floated as good as a life jacket. It would easily hold him up. He put his head between the pant legs so the knot in the legs was behind his head. As long as he held the waist down underwater the air didn't bubble out. Holding the waistband against him with his arms he swam alternately on his belly or his back using his legs to propel himself.

As he swam the sun set behind the hill. He had to hurry. Even with the make-shift lifejacket Joey was scared when he got to deeper water. Panic swam right beside him, but he wouldn't give it his attention. He focused his thoughts on his family.

"Mom," he said. He breathed and kicked, "Glory." Breathe, kick, "Story." Breathe, kick . . . he hesitated, "Dad!" He repeated this as he slowly worked his way to the place he last remembered seeing the map.

The water was clear. He could see the bottom. There were rounded boulders down below. He got to where he thought the map was and didn't see it. Panic almost got the better of him. His hope was sinking with the sun.

"Henrietta wouldn't have come if there wasn't a way," he said. He didn't know how he knew, but he knew. The thought buoyed his hope.

"Sometimes you know things without knowing," Beezer had said.

The life-jacket made it hard to look down. On his belly he couldn't lean too far forward without losing the air from the jeans. Leaning to one side he was able to glance sideways down into the water.

His heart leapt when he saw it. The map lay unfolded next to a large rock ten or twelve feet down. Joey's excitement faded when he realized what would come next. He was going to have to let go of the life jacket in order to swim down to the map. When he did the air would escape and the life jacket would be no use anymore.

Joey was numb with fear.

"Oh, Henrietta," he said, voice shaking. "I wish there was another way." In his mind's eye he saw Beezer watching him in one of the colored bubbles. He wondered if Beezer was as nervous as he was.

"Here I come, Beezer," he said.

With that he took a big breath and let go of the jeans. The water was so much colder when it closed over his head. Joey pulled with his arms and kicked. At eight feet under his progress slowed and his ears began to hurt. In fear he began flailing. Wasn't going down supposed to be easier than this? With an almost overwhelming desire to breathe he turned back toward the surface. The old air in his lungs helped him back up. When the air touched his face he took in great gulps. He looked desperately for his jeans and saw them about ten feet away just under the surface of the water. They were slowly sinking.

Joey looked toward shore. It was too far away. He would never make it back. He saw the doll serenely staring out at him. He remembered Glory's smell on the doll. He would see Glory again or die trying.

Taking another gulp of air he went down again. Joey knew this would be his last attempt. An unexpected calmness came over him. In a minute he would either reach home or die. Either way the adventure would end.

His eyes focused on the map. He kicked and pulled as hard as he could. Again, at eight feet there was a sharp pain in his ears and his progress slowed. This time he pushed air out of his lungs. Bubbles rushed past his face. With the buoyant air gone he made three more feet in one stroke. He was just seconds away from drowning.

The map was just one foot away. His mind was fogging. He was dying. Through the fog he saw the home heart in bright red on the map.

"Home!" he thought. He gave one more kick and reached. The light grew dim. The weight of the water pressed hard on him. Everything faded. His last thought was that dying was a lot like using the map.

Chapter 16

Joey slowly regained consciousness. He became aware of water all around him. Was he lying face down at the bottom of the lake—dead? Something was odd. The water felt warmer, softer, and he was breathing. Did you breathe when you were dead? With each sweet breath he smelled mud and wet grass.

When he opened his eyes he saw water everywhere. It wasn't the lake. This water was splashing bubbling like it was boiling. He caught glimpses of grass and mud sticking out above the surface. There was noise, too—a great rushing din. With an effort Joey raised his head. He was weak and his head felt heavy. Rain. It was pouring rain. He turned his head and stared disbelieving for a moment. It was the garage!

With effort he rolled over and sat up Indian style. The rain pounded down. The limbs of the weeping willow hung wet around him. Through the sodden limbs he saw the mansion. Joey was home.

The transition from the bottom of the lake to the watery backyard was confusing. He didn't remember actually touching the map. He had been a blink away from death at the bottom of the lake. Joey still wasn't convinced he was alive.

His right hand was tightly closed. He opened his fist and stared. It was crumpled and torn, but there was the bottom corner of the magic map. The bright red heart glowed through the rain. The words were still clear, *Home is where the heart is.*

Tears rolled down his face with the raindrops. This time they were for pure joy. Something wonderful had happened to him; something even bigger than coming home. Gratitude and love were the cornerstones of the joy he felt He thought of Henrietta and Beezer. He thought of Captain Call and Tahee. He thought of his family. He recognized a love as deep as eternity. Joey couldn't contain the joy he felt and sobbed out loud in the din of the rain.

A voice came to him through the rain.

"Henrietta?" he said, looking around.

It wasn't her. It was Mrs. Johanaby. She called to him from the back porch. She was still wearing her cut-off sweats and Scooby Doo shirt. She was barefoot. To Joey's eyes she looked as beautiful as Henrietta in her curls and hoop skirt.

Mrs. Johanaby spotted Joey sitting in the rain. She leapt off the porch and ran to him with muddy, splashing steps.

"Joey. JOEY!" Ignoring the rain she knelt down in the mud in front of him, felt his forehead, and then cupped his face in her hands. "What are you doing sitting in the rain? Are you all right? I thought you were still in bed. When I checked, you weren't there." She looked into his face and somehow detected his tears in spite of the rain.

"Oh, Joey," she said, not understanding it was joy he felt and not pain. She pulled him close. He lifted his heavy arms and put them around her. In her embrace he felt such contentment he never wanted to let go. When her hold loosened and his didn't Mrs. Johanaby tightened hers again. She pushed her cheek against his ear and ran her fingers through his wet hair.

"Let's get you in out of the rain," she said into his ear. Still on her knees Mrs. Johanaby tried to lift Joey in her arms to carry him to the house just as she had with Glory. Joey was far too heavy for this.

"Mom, I can walk. I'm okay," he said.

Mrs. Johanaby let him slip to his feet. Unwilling to fully let go she put a supporting arm around him as they walked to the house.

Under the protection of the porch roof they stopped and looked at each other. The rain drummed a dull roar on the roof. Her hair lay tangled and flattened on her head. Water dripped down her face and off her chin. There were dark circles under her eyes.

"Aren't we a sight?" Joey said.

Mrs. Johanaby laughed, and then cried. She pulled Joey close for another soggy hug. Joey patted her back. This time she didn't want to let go. In no hurry Joey laid his head on her shoulder.

"I missed you, Mom," he said. He felt her body stiffen slightly in a question.

"Missed me?" she said, loosening her hold and meeting his eyes. "You mean, last night when I was at the hospital with Glory?"

Last night? Joey thought. *This is the morning of the same day I left on my adventures?* He didn't understand how that could be. If no time had passed had he really gone on any adventures at all?

Joey opened his hand. The map fragment was still there. His memory of the adventures was clear. He felt the difference his adventures made inside him. Yes, he had gone.

Mrs. Johanaby looked at the fragment, too. Thinking he was offering it to her in answer to her question she gently took it. She studied the heart and read the words; *Home is where the heart is.* She looked into Joey's eyes. Not understanding what it meant her eyes flicked nervously to the left. Joey recognized the nervous habit. She did this when she was uncomfortable.

"Why were you sitting in the rain," she asked. It was a question meekly asked. She was afraid of something, Joey could tell.

He thought for a moment, and then he answered. "I went to see Beezer in the garage, and . . . and I fell." Both of those things were true if not completely accurate.

His mother's eyes flicked nervously to the left again. She knew he was holding something back and was afraid of whatever it was. She was trying to find courage to face it. Joey understood this. He also knew what it was she was afraid of. It was there in her eyes, a hint of the same look he had seen when she realized that she hadn't gone back to the pond for him. Even though he was alive in her arms at that moment she was afraid that she had lost him in some other way.

"I am sorry, Joey," she said. "I am so sorry." She pulled him close again and held him more tightly than was comfortable. She was crying.

Joey again laid his head on her shoulder, this time with his face in her dripping hair. "I love you, Mom," he said. His thoughts were a jumble. Those were the only words to reach his mouth. They made Mrs. Johanaby cry harder. Joey cried with her. Finally, with a hiccup, she stopped crying and loosened her grip. She smiled embarrassedly and wiped her face with her hands.

"Go get some dry clothes on. Then come back down to the kitchen. I'll have Cream of Wheat ready with gummy bears," she said. "I have something I want to read you."

On his way to the stairs Glory and Story stepped out of the TV room. Joey recognized the sound of the same show they were watching when he left for the garage. They looked at him curiously as he stood dripping on the floor.

"Mom's going to be mad," Glory said. Her voice was soft and threatening. This was her way of telling him she was going to tell— *maybe*. It was a power play she used often.

"No she's not." Joey said it calmly and with authority— authority that comes with speaking the truth. A troubled frown formed on her lips. She wasn't used to being resisted.

Looking at Glory Joey remembered her doll. It was sitting all alone on the rock looking out across the lake with those unblinking eyes. Those serene eyes—it was like the doll had known all along he would make it. Thinking of the doll and how much it had meant to him to find it by the lake, Joey felt a wave of love for Glory. He stepped forward to give her a hug.

"Eww," she said, darting back into the TV room. "You're all wet."

Joey looked down at the puddle that was forming around him. *Fair enough*, he thought.

Story still stood there staring dubiously at him. Joey made as if to give him a hug. Story screamed in delight and darted after Glory.

Upstairs Joey studied the ripped corner of the map. His mother had given it back to him. He was glad the paper was so thick, almost like cloth. Otherwise it wouldn't have survived the soaking it had taken. The Home Heart was more precious to him than anything he owned. He laid it on his desk under a book to flatten it as it dried.

He peeled off his wet clothes, dried himself with an old t-shirt, and pulled on dry clothes. He sighed with pleasure when he finished dressing. Sitting on his bed he looked out the weeping willow window. He could see the branch Henrietta and he sat on—was it last night?

A sudden intuition saddened Joey. He was never going to see Henrietta again. Her job here was done.

"No!" he said in disappointment. "I didn't get to say goodbye." After a moment he added more softly, "I didn't get to say thank you."

A feeling of depression and unfairness threatened his joy. He leaned forward and put his face in his hands. Betraying his disappointment an almost playful thought came into his head. "Why not say it now?"

Joey closed his eyes. He smiled. *Yes, why not*, he thought.

"Thank you, Henrietta." He spoke the words as if she were there. "Thank you." Tingles spread across his chest and arms.

Joey found a bowl of Cream of Wheat sitting at his spot at the kitchen table. A bag of gummy bears and brown sugar sat next to it. Mrs. Johanaby sat in her bathrobe wearing a towel around her head like a turban. She was reading from a sheaf of papers.

"Thanks, Mom," Joey said, sitting down.

Mrs. Johanaby looked up and smiled her too big smile. Joey drank it in like sunshine.

"I stayed up all night writing this," she said.

"Is it a paper for your class?" Joey asked.

"No, it's a story about one Joey Johanaby, my son," she said. She looked at him almost shyly. "After yesterday at the pond . . ." Her voice wavered and her hand went to her mouth.

Joey squirmed in his seat. He didn't like seeing his mom vulnerable.

"It's okay, M—" he started to say.

"NO, it's not," she said. Taking a big breath she blurted out, "Joey, I forgot to come back for you yesterday!" She put her hands over her face this time. Tears dripped off her palms. When she lowered her hands her eyes were red and swollen. "There, I said it.

I actually said it." Her voice wavered. Joey heard a hint of relief in it.

"What kind of mother forgets one of her own children?" She was looking at Joey, but she wasn't asking him the question. "Every time I look at you for the rest of my life I will relive that moment."

She looked at him now and Joey could see it in her eyes—she was reliving that moment of horror.

That moment had stayed with Joey, too. She had pulled Glory from the pond and left him. He was aware that this was wrong, but he hadn't dwelt on it. The guilt he felt about abandoning the twins, and then his hesitation to jump in to save Glory made Joey feel like his Mom had a right to punish him. Joey started to understand that maybe this wasn't true.

Joey sensed the power he held over his mother. The fact that she forgot him would be a fact for eternity. For the rest of her life he could bring it up whenever he wanted. This idea appeared in Joey's mind for only a moment. He let it go like a child lets go of a balloon to watch it float away in the sky.

His mother had made a mistake. Beezer had been there to save her from the consequences of her mistake. Captain Call had made a mistake. Joey had been there to help soften the consequences of his mistake. Since his father's death, Joey thought of his whole life as a mistake. Beezer and Henrietta showed up to help correct this thinking. Mrs. Johanaby needed his help now.

Joey slipped out of his chair. He went to Mrs. Johanaby and put a hand on her shoulder. She didn't respond. Joey reached under her hands to her chin. He gently turned her face toward his and looked into her tired, brown eyes.

"Mom," he said. "I know you love me." In guilt she tried to turn her head back to her hands. Joey wouldn't let her. "When you look at me the rest of your life, all you should see is a son who loves you more than anything in the world."

Mrs. Johanaby broke down in a storm of emotion that washed over Joey like the pouring rain. She hugged him and kissed him and then hugged him more.

After a time she let him loose. "I wrote this for you," she said. She handed him the sheaf of papers. "Excuse me." She got up and left the kitchen.

Joey felt a little dizzy from emotion, or hunger, maybe both. He set the papers in his spot at the table. He dropped gummy bears into his cereal followed by brown sugar. He was going to read while he ate. When he put the first spoonful of hot cereal in his mouth he couldn't stop eating until he scraped his bowl clean.

"Oh, that's good," he said.

His hunger satisfied Joey picked up the papers and started to read. It was a story of sorts. At first he thought it was about his mother. Then he thought it was about him. Finally he realized it was *their* story.

He read about his birth and the first time she held him. She was only eighteen. Being a mother terrified her. He read of diaper changes and throw-up. He felt her disappointment when he said "Dad" before "Mom." There was her hysteria when they couldn't find him one afternoon. Finally they had found him in the car where he had been playing and fallen asleep. She wrote of the only time she had ever spanked him. She felt so bad that she never did it again. She had remembered her first day of school when she took him to kindergarten. She was overwhelmed when the twins were born. She knew he felt left out, but didn't know what to do.

Joey smiled broadly as he read about these first years. Mrs. Johanaby had told him some of these stories before. On paper they became more real. His mother became more sharply defined in his mind. His smile left as he read on.

Her husband and best friend in the universe got sick and died. There was no going on after that, except for the kids. She wrote of fear and loneliness in a way that nearly broke Joey's heart. She wrote of how much she depended on Joey—so much that she almost forgot he was only twelve-years-old. She described her feelings of horror at the pond when she realized what she had done. She wrote that if she had lost her husband *and* Joey she couldn't go on. Even if he forgave her she would always be guilty of what she had forgotten at the pond.

"Not guilty, Mom," he mumbled. "Not guilty."

She finished by professing her love and promising before God she would never forget again.

Mrs. Johanaby was still "Mom" to Joey, but after reading her story there was much more Molly to her.

"Molly," he said out loud. "Molly." He thought it was a pretty name.

Story and Glory came running into the kitchen.

"Not fair," Story said. "You got gummy bears."

"I get gummy bears, too," said Glory, grabbing the bag.

"You get four," Joey said, sensing that winning a battle by giving up some would be easier than giving up none.

"You're not the boss of—"

"You get four," Joey interrupted, looking into her eyes and raising an eyebrow.

Glory, annoyed, frowned. Then she giggled and said, "Okay."

Not letting Story get his own she gave him four, took four for herself, and then led the way out of the room. Facing down Glory wasn't as noble as facing down pirates, but he liked the way it felt.

It rained for the next two days. They were all stuck in the house fighting cabin fever. Joey often thought he heard chimes through the sound of the rain on the windows. It was always just his imagination. Joey wanted to discuss his adventures with Beezer. He looked out of his window at the garage hoping to see colorful, glowing bubbles rising through the roof. Beezer's windows remained dark. He never showed up at their door. Joey read, drew pictures, and played Uno Poker with Glory and Story for chocolate coins. The poker games ended when they ate the last of the winnings. Chocolate smudges remained on the cards.

The third morning the sky was clear with sunshine imminent. Joey, Glory and Story went outside after breakfast to introduce themselves to nature again. They immediately started a game of puddle jumping. This quickly turned into puddle splashing and mudslinging.

Joey escaped by going to the garage. He wanted to see if Beezer was around. As he slid the door open he smiled at the smell of oil and old engines. He felt he was returning after a long absence. Feeling none of his usual fears of the dark and oily interior he went straight to Beezer's door. He knocked and the door swung open. It hadn't been shut all the way. Joey stared in dismay. The room was empty. There were no trains or swords.

There were no models or kites. The room was empty. Beezer was gone.

Joey stood trying to control a feeling of despair. Henrietta and Beezer were gone. It left a hole in Joey's heart right next to his father's.

"Why do people have to leave?" he said. He could almost taste his disappointment.

Joey stepped into the empty room. Bright sunlight streamed through the three back windows. Dust floated in the sunbeams. Even in its emptiness there was something lovely about the room. When he turned around to leave, he saw it—the rocket that had hung so long in the tree. It was leaning against the wall behind the door. He stared at it a long time without moving. Beezer hadn't left it by accident. Joey took comfort in its presence as if it were Beezer himself. A small envelope was taped to it. Stepping over he took out a folded piece of paper. Opening it he read:

Nobody leaves forever.

Joey stared at this sentence and smiled. It meant so many things. There was another line written further down the paper.

If you ever need me. Use the rocket!

As Joey thought about what that might mean he heard chimes. They were more distinct than he had ever heard them before. His first thought was of Henrietta. There was something different about these chimes. They actually sounded like they came from this world.

Joey ran out of the garage and looked toward the house. Glory and Story, dripping with mud, stood under the weeping willow near the house. They were staring up through the limbs.

"Have those always been there?" Glory asked, as Joey approached.

"We would have heard'em before," said Story. "But I've never looked up there before."

High above, tied to the limb Joey and Henrietta had sat on, were a set a chimes. Joey knew for a fact they hadn't been there

208

before. Their appearance brought brightness to his heart. Only Henrietta would have left such a gift in such a place.

Glory gasped. "Is that my doll?"

Joey looked again. A doll sat leaning against the trunk on the same limb the chimes were tied to.

"Would you look at that," Joey said. *Was* it the same doll he had left at the lake? It didn't look like it.

Glory ran to the tree. She couldn't reach the lowest limb. Looking at Joey and asked, "Can you get it?"

"Yes, I can." Joey started up the tree while Glory and Story hopped and twirled in excitement below.

"Careful!" Glory ordered. "Don't knock the doll off."

As he got closer he caught his breath at the beauty of the chimes. Hanging from a polished circle of dark wood were eight narrow tubes that tinkled happily. Between each tube hung tiny decorative figurines. There were two sailing ships, four colorful birds, and two pine trees. A smaller circle of wood hung in the middle of the tubes to knock the tubes and make them ring when the wind blew. Hanging underneath the knocker was a likeness of Beezer's coke bottle glasses. This made Joey laugh.

"What's so funny?" called Glory.

"Nothing," Joey answered.

The chimes hung on the limb not too far from the house. They were near his attic window. He would be able to hear them in his room. It would be like Henrietta was always with him.

"I love you, Henrietta," he said.

Joey stopped and stared as he approached the doll. He carefully picked it up and sat on the limb to study it. Was this the doll he left beside the lake? He wasn't certain. The wild hair had been tamed into curls like Henrietta's. Instead of a little white slip of a dress the doll now wore a hoop skirt with beautiful detail. Little, dainty boots were on its feet with real laces. It was lovely.

The eyes gave it away. They were blue and looked at him with a serenity that spoke of cool mountain air and the scent of pines.

"You clean up better than I do," Joey said.

"Hurry! Bring it down." Glory called.

Joey put the doll up to his nose and breathed in. He smelled plastic, fake hair, a hint of Glory . . . and lilacs.

It was hard climbing down the tree with the doll in one hand. "You could have put the doll lower down," Joey said with a grin.

Glory's mouth fell open when Joey showed her the doll. She moved to grab it, but Joey, held it away.

"Uh uh. Mud!"

Glory looked at herself and groaned with impatience.

"Ohhhh!" she said. "Did you do this?"

"Henrietta did," Joey said.

"Henrietta? The ghost?"

Again she reached to touch. Joey held it away.

"I won't touch it. I promise. You think I want to get her dirty?" Joey brought the doll forward. Glory traced the dolls body with her finger without actually touching her.

"How do you know Henrietta did this?" she asked. Joey noticed Glory didn't question Henrietta's existence.

"Because it looks just like her," he said.

"You've *seen* her?" she asked.

"Yes. It's a good story," Joey said. "Maybe I'll tell it to you out here under the tree tonight."

Glory looked at him, a spark of excitement in her eyes. "Story! Joey's going to tell us about Henrietta tonight."

"Alright!" Story called. He had tired of the doll and was floating sticks in a puddle.

Glory looked serious. "I gave her to you," she said, not asking the question that was on her mind

"She's the most beautiful gift I've ever received," said Joey.

Glory nodded. She knew that.

After what was an agonizing pause for Glory, he continued. "But I don't know how to take care of such a fine doll. Would you take care of her for me?"

"Yes! Yes! Yes!" Glory said jumping in a circle. "Henrietta," she said, again bringing her hand lovingly close to the doll without touching her. "That's her name. Oh, I've just got to hold her," she squealed. "You hold her until I get cleaned up," she ordered. The screen door slammed as she went through. In a moment she stuck her head back out.

"Nicely!" she yelled. She saw Joey holding the doll in the crook of his arm like an infant. "Okay, that's weird," she yelled and disappeared inside.

At lunch over grilled cheese sandwiches Mrs. Johanaby read a note Beezer had left them. She had found it on the kitchen counter.

Dear Johanabys. It may be a while before you see me again. I have some friends who need my help. They live quite a ways from here and I don't know how long I will be gone. Mrs. Johanaby, you are a fine woman and mother. With Joey's help you and your family are going to be just fine. I'll be in touch. God bless you.

Beezer

"Ohhh," Story whined. "Beezer was so much fun." Story was thinking of treasure chests and golden chocolate coins.

Joey watched Mrs. Johanaby read the letter again to herself. She looked at him when she finished. "He sounds pretty confident that we'll be fine," she said.

"Sometimes you just know things without knowing how you know, you know?" Joey said.

"I'll have to puzzle that one out," Mrs. Johanaby said with a smile.

That night Joey kept his promise. With Mrs. Johanaby's permission they got to stay up later than usual. She even gave Joey permission to build a fire using a garbage can lid as a fire pit. He used his new-found flint and steel skills to build the fire. Glory and Story were impressed.

As the stars came out, Joey started his tale. He wondered if they would make fun of his story. They didn't. They listened almost reverently accepting every detail of his story as the truth.

"I knew Beezer was magic," Story said when he heard about the magic bubbles. "How else could he turn gold into chocolate?"

Glory was sad when she heard Joey's version of how Henrietta had died. She almost cried when she understood how bad Colonel Horsebaum felt about what happened.

"Poor Colonel Horsebaum," she said. "Henrietta forgave him, didn't she?"

"Yes," Joey said, knowing that Henrietta wouldn't have been able to help him if she hadn't.

Glory and Story covered their faces with their hands at the parts about the pirates and the eagle. They clapped when Henrietta appeared to Joey in the forest. They were "wowed" by his life jacket and dive to the map.

"They're gone now, aren't they," Glory said. She seemed to sense it, like Joey did.

"Gone is the wrong word," Joey said, thoughtfully. "'Gone' is for that ice cream you ate last week or for that dollar you spent at the dollar store for that squirt gun that broke the next day. 'Gone' is never for people, especially people you love. They are never 'gone.' They are just somewhere else at the moment."

"Dad," said Story, quietly.

"Yes, Dad's not gone," Joey said. "I know that now."

"Do you think Dad sent Henrietta?" asked Glory.

"I don't think so, but I know he's going to be happy to meet her when he does."

Mrs. Johanaby came out the screen door. "Look what I found," she said, holding up a bag of marshmallows. "They're getting a little hard, but they might still puff up over the fire. Joey, can you cut some willows from the tree?"

Joey got up and walked around the tree searching for suitable branches. They hadn't roasted marshmallows since Mr. Johanaby had died. He paused and looked at his family on the other side of the tree. They were happy tonight. Story and Glory leaned forward on their hands and knees to try to light the ends of twigs on fire. Mrs. Johanaby, her face glowing in the firelight, smiled as she watched them. The "don't play with fire" warning was barely restrained in her throat. The only one missing was his dad.

He's not here, but he's not gone, Joey thought. Joey felt as happy as he had ever been in his life. Maybe happier. A little breeze moved the warm, night air. The chimes high above tinkled. Glory and Story both looked up and said together, "Henrietta." To Joey, Henrietta or not, it was a beautiful sound.

ABOUT THE AUTHOR

Although an avid reader all of his life, Tory Anderson didn't discover the magic of writing until he was in college. By the time he graduated with a master's degree in English he had plans of doing nothing but writing for a living. However, his own story had surprises in store. The need to support a wife and eight children distracted him from writing for many years. The hundreds of stories he read to his children inspired him to pick up the pen once more. He lives in Levan, Utah, with his wife and five of their eight children who still remain at home.

You can contact Tory at Tory@ToryCAnderson.com

CPSIA information can be obtained
at www.ICGtesting.com
Printed in the USA
LVHW041457040919
629924LV00011B/752